# Hark

## John R Gordon

TEAM
ANGE
LICA

Published September 2020 by Team Angelica Publishing,
an imprint of Angelica Entertainments Ltd

Team Angelica Publishing
51 Coningham Road
London W12 8BS

**TEAM**
ANGELICA

www.teamangelica.com

A CIP catalogue record for this book is available from
the British Library

ISBN 978-1-9163561-1-5

*Cover art by John R Gordon*

# Hark

## John R Gordon

*Thank you to Tanya McKinnon, who first urged me to write this book; to Diriye Osman and Rikki-Beadle-Blair for their unflagging love and support; to Patrik-Ian Polk, Kate Farquharson, and to Isabel, my mother, and Peter, my father.*

# Chapter One

"You ever been inside a haunted house?"

That was how it began, the summer when Cleve met Roe, and Roe met Cleve, and they both met Hark: with a cornball question that was really an invitation to something else a lot more interesting. Hark doesn't come into the story until later, though he's by far the strangest part of it, the magical part maybe, although afterwards neither Cleve nor Roe could decide whether anything he told them was true.

The story doesn't really begin there, to be truthful. It starts two nights before, with what happened to the statue of Colonel Tyler. He was described by the local paper, the *Welt County Times*, when it reported the story, as "a Confederate Hero in the Northern War of Aggression," which probably tells you everything you need to know about the town of Claypit.

The statue was made of bronze, and like everything else on Coleman Avenue, it was dulled by a patina of dust, grit and vehicular particulates. For as long as anyone could remember, it had stood at the intersection of Coleman Avenue (usually called Main Street by the locals), China Row and Paper Street. Though it was seven feet tall, and stood on a plinth the size of a tomb, no one paid it much attention. There was indeed nothing to distinguish it from other, similar statues in many Southern towns – except perhaps the somewhat effeminate way the Colonel held his gloves against his left hip. His right hand rested limply unmartial on the pommel of his sword hilt, and the lips below the handlebar mustache were pursed and prim.

These were the sorts of – possibly accidental – details kids always notice, and comment on snarkily while their elders pretend not to see them.

The granite plinth on which the statue stood was dedicated To the Fallen Soldiers of the Confederacy in six-inch high, incised letters.

Most of the stores around the intersection were closed down. The hardware store went a couple of years ago. Bubbles, a Laundromat with dead flies piled so high behind its grimy window you thought there must be bodies hidden in there, closed in the nineties, which was before Cleve was born. Rayleen's, a dressmaker's, in the window of which the same taffeta prom gown had been on the same headless dummy for as long as Cleve could remember, a strap forever forlornly hanging off one shoulder, had never been open, or so it seemed to him. An ice-cream parlor, a sooty fiberglass cornet thrust out above its boarded-up entrance like a cavity-inducing Statue of Liberty torch, he vaguely remembered still being in business when he was a toddler.

"Bring us your diabetic, your massive huddled," Cleve would murmur to himself every time he passed it.

Only the gun store, the liquor store, the tattoo parlor and three bars were still going strong. Morgan Cole, the owner of the gun store, had once been a Hell's Angel, but after a bad smash-up he had been bedridden and had piled on the weight. When he hit five hundred pounds he traded his Harley for a Rascal that most days stood where the Harley had, pulled in neatly between the white lines that marked the nowadays rarely occupied parking spaces along Main Street. Cleve's dad had given up dirt-biking around the same time as Morgan played dare with a ten-ton truck and lost, and Cleve had a sense the two events were connected, though as far as he knew his father had never been a Hell's Angel.

Morgan had decked his Rascal out with Confederate flag pennants. His store, Family Firearms, was on the south side of the street, and that was no accident. Though there was some mixing in in Claypit, and for sure Morgan would sell a weapon to anybody with the money to buy one, white, black or brown, in the mid noughties Coleman Avenue had featured on national TV as a "racial faultline," and not much had changed since then.

West of the intersection, in the direction of the free-way that had carried off so much of the town's trade since it opened in the 1980s, just this side of a succession of disused basketball courts and almost facing each other, were the bowling alley, where the white kids hung out, and the pool hall where the black kids hung out – the roughest of whom were called the Paper Boys and the Pit Boys, respectively.

The Paper Boys, sometimes also known as the Milltown Boys, were named for the closed-down paper mill that rusted on the banks of the Nooseneck River to the south of the town; the Pit Boys for the worked-out china clay mine to the north. Cleve had never been inside the pool hall, but wondered about it sometimes: did anything go on in there that was different from what happened in the bowling alley? If so, what?

When young white and black men interacted on Main Street, which did happen sometimes, there was always an air of criminality about it, a sense of deals being done of the sort you didn't talk about out loud. Or so Cleve thought, looking on.

In the bowling alley, Barney's Balls, a name so groan-inducing you made sure you didn't think about it, an outsize Confederate flag covered most of the wall behind the counter where you exchanged your shoes. The burgers and fries and Cokes were cheap there, even if the Cokes were the sort that came out of nozzles, not cans or bottles. Everyone called them "slurry," even the servers: "You want a slurry with them fries, hon?"

Girls mostly asked for a Diet Slurry, especially when they were on dates with boys, though when no boys of consequence were about they might sigh and say, "Fuck it, I'm goin' full fat tonight."

As it didn't serve alcohol, Barney's Balls was one of the few places young people could go instead of just hanging around their families' homes all the time, and mostly the servers didn't mind you sitting all evening over a single portion of fries and not even bowling. Older teens smuggled in whisky, which was known as "spiking the slurry," and sometimes there were fights, often over girls, and sometimes between girls.

"Nice" girls and boys didn't go to Barney's. Cleve did, though not often, his parents' home being five miles east of town. Though he had got his license earlier in the year, he couldn't afford to run a car or motorcycle, and only rarely had the loan of his dad's pickup. When he did go, he mostly went with Spider. Karen would join them after she finished work at the tattoo parlor.

Karen was one of the girls who got in fights. Cleve's parents thought Karen was trouble, and he had to admit they were right. On his sixteenth birthday she had gotten him drunk and given him a tattoo.

"Just real small. You tell anyone, I'll lose my license," she had said, smoking while she worked, concentrating on filling in a dime-sized heart at the top of his hip-bone. The clattering needles were oddly loud, and the sensation was like creeping sunburn. Through the latex of the glove she wore, the heel of her hand was warm against his pelvis, its presence almost, but not quite, arousing.

Spider had watched from under greasy black bangs, swigging whisky from the bottle, amused. He too was a bad influence: "wild," for all he had served his country and lost two fingers in Faluja or somewhere else deserty, and been honorably discharged as a result. Cleve noticed that Spider shifted the locale of his loss of digits to wherever was in the news that week, so he knew people would have heard of it.

"You know which two," he would say, grinning, making a gesture the meaning of which was clear despite the middle finger's absence. At twenty-three he was old enough to go in the bars, but at nineteen Karen wasn't, so they would go as a couple to Barney's, and sometimes they would invite Cleve along. Spider had a veteran's pension, so he was better off than many, if not most, in Claypit.

Whatever you heard about the state of the economy nationally – supposedly it was doing better lately – money and jobs were in short supply in Claypit, and behind everything was a sense that the town, if not the whole county, was in terminal decline. Like, say, Tanner's Peaches used to be a big thing up until the seventies. All the white kids roundabout – Cleve's and Spider's and Karen's parents and many others – used to pick for Tanner's in the summer. But the paper mill, at that time one of the biggest employers in the area, was slowly poisoning the soil, and the peach farms, which were downstream of the mill, started to die off.

By that point – Cleve never quite figured out why – no white people wanted to pick the peaches anyway, and old man Tanner had to get in migrants, mostly Hispanic. That made some people mad, though Cleve couldn't see why. Who cared if someone else came in to do a job you didn't want to? It wasn't like they stayed, or not more than a handful, anyway. Most of that handful attended the school he went to, Welt County High, Claypit's main high school.

In the frowsy thrift stores along the backstreets – those mysterious places, rarely open, that never seemed to actually sell anything, ever – you still sometimes saw old signs for Tanner's Peaches, made of enameled tin. Cleve's mom used to collect that kind of stuff at swap meets, and would put them up around the kitchen walls. That was when she could still get out of the house.

Around 1900 valuable china clay deposits were discovered to the north of the town, (then known as West Tanner), just past the crummy land the black people were given to sharecrop after the Civil War was lost. The soil, never good, was pretty much worked out by then, so they went to work in the mines instead. Between 1920 and 1950 they were out-earning a lot of the white people in the town – rezoned and renamed Claypit in 1922 – which led to ill feeling.

In 1940 the paper mill opened, bringing jobs and moderate prosperity to the white people, and that eased tensions somewhat. By 1950 the good quality clay had been mined out, and the works closed down. The jobs lost were never replaced with anything else, and the Pits was reputed to be the most violent and crime ridden part of town, and was certainly the poorest. The local paper often identified it as Claypit's most pressing social problem. Black councilors lobbied for increased resources and inward investment, but in the middle of what seemed an unending slump these were not forthcoming.

The Pit Boys were the scariest gang in Claypit, even scarier than the Paper Boys, the white gang from Milltown with which Spider was casually affiliated. Brawling, knifings, robberies and drug dealing were all blamed on them, but it wasn't the Pit Boys who Cleve saw pull down the Tyler statue one sweaty night that first week of the summer break.

The business over the statue was the first time in forever that Claypit became a part of "the national conversation" – or at least that was the way both Cleve and Roe saw it, though they hadn't met yet.

When it came to social progress Claypit had never been an early adopter: there were other towns where Confederate statues had already been taken down. Sometimes this was done secretly at night, to avoid trouble from the Klan, neo-Nazis, and Southern Risers generally. Sometimes it was done in bright daylight, before TV cameras, accompanied by impassioned speeches delivered to a cheering, mostly black crowd, and much hopeful talk about how the South was finally facing up to its past. Flush-faced white protesters were kept out of view.

Cleve had noticed these stories on the national news, mixed in with Black Lives Matter protests and phone footage of police brutality against black people, but hadn't connected them with the campy, begrimed statue at the Main Street intersection: it was just a thing that was there that, so far as he knew, no one had any strong feelings about one way or the other.

He was wrong, of course – though he was right that the statue of Colonel Tyler wasn't much loved by anyone. If it had been, it would have been moved a few blocks east, scrubbed down, burnished, and given pride of place in front of Claypit's historic town hall. Its being abandoned at the intersection had to do with some sort of interminable feud between two old families of standing in Welt County, the Tylers and the Oglesbys. The current mayor was an Oglesby, Lee Hunter Oglesby, and any leftover Tylers were dead, or too flat broke to get their voices heard on the matter.

Cleve had never seen the statue as anything anyone should do something about. It was just a drab lump of brass, about as drab as everything else in his dead end hometown, and he wasn't thinking about it the night it was pulled down. Instead he was thinking about robbing a liquor store.

# Chapter Two

The robbery wasn't Cleve's idea. It was one of those things suggested by someone – afterwards you could never remember exactly who – that you all kicked around, nobody knowing how seriously anyone else was taking it. After a while, without anyone actually making a decision, you realize it's turned into something you're going to do for real.

The discussion took place at Spider's house, of course. Cleve and some of his other friends were in the habit of hanging out there. This was because, owing to his veteran's allowance, unlike the rest of them Spider could afford a place of his own. It was single story, with a chain-link-fenced, weed-infested back yard, and was one in a vast grid of interchangeable, low density tract houses that in the early 1950s had been thrown up over what had once been farmland. Intended as cheap homes for mill workers, the houses were also built in anticipation of the arrival of other industries that never showed up. Then the mill folded, leaving the area almost as badly off as the Pits. A good many of the houses stood unoccupied, and the rent was cheap.

Spider's house faced onto Paper Street, which was the western boundary of the Milltown district, and ran up from the mill to the Main Street intersection where the statue stood. He was disliked by his neighbors for throwing empty beer cans, bottles, mattresses and other trash out into his backyard, leaving them piled there among the waist-high, never-trimmed weeds; for fixing up motorbikes in his front yard, especially on Sunday mornings; and for practicing anytime he felt like it with his thrash metal band, Defibrillator. Karen sang backup and waved a tambourine about. The aim of the band, she said, was to shock Claypit back to life. Mostly they covered any song they thought was particularly lyrically obnoxious. Stuff by Cradle of Filth was a favorite.

Cleve drummed with them sometimes – he could keep a beat – but he wasn't much good really. To be fair to Cleve, nor was Spider (yelling lead vocals; limited lead guitar), but it was his band. Karen couldn't, as Cleve's mom would put it, carry a tune, but she was the lead singer's girlfriend, so she got a free pass and no one said anything.

They were yet to play an actual gig: so far it was all at the planning stage, like everything in Cleve's life that summer, or that was what it felt like. Rehearsals were mostly an excuse to hang out at Spider's, something a parent would just about buy as an acceptable activity – useful when you'd conspicuously failed to get a summer job, and your idling presence in the family home would constantly remind both them and yourself of the fact, and stoke up resentment on both sides.

*Jobs.*

If they'd had jobs themselves, Spider's neighbors might have been more forbearing, but like most in Milltown they struggled along on social security. As a consequence, they were home pretty much all the time, slumped in front of their TVs or computer screens, filled with impotent rage, escaping their shut-in lives only once in a rare while to supplement their incomes with bits of semi- or actually illegal (and certainly never declared) work on the side – which, being the kind of work you can never count on, never really solves anything. Prescription drug abuse had become rife in the past five years, and it was as an opioid hotspot that Claypit had resurfaced in the national press most recently, albeit not with a starring role this time. It was just one place among many others that were similarly blighted.

It seemed like everyone knew someone with a problem, and Cleve was no exception.

"It's the new normal," his dad had said after reading the article, sad and angry at the same time. "We're the new normal."

Cleve's last year of school was coming up, and then what? His parents couldn't afford college fees, and, though intelligent enough, he sure wasn't in line for a scholarship anywhere. His prospects seemed pretty much nonexistent, and that made him more open to the idea of the robbery than he would otherwise have been.

Claypit and crime sort of went together anyway, even if only in a leaves-getting-sucked-down-a-drain kind of way. His twenty-seven year old cousin Vince was in Welt Penitentiary, doing what he called "a stretch" for a botched home invasion up in Tanner's Cross.

Tanner's Cross was a well to do white suburb on the northeastern side of town. Comfortably beyond the stifling, bell-jarred alluvial plain, it wound its way up into the curve of cooler hills beyond. Cleve cycled past the bottom of it on his way to Welt High or Barney's Balls or Spider's house. There was a private school there, the Tyler Academy, named for the same unloved colonel whose statue stood at the Main Street crossroads. Houses in Tanner's Cross were larger and more varied in style than those in Milltown, often shaded by large old trees, and the air up there had no tang of pollution.

Spider was there that afternoon, of course, sprawled on the couch with the duct-taped rips in its sage-green draylon covering. Karen sat by him, shoes kicked off, her bare feet curled under her. Spikily cut black hair jabbed at her heavily eye-linered eyes. It was a Monday, her day off work.

"Nobody gets inked on Mondays," she said, cryptically. "Not ever."

She had a scabby new rose on her shoulder, covered by Saran wrap until it healed. Cleve didn't tell her his mom had finally noticed his tattoo. He usually hid it with a band-aid; last week he forgot, and she saw it when he came down in just his shorts with a tee shirt for the wash.

"I'm gonna call the cops on that bitch," Myrtle had wheezed, trying to pull herself up from the couch in a series of wrenching wallows before giving up and sinking back, too breathless to carry on. She flapped her plump hand panickily as the couch sagged and creaked under her, and Cleve wheeled the oxygen cylinder over and helped her get the tube clipped in under her nose.

Also at Spider's that afternoon were Choc, who was a year or two younger than Spider and part Choctaw, hence his nickname; and Rick and Rob, twins who were in the same year as Cleve at Welt High. Rick was in the basketball team. Owing to being tall and rangy Cleve had been in it too for about five minutes, and that was how he got to know first Rick and then, through him, Rob and the others.

Rob had been born with a short leg, something congenital. Both brothers blamed it on heavy metals contaminating the water table – they lived practically in the shadow of the rusting paper mill – but Rob got about fast with a crutch, and was smart-mouthed to compensate. Then there were Patty, a girl as plain and nondescript as

Karen was sexy and distinctive, and who had a crush on Rick; and Tag, a small, eager, tow-haired, buck-toothed boy with an especially violent, alcoholic father. Patty and Tag were, respectively, a year and two years below Cleve at school. All of them saw Spider and Karen as their springboard into a wider, wilder world.

Even so, to Cleve hanging with Spider was a balancing act that involved being open to doing exciting new stuff while avoiding marking your permanent record with the school, the cops, the world. Beers sometimes, yeah, that was cool; cigarettes sometimes, yeah, okay; whisky, no; dope – smoking, snorting, pills – no way. Stuff that could be pranks, yeah; stuff that was obviously criminal, like actual shoplifting (which Patty claimed she did "all the time, including weekends and public holidays"), no. But overall, Cleve's feeling was: better dangerous than dull. And since he had no money – his weekly allowance was a measly ten bucks – and nowhere else to go, he had to earn his place, earn the beers and cigarettes by being up for whatever. Spider and Karen were older. He was learning all the time. To be with them was a privilege, kind of.

Knowing the neighbors couldn't stand him gave Spider energy, but it made being there kind of claustrophobic, because he always had the blinds pulled down so no one would know what he was up to.

Having grown up in Milltown, and dropped out of school early, and been in the army, and gotten in trouble he didn't talk about much that might or might not have involved, but probably did involve, jail time, Spider was an honorary Paper Boy, but he wasn't one of them really. This was because, despite the Confederate flag that hung above the mattress in his bedroom, Spider despised racism, or at least racists.

"They got Trump, they got their White Power president. What they got to whine about?" he would object whenever some right-wing pundit appeared on TV, and he would start a fight with anyone – even actual Hell's Angels – who tried to hang swastikas on any kind of American flag, which was a thing in Claypit. He would stalk up to the offender, get in his face and say, "What the eff you doin', man?" – looking so crazy that 99% of the time the other would back off straight away.

"Nothin', man. What the fuck, man?"

"You fought for that flag, man?"

"What?"

"You fought against America for the Nazis?"

"Naw, I –"

"Then what the eff you wearin' it for?"

To watch this kind of encounter was both scary and exhilarating, as was knowing Spider's ace in the hole: "See this hand. I lost this hand fightin' for America. What price you paid to wave that Nazi shit around?"

Sometimes Spider would add a contemptuous, 'You – you're an enemy alien, man. An enemy alien" – which was usually leftfield enough to confuse his opponent, and defuse the situation as Spider turned and went back to whatever he was doing. Sometimes he did get beaten up, though, because he was skinny and short and didn't care how big the other guy was.

Despite this, Spider didn't have any black friends, though he did have shady "business" interactions with black men sometimes, round the side of the pool hall across from Barney's Balls.

The pool hall was called O'Flaherty's. The letters making up the name on the sign outside were incised vertically into an Irish green hardboard box and lit from within by light bulbs, a cheap-jack version of neon. One time a bird got in through one of the holes, and Cleve had watched as it banged about in a panic inside, and the heavyset black manager came out with a ladder, climbed up, reached in, and eventually dragged it out. He threw it up in the air. A jackdaw, it flew off raggedly.

Rick had black friends on the basketball team. One of these, Jackie Temple, Cleve had developed a crush on in an abstract kind of way after coming in for a couple of tryouts. He hadn't made the cut, and had probably pissed Jackie off by acting weird around him. Or more likely Jackie hadn't even noticed – if you don't know how someone is normally, you can't know if they're acting weirder than usual – and had never given Cleve a second's thought, which would be a relief and disappointing at the same time. Jackie had a wide smile, a messy afro, feline eyes, freckles, a small, flat nose and an easy, rangy build. Rick said he had two girls on the go. Rumor was he was already a father.

Karen could be kind of racist, though mostly, Cleve thought, to wind Spider up, and Choc said racist stuff sometimes, maybe to prove his heritage didn't mean you had to watch what you said around him. On the other hand Karen was pretty much pro-gay, with Spider taking a "the more guys are gay, the more girls for me" line that forgot lesbians existed – and that he had a girlfriend already.

This didn't make Cleve want to come out to them, though. It was too abstract, and Karen was prone to say stuff like, "Fags are cool. They've got female spirits and the best dress sense."

Patty and Tag never seemed to have any opinions. Probably they were afraid of getting kicked out of the group for saying the wrong thing, and having to go back to hanging with kids their own age.

"I'm a bohemian," Spider would say, when asked about his politics or beliefs, and because of that they called themselves the Bohemians. Cleve had suggested they change the name of the band to the Bohemians on the grounds no one could say "defibrillator," but Karen blocked him.

"Look at Chiwetel Efiofor," she said. "If you're cool, they learn it."

"It's Ejiofor," Spider said, rolling a joint, and Karen punched him on the shoulder.

Running down from the northeastern hills, the Illitabi River slanted through Claypit on its way to join the larger Nooseneck to the south of the town, meeting it where the closed-down paper mill stood. Mostly it was covered over, but south of Main Street a stretch of it was open. There it looked like a huge storm drain, and was overlooked from the Milltown-side bank by Cleve's high school.

Owing to quirks in zoning that were the result of attempts to break up black voting blocks, the school was attended both by white students from Milltown and by those black students who lived in the first six streets north of Coleman Avenue, an area generally known as Coleman. Superficially Welt County High was well integrated, with a ratio of about 70:30 white to black plus a few others, but somehow as the kids got older they began to self-segregate. It was like either they started seeing something that was true, or they started being blind to it.

That felt like a bad thing to Cleve, but what could he do about it?

Cleve's life was mostly made up of things he couldn't do anything about. He couldn't get more than middling grades. He couldn't excel at basketball. He couldn't get a decent summer job or even a lousy one. He couldn't get a scholarship for sports or academic attainments.

His dad floated the idea he might try and join the army after his schooling was done, but Cleve would look at Spider's mutilated hand and feel repulsed. Nothing about IEDs blowing your balls off when they exploded under your jeep, or torturing-slash-patriotically-interrogating Iraqis or Afghanis or Syrians or whatever, or posting phone footage of dropping camel spiders down the back of your best bud's shirt, made him want to sign up.

Cleve had known he was gay since he was fourteen – another thing he couldn't do anything about – but didn't feel he could come out at school, not without risking becoming a pariah, and for what? There wasn't a Claypit Pride Parade to wave a rainbow flag at; there wasn't, so far as he knew, a community to become a part of.

If he had a boyfriend's hand to brandish in a "dare we attend the prom together, let's sue the school" kind of way, something heroic and romantic where you ended up defiantly pinning corsages on each others' lapels before running up the steps into the dancehall, that would have been different. But just *saying* it? Dude, what *for*? He was tough enough, tall enough, fit enough to not get too much of a kicking, probably, but he didn't enjoy fighting, not the way say Spider did. Spider got turned on by it, or charged up, or both. Plus Spider had actually killed people, so brawling probably didn't feel like a big deal to him.

Despite its being pretty much a typical Southern high school in a typical, mid-sized Southern town, there was actually a self-proclaimed queer contingent at Welt. Maybe it had to do with the mix of different races there. Black Protestantism and Hispanic Catholicism were quite different from white Evangelism, and white conservatives (the majority) were often overtly racist, so there wasn't a united front against the sexually non-conforming. Straight students quickly worked out that if you wanted to annoy your parents, it didn't matter what your real views were, nothing succeeded like loudly declaring you supported gay marriage. This was something even the jocks noticed – at the same time as they noticed that girls tended to like liberal-leaning guys who were prepared to show they were "sensitive."

The queer kids were all white, mostly girls with blue or pink hair cut shorter than the other girls', and a few limp boys with bangs in their eyes. They would throw *RuPaul's Drag Race* parties at each others' houses, and occasionally got scolded, usually by black girls, for saying "Yass" or "Slay, gurl" too loudly in the canteen, thereby committing the crime of cultural appropriation.

Cleve suspected a lot of them of posing, but not in a mean way: he just didn't feel he had anything in common with them. It was the same with the Goth contingent. He liked their willfully apathetic performance of alienation; liked the way they said, "They'll grow out of it," about the queer kids while listlessly reapplying black lipstick, boys and girls alike, but their style wasn't his, and Goth music depressed him.

The only thing that flat-out alienated Cleve was being gay.

He found school okay, mostly, and had friends, though no one he was particularly close to. Rick and Rob, maybe, but they had gotten subsumed into the Bohemians, and he felt awkward with the jocks, who talked endlessly and sometimes unpleasantly about girls, joking about Cosbies (which were what they called date rape drugs) and making girls into MeToos – their name for girls they could pressure into going all the way, and who then got upset later when the word went around. It was ugly stuff, though he didn't know how much, if any of it, the jocks actually did. Some girls did have to take time out for pregnancy, but it was never clear if they'd been Cosbied or it was just through not taking care with a guy they were into.

Girls would smile at Cleve, who was tall, fit and nice enough looking, but they always wanted the guy to make the first move, which of course he never did – he wanted a guy who made the first move too. He avoided close friendships with girls in case they tipped over into something awkward and exposing. With his family situation it was easy not to invite anyone to his home, and nice girls didn't have boys over, or not when no parents were there, anyway.

Sometimes, just occasionally, Cleve felt an odd connection to blackness. His cousin wrote him every once in a while from prison, and Cleve always wrote back – Welt Penitentiary was a two hour drive away, so visiting wasn't practical. Vince said 80% of the inmates were black, and he thanked God he'd never had any pro-Confederate type tattoos done or he would have been dead on day one. Vince said there was solidarity between black and white prisoners against the guards. "They got the power," he wrote. "We don't, except if we're together."

Cleve had started to notice that the black kids got harsher responses from the school authorities if they did something wrong. Like if you were white, especially if you were on a team, they would probably hush it up if you got caught smoking a joint. But if you were black you would likely end up in court, and you couldn't even complain about it because you had broken the law. If you were white and you got trashed on beer and tore up someone's front yard and threw all their prize-winning begonias into the street (a real-life example) and got caught puking in the gutter, you were "high-spirited." If you were black and did something like that, you were guilty of vandalism and criminal trespass and got a record. It was the same thing with fights and, for girls, shoplifting, and was another Claypit thing you couldn't do anything about.

"Goddamn Klan," Spider said, lolling back on the ripped-up couch and chugging a beer. He was looking at an article on his laptop about how many southern police officers were known to be in the Ku Klux Klan, and turned it round to show the others a map spattered with red dots like blood at a crime-scene. Each dot indicated an officer. As if gravitationally, they clumped more thickly the further south you looked.

"Zoom in," Choc said.

With some pulling about of the map, Spider managed to find Claypit. "One, two... three," he said, jabbing a blunt forefinger at the screen. "Three pigs."

"Do they say names?" Cleve asked.

"Nup."

"Is that a naw or a yup?" Karen asked, not looking up from fiddling with her phone. Her plum nail-varnish was chipped, and as always her fingers were crowded with rings.

"Naw."

"So who cares?"

"It's pretty sick is all," Spider said.

"So what are you gonna do about it?"

Spider shrugged irritably, closed the laptop and put it down on the floor, almost knocking the overflowing ashtray off the arm of the couch as he did so. "So we all on for tonight?" he asked. Even in private, discussion of the robbery was indirect.

Cleve, Rick and Rob exchanged glances, each daring the others to punk out. No one did, and as one they nodded. Choc, Patty and Tag nodded too.

"Okay, then." Spider twisted round, reached over, lifted a corner of the blind and lobbed a now empty beer can out into the backyard. Some unseen animal, likely a rat, scurried away rustlingly through the straw-dry undergrowth.

The sun was by then low in the sky, the late afternoon heat intense and smothering.

# Chapter Three

They all knew the liquor store from the outside: it was one of a row of featureless, two story brick-built units on the south side of Main Street, fifty yards or so east of the intersection where the Tyler statue stood. It opened daily at 8 a.m. From Monday through Saturday it closed at 11:45 p.m.; Sundays it closed at 11:30 p.m., and today was a Sunday. Mesh shutters over the grimy front window obscured the interior, and of the Bohemians only Spider had ever been inside.

The proprietor, who most of the time also manned the cash register, was a chunky, taciturn man with cropped silver hair named Cal Berry. He didn't seem to have any friends, and generally headed straight home after locking up, walking rather than driving. He lived somewhere in Milltown, and presumably crossed the river by the narrow footbridge close to Cleve's school.

Back of the store was a small yard with ten foot concrete walls topped with razor wire. It was accessed through a metal door that was bolted, Spider said, from the inside, and would be impossible to break down quietly. The neighboring unit, however, was unoccupied, had an unpadlocked plywood back door, and a flat-roofed single story rear extension from which it would be easy for someone to drop down into the liquor store's backyard. It would then be the work of a moment to pull back the bolts and let the others in.

The plan was for them to drive past the store, park one street south and one block along, then sneak back on foot. Patty and Rob were to keep watch – "If anyone notices you, just French kiss till they go," Karen advised, and both of them blushed furiously – while Cleve and Rick climbed over via the extension. Spider, Choc, Tag and maybe Karen – she was keeping it vague as to whether she was even going to come along – would then hurry round with a crowbar, tools and bags, and slip in through the unbolted door. They could take their time quietly getting the liquor store's back door open without worrying about being seen from the street.

Spider had chosen Sunday because 1) the store closed slightly earlier, 2) the entire weekend's takings would be in the till, waiting to be paid in first thing Monday morning, and 3) working folks would be in bed early. He seemed to know Cal Berry didn't have a safe.

The Bohemians had agreed to split whatever profits they made equally, and the thought of having real money in his pocket for once made Cleve feel giddy with possibilities, even though he'd have to be careful his mom didn't find it, or his little sister Terri, who had a habit of going through his things when he was out.

At least she hadn't figured out the password to his computer, even though he did always clear his browser history.

As they went over the details of the plan for the zillionth time Cleve was struck by the realization that crime was work just like regular work, which was disappointing. He felt bored and increasingly sick with dread, but there was no getting out of it now.

One of the few stores along Main Street that was still in business sold army surplus clothing as well as work overalls, steel capped boots, and spare parts for farm machinery. Cleve's dad took his chainsaw there to be sharpened, and Cleve had noticed they sold balaclavas. He said so to Spider, but Spider decided to buy off eBay, so no one would trace them back to him if things went wrong somehow.

Cleve felt both sheepish and suffocated as he tried his balaclava on. The stifling humidity was, if anything, growing worse as dusk closed in, and he wished he could come up with a reason for backing out without losing face. Then he imagined buying his mom flowers, a bunch of cabbage sized blooms collared in cellophane and tied with a scissor blade-curled ribbon, and her smiling, with any luck too pleased at that moment to ask where he got the money from.

Maybe he could even make a down payment on a dirt bike.

Dusk drifted into evening, then night, in twists of cigarette smoke and chugs of beer. An old film played on Spider's wall-mounted, widescreen TV. The picture was framed by black pillars because it was from when they didn't know how to make televisions the same shape as movie theater screens. Cleve wondered why wide and narrow was cooler than square. It wasn't like you saw more, not really.

After what felt like forever it was finally midnight, and in a subdued mood they trailed out to Spider's pickup. Spider was driving; Choc rode shotgun. Karen, having shrugged lazily to indicate that she had decided to come, "obviously," clambered over Choc and positioned herself between him and Spider. She was wearing short-shorts and a crop-top, one strap of which kept slipping down, and sandals you couldn't run in, like they were going to hang out at Barney's Balls, not carry out a robbery.

Rick, Patty and Tag sat in a row in the backseat. Cleve and Rob sat on the flatbed, which Rob preferred because he could stretch out the backwards bones in his short leg – "my bird-leg" he called it – instead of keeping it folded under him, as he would have had to if he sat inside.

Between them lay a long, bulky black tool bag Spider had placed there personally. "Don't touch," he said, grinning gap-toothedly. It was the size and length to hold a broken-down fishing rod or maybe pool cues.

Spider drove up Paper Street not too fast, not too slow. Just before Main Street he took a right into the tangle of backstreets known as the Triangle, so-named because it was framed by Paper Street to the west, Coleman Avenue to the north, and by the open storm-drainage of the Illitabi on the hypotenuse.

Once upon a time, during Prohibition, a period that fascinated Cleve's dad, it had had a whorehouse, then called a "fancy house," and more recently, but still back in what Cleve thought of as the pre-internet Stone Age, there had been a store there called Bluebusters that sold porno mags and videotapes. Bluebusters had been burnt out, by the Klan, Cleve had heard, for selling stuff featuring race-mixing and homosexuality, maybe even both at the same time.

If you were a mixed race couple, you probably lived in the Triangle, and there was even a gay bar there, called Discretions. "A real dive," Cleve's dad had called it the one time he mentioned it. It had no windows, and you needed to knock and show your ID when the slot opened, or so Karen had told them one idle afternoon, and Cleve had had to act like he wasn't particularly interested, and stop his face from flushing as Choc asked crude questions.

The Triangle was maybe forty small blocks of mostly two-story, mostly clapboard row houses. Its crisscrossing streets, some of which had no names, were narrow, often dwindling into alleys that dead-ended in backyards, and there were few streetlights.

"You really into this, man?" Cleve asked Rob as Spider drew up behind an abandoned car with four flat tires, and cut the engine. His gut was tight.

"Sure, why not?"

"Um, getting caught?"

Rob gestured with his crutch. "I'll play the sympathy card."

"I don't have a sympathy card."

"Sure you do: your mom."

"My mom's doin' okay."

"If you say so, dude."

Rob gripped the side of the truck and rolled himself over, fanning the crutch round so he landed like an acrobat dismounting from a pommel horse. Converse sneaker-sole and rubber crutch-tip hit the tarmac simultaneously for a perfect 10.

Cleve clambered out after him. No lights were on in any of the houses overlooking them, but somewhere old-school country and western was playing, the stuff Cleve's grandpa used to like. An intimidating old man, he lived in a senior facility out west by the freeway, and Cleve didn't see him often.

The front doors of the pickup swung open and Choc and Spider got out. Karen stayed inside. Quietly they closed the doors on her, and the dome light went off. In the darkness her face was illuminated as she bent over her phone, as if in prayer or contemplation.

The others slid out from the backseat, looking very young to Cleve then, and he noticed that Tag was nervously twisting his balaclava in his hands. Spider did too. "Put that away," he said tersely. Turning to Cleve he said, "Pass the bag."

Cleve reached over for it, pulling it towards him by the strap, took hold of it and lifted it. The material was soft and he could feel the weight and shape of what was inside. A shotgun. By its length the barrels had been sawed off.

*Naw.*

I gotta say something.

But his mouth was filled with cotton wool as he handed the bag to Spider.

# Chapter Four

Leaving Karen in the truck, they followed Spider, going back the way they had come. Cleve wondered if Choc knew about the shotgun. He was sure Patty and Tag didn't, or Rob or Rick. Rob would have said something about it.

Spider turned up the first alley they came to that led towards Main Street. Trash cans stood outside back doors and a gutter ran along its center. Where the asphalt had cracked, weeds flowered colorlessly. At its far end moths looped and bumped around a single streetlight. Nobody was about. The air was gauzy and asthmatically hard to breathe.

Why had Spider brought a gun, FFS? Wasn't the shop supposed to be unoccupied? And if Cal Berry *was* there, would Spider stop at threatening him with the gun, or would he shoot him for real? Had being in the army made it easy for him to kill someone just like that? What if Cal had a gun under the counter and went for it?

Uneasily Cleve began to think this was about something other than getting money. Like revenge or something. Or like Spider and Cal Berry were part of some underbelly thing, maybe to do with drug deals. Cleve had always known there were dark currents in Claypit he didn't understand. Now he was being pulled down by them.

He thought of cop shows like *Law & Order*. If you went along with a crime then you were guilty too, unless you could prove you really didn't know what was going to happen. He thought of his cousin Vince, stuck in prison for five years, and of his mom and dad, and Terri. Even supposing the Bohemians got away with it, what would the money solve really? Even thousands would be gone soon enough. Now the idea of it made him sick.

"I can't," he choked as they reached the streetlight, and his voice was so thick Spider looked round, not understanding.

"What?"

"I'm sorry, dude. I can't do this."

Spider's eyes were black and glinting. Cleve thought he was going to vomit. It was so hard to not just go along with things; to be the uncool one. The others looked away, faces blank or in shadow, waiting on Spider. Cleve fought a rising urge to apologize; to beg to be allowed to change his mind and offer to carry the gun-bag to prove his commitment to the Bohemians, to the thrill. The image of Spider repeatedly smashing the rifle butt into his face flashed up in his mind.

After what felt like about a week, Spider shrugged. "So go home, dude."

"I left my bike at yours."

"So walk."

Cleve licked his papery lips and nodded, feeling a thin relief trickle down inside him like urine down a little kid's leg. Because Spider could have told him to go wait with Karen, and Cleve would have done, and right now Karen was an accomplice, and Cleve would be an accessory too, even though he had partway punked out, if he was with her. If they got caught.

Still he couldn't just go. These were his friends, and the moment he turned his back on them he wouldn't have them anymore, and that was frightening, and the summer break had only just begun.

After a while Choc murmured tensely to Spider, "We doin' this or not, man?"

Spider nodded, gave Cleve a last look, and led the others away. The only sound was the soft clicking of Rob's crutch. At the corner Tag looked back, and Cleve thought he looked scared. Then he was gone.

The moment was broken, and in a way the world was too. Cleve was not a robber, he was a teenager alone in a nameless alley off a seedy backstreet. A good boy who ought to be home in bed. A young man with no friends.

The thought came to him then that Spider couldn't fire the shotgun, not with those missing fingers. That meant he was planning on someone else using it. The thought was ugly. Cleve had never really considered whether Spider and Karen were good people; it had only mattered that they were cool and made things happen. Now he thought actually it did matter, maybe a lot. Not good on the "s/he never curses" level: deeper down.

Lifting the lid of a nearby trash can, he tugged the balaclava from the back pocket of his jeans and dropped it in, replacing the lid carefully so it didn't clang. The thought of the long, in a way defeated, walk back to Spider's depressed him, and then he would have six humid miles to cycle home.

It seemed like a bad idea to risk being noticed by passing cars ambling down Paper Street on the night of an armed robbery. Instead he decided to make his way through the backstreets of the Triangle to the footbridge, cross over, then cut across and round to Spider's from the high school. Paper Street bent east on its way to the mill so the distance would be about the same.

An aching need to be someone else, somewhere else, rose up in him then, and he felt absolutely alone.

Avoiding the street where the pickup was parked, he followed a narrower one that slanted, then curved, farther into the Triangle. This was the only part of Claypit where the streets weren't laid out in a regular grid. Cleve liked that – it was more human, less Camazotz-y, than Milltown – but it meant you could quickly get lost in what was in fact quite a small area.

So it was that he found himself drifting to an uncertain halt in front of a funeral parlor. Across the street was a nameless, featureless storefront that had tarred boards up in place of plate glass. Above an entry-buzzer by its windowless door was a pink neon triangle not much bigger than a kid's night-light, and a surveillance camera angled high in the frame looked down on what Cleve realized was the intimidating entrance to Discretions, Claypit's only acknowledged gay bar.

While some bars might bend the rules, or accept obviously bogus IDs, Discretions didn't, and it wouldn't admit the jocks from the college who occasionally tried to bluff their way in for (they claimed) the scandal value. Cleve knew the pink triangle was the symbol the Nazis sewed on gay men's clothes before sending them to the gas chambers, and he didn't get why a gay bar would want to use it, even if it was ironic somehow. He imagined sadness and ugliness inside. He couldn't connect the gay porn he'd seen online, which was all brightly-lit six-packs and waxed chests, with that, or with anything that was real in his life, or reachable.

People were real in porn, obviously. That was the whole point: they were *really doing it*. But it was fantasy too, with all the untidy, scary stuff tidied away – the stuff that showed how you got from A to B; from a lonely gay boy in a dying southern town to a confident gay guy rolling around with other hot guys, probably in LA, possibly next to a swimming pool, mostly only wearing shorts and trainers, or Speedos.

And then it didn't give any clue as to how you found someone to love.

Cleve couldn't imagine ever buzzing on that door. It was one of the many things he couldn't imagine about his adult life. He ran a hand over his buzz-cut scalp. The back of his neck was damp with sweat.

Just as he was about to go on, the club's door opened. Purple light spilt onto the sidewalk as a man came staggering out. Older, heavyset, in a check shirt and blue jeans worn over Cuban-heeled boots. His face was illuminated briefly before the door closed again. It was Cal Berry.

Cleve moved back into the doorway of the funeral parlor. Being seen by Cal the night his store was robbed seemed like another really bad idea, and Cleve didn't want Cal to know that he, Cleve, knew Cal went to Discretions. If Cal found out, then it felt like Cleve would have to share with him that he was gay too, or it would be unfair, and he really, really didn't want to have to do that.

Cal was obviously drunk – he was now leaning heavily against the boarded-up storefront – and Cleve had to decide whether to try to get past him, which would mean risking being seen but reaching the bridge ahead of him, or sneaking along behind, which would be safer but would take about ten times longer, judging by Cal's unsteadiness.

Cal dropped a bunch of keys, squatted with a grunt, felt about for them in the dark, found them, stood up, dropped them again, squatted again, groped again, stood again. To watch all this was painful, but Cleve realized that once Cal got to the end of the street he could catch up to him without giving away that he'd seen the older man coming out of the Claypit gay bar.

Instead of heading homewards, however, Cal Berry

lurched off in the direction of his store. Cleve swore under his breath. The instant Cal turned the corner and was out of sight, Cleve hurried down the cross-street in the opposite direction, breaking into a run as he reached a street he reckoned ran parallel to the one Cal had turned onto, aiming to get ahead of him and cut across in time to warn Spider and the others.

It was strange how fear distorted distances: he came to the street behind the liquor store quite suddenly, and at right angles to where he was expecting it to be. The backyard door was closed, no one was on watch, and there were no sounds from inside. Had they been and gone already? Surely there hadn't been time.

"Spider!" Cleve whisper-called, cupping his hands round his mouth to channel the sound and stop it spilling out more widely. "Spider! Choc! Berry's comin'!"

From somewhere above came the squeaky sound of a window-frame being forced up. Then a light came on. Looking up at the house he was standing in front of, Cleve saw there were no curtains in the window, or blinds.

*They lean out and look down, my face is gonna be the one gets connected to the robbery*, he thought. *Not the others: me.* He slipped away quickly, his heart hammering.

Not wanting to bump into Cal Berry, who, drunk as he was, might still remember him well enough to pick him out later in an ID parade, Cleve headed in the direction of the intersection where the Tyler statue stood. He had a vague plan to go up onto Main Street, check out the front of the liquor store, and if there was nothing to see, make his way back to where Spider had parked the truck. If it was gone that would mean they had cleared out in time and everything was cool. If not, he could at least warn Karen.

A glance at his phone told him it was nearly one a.m. They had planned the robbery for then because late on a

Sunday night the center of town was supposed to be dead. For somewhere dead it was pretty lively, however, because now he heard sounds up ahead: soft male voices calling to each other – "No, you"; "C'mon now"; "Your way"; "Ssh!" – and furtive clonks of things knocking against something hollow and metallic.

Cleve slowed to a dawdle. Cal Berry was likely still staggering along somewhere behind him, so he didn't want to turn and go back. Also, he was curious: who were these other people out in the night, and what were they doing?

Where the side street met Paper Street Cleve stopped. He was one small block south of the Main Street intersection. The sounds were coming from there. He leaned forward and looked round the corner.

A surreal sight met his eyes.

# Chapter Five

There, in the middle of the intersection, were four men in balaclavas. They wore sneakers, jeans, dark vests or tank tops and small backpacks, had the slender build of teenagers or young men, and the skin of their bare arms was various shades of brown. Some had bangles on their wrists. One wore fingerless black leather gloves.

Like cowboys at a rodeo they had lassoed the statue of Colonel Tyler by the neck, and had gathered together to pull it sideways, leaning back and out, bracing themselves as if to bring down a steer. Suspended overhead, the junction stoplight gave the scene an artificial quality as it cycled through red, amber and green, like something in a film or a play.

Though their faces were covered, Cleve didn't think any of them went to Welt –at least there was nothing in their physiques or physicality he recognized – and his first thought was they must be Pit Boys, but there was something about what they were doing that was more like a prank than a real crime, and the Pit Boys didn't play.

His mind flashed then to the real crime he had almost

been involved in, that might still be happening. Sneaking along Main Street to check the liquor store from the front would be impossible now.

With a screeching, tearing sound the statue of Colonel Tyler started to bend towards the tugging, grunting youths. Evidently it was not only hollow, but the bronze from which it was cast was thin to the point of flimsiness, because, though the booted feet remained welded to the base, the ankles folded in on themselves. Abruptly it tilted over and, with a metallic clang that echoed along Coleman Avenue, up China Row and down Paper Street, plunged headfirst down onto the asphalt. There it split open like a chrysalis.

"Shoulda filmed it," one of the youths said to the others, breathless, excited.

"How we pull it down and film ourselves at the same time?" another objected.

A third produced a phone from his pocket and began to film the fallen Confederate hero where he lay. Soon all four balaclava-clad young men had their phones out. One – the one wearing fingerless gloves – placed his foot on the bronze chest, posing like a hunter on a trophy kill. "Slave owner," he said, and bent over and spat on the unseeing bronze face. Another laughed, dancing as he filmed, jerking his hips joyously, and the rest joined in, and strange sensations lanced through Cleve as he watched this.

Then – and this was the true beginning of all the weirdness that summer – the air around them compressed and blurred, and a single bolt of lightning cracked down from the cloudless sky. It struck the stoplight, sending it swinging and bouncing on its wire. A burst of white sparks scattered from the top of it, making the boys below hunch, and the surrounding streetlights cut out, plunging the intersection into darkness.

That was all strange enough – no way had the air

been heavy enough for a storm, even a dry one – but then Cleve had the impression that a door had opened in one of the unlit buildings across the way. It appeared as a floating rectangle filled with blue-white light. Something dark moved across it or stepped through it, and the door closed, or the rectangle thinned, narrowed to a line, then vanished. It left no floater on Cleve's retinas, so maybe it had just been the burn from the lightning flash, an optical illusion.

The young black men were now hurriedly unlooping the ropes from around the statue's neck.

Then sirens began to wail as two or more cop cars came speeding towards the intersection from the east, therefore inevitably passing the liquor store. Would they notice a robbery in progress and peel off to investigate?

*Shit.*

The black youths broke up and pelted off in different directions. Cleve turned and ran back the way he had come. His main thought, apart from getting away from the immediate danger, was to go help his friends – if they hadn't already shot through, that was – even though it would mean putting himself right back in the trap he thought he had escaped. He had no excuse to offer if he barreled into Cal Berry talking to the cops round the back of the store.

At least he had got rid of his balaclava. But what if they searched the trashcans, found it, and tested it for DNA? He had sweated into it for sure.

Maybe he should go get it.

As he reached the rear of the liquor store the whoops of the sirens fell silent: the cops had pulled up somewhere close by.

Finding the back of the store as it was before, Cleve hurried on. An alley a couple of units along cut through to Main Street and he made his way up it. Peeping round the corner he saw Spider and Choc, their hands cuffed behind them, standing between two hulking uniformed officers, one of whom had his weapon drawn and held loosely at his side. Choc had been mouthing off by the look of it, because just then one of the cops yanked on his cuffs sharply to shut him up. Tag was face down on the sidewalk, being cuffed by a heavyset officer who knelt on the small of his back. A woman officer gripping her by the elbow, Patty stood to one side, crying into her hair for all she was worth.

The gun bag lay on the ground between Choc and Spider, still zipped up but radiating criminality. Two cop cars were pulled up on the slant in front of the store, their lights revolving silently, and an officer sat in one of them, radioing the robbery in. A dazed-looking Cal Berry was talking with one of the arresting officers, shooting glances at Spider. Cleve now saw Rick and Rob were in the back of the other car. Rob's crutch stood between his legs, and he and Rick leant forward as though their hands had been cuffed behind them.

No sympathy for the disabled, then.

Cleve looked past the sorry scene. A third cop-car was pulled up at the intersection, next to the fallen statue. Hands on hips, and wearing sunglasses at night, a police officer looked down on it, then looked around him, a sentinel of the law who mostly couldn't be bothered. He squatted on his haunches and examined one of the abandoned ropes, maybe trying to figure out whether this or the robbery was the more prestigious case.

Now two pickup trucks came sculling along, Confederate flags on poles billowing behind them. Hardcore Milltown Boys with gleaming eyes and flushed faces spoiling for a fight, preferably an unfair one, on Claypit's "racial fault line." Cleve hoped the black boys had got off the streets: he was sure not all of them had run north.

One of the cops put his hand on Spider's head as, with his hands cuffed behind him, he awkwardly got in the back of the nearer car. Tag was now crying as hard as Patty, looking more like he was nine than fifteen.

Coulda been me, Cleve thought, and in the warm air his hands turned cold, and his fingers cramped up.

He turned from the sight and went to go warn Karen, but when he reached the spot where Spider's pickup had been parked it was gone. Cleve hadn't seen Spider give Karen his keys, but supposed he must have done: Cleve knew she could drive. Maybe the sound of the sirens had spooked her. Maybe Cal Berry had walked right by her, even (though he couldn't imagine why) spoken to her, and she'd freaked. She didn't seem the type, but then how keen had she been on the whole robbery idea in the first place?

Several windows were lit up in nearby buildings that hadn't been before, though no one seemed to have come out to see what the fuss was about.

No way Cleve could risk Paper Street now. A teenager who didn't even live in the area, and one who it turned out knew all the suspects, getting let go by the cops after being stopped walking away from the crime scene? Even Johnny Cochrane couldn't swing that one.

No: he would follow his original plan and go to Spider's the back way. Tempting though it was to head straight home, even though it would be a long walk, he didn't want to risk leaving his bicycle at Spider's. Better to go collect it before the cops showed up to turn the place over and make connections. His mom had made him get it invisibly marked at an anti-theft event the police had organized at his school, and the irony of that putting him in the frame for armed robbery would be too painful, the consequences too totally unfunny for it to ever be a cool anecdote.

He came to a skewed intersection he didn't recognize and tried to figure out where he was. There were no streetlights to help or street names to prompt him. The image of the curious blue-white rectangle he thought he had seen after the lightning bolt struck came back to him then: the sense of someone stepping through a door; and his hackles rose, in response to static, maybe, or from a sense of being watched. No lights were on in any of the houses here, but someone could be standing unseen in the dark, looking out.

Off to his right he heard a low rumbling sound, familiar but he couldn't think what it was until the skateboarder rolled into view. A young black man, dark skinned, lean, almost slight, and Cleve's exact same height, he wore a cut-off tank top that showed off his arms and shoulders, a black backpack, a studded leather wristband on one wrist, black rubber bangles on the other, fingerless black leather gloves, tight black jeans and red Cons.

He was the one who had been posing big game hunter-style with the fallen statue.

The black balaclava he had had pulled down over his face earlier was rolled up into a skullcap now, and his large eyes were dark with fear. His lips were full and his chin was small, and he rolled to a halt ten feet from where Cleve stood, stepped on the board's tail and jumped its nose deftly into his hand. Perhaps he thought Cleve was a Paper Boy and that he might be able to use it as a weapon if he had to.

On the board's underside was a portrait of Prince with a Ziggy Stardust lightning bolt on his face. Prince and David Bowie were two rock stars Cleve had only learned about from the documentaries that came on TV after their deaths a couple of years ago, but he had instantly found both of them intriguing because of what could only be called their queerness, and because they were men.

"Cool board," he said.

The other boy nodded, then shot a look back the way he had come.

"Cops won't come down here," Cleve said. "They got

distracted."

"By what?" Though it had a nervous crack in it, the young black man's voice had a pleasing grain, like maybe he was a singer or something. Just two words, and he sounded way more educated than any kid at Welt County.

"The liquor store gettin' robbed. Maybe you should get rid of that, though" – Cleve pointed at his rolled-up skully. "It's kind of a dead giveaway. I'm Cleve."

"I'm Roe," the other said, touching the balaclava uncertainly but not removing it, and Cleve at that point assumed it was "Row" as in boat, but was to find out later it was short for Monroe, and Roe shook Cleve's hand when Cleve came forward casually and offered it, but didn't provide a way into any sort of soul handshake or hip hop style lean in like the black students at Welt County usually did. Looking around him, Roe added, "And I'm like, totally lost."

"You tryin' to get back to the Pits?"

"Hardly."

"Where, then?"

Roe hesitated, then said, "The Side."

"Okay." Cleve knew that was the better-off part of black Claypit and was to the northeast, up Pine Bluff and next to where the Illitabi ran down, though he had never been there and had no picture of it in his mind. "And you want to get round to there without being seen on Main Street?"

"I do."

Out of nowhere Cleve imagined kissing Roe, and Roe responding, and his heart lurched. On this weird night anything seemed possible, even something like that, something good. An averaging out of luck, maybe, after all your friends had been dragged off to jail. Cleve didn't really believe in God, or not a God that actually did anything, but he did believe there had to be a balancing of fortunes, some sort of cosmic fairness.

"Best way is over the footbridge where it crosses to just by the high school," he said. "Then you kinda follow the storm drain along – the river, I mean. Back alleys run behind yards most of the way: you can go down 'em. They'll bring you out pretty much opposite where you want to get to." Off Roe's look he added, "I know, dude. It's Milltown, and the Milltown Boys are out for blood tonight. But we ain't all like them."

"You live there?"

"Friends do. I live in Coleman East, out past Tanner's Cross."

"Okay." Roe ground his jaw. "Okay."

"I can show you the way."

"And why would you do that?"

Cleve smiled. "Couldn't leave a stranger in distress, I guess."

"Very *Streetcar Named Desire*."

"Is it?" Cleve smiled more broadly. "I guess that makes you Blanche."

"Hardly."

"We can go this way," Cleve said, blushing. He had figured out where he was while they were talking.

# Chapter Six

Skateboard in hand Roe fell into step beside Cleve, and they turned down a side street that Cleve reckoned ran parallel to the one Discretions was on. He half wished they had had to go past it: the gay bar would have been an excuse to start a conversation that might have gotten interesting.

Cutting through back alleys, they zigzagged south east. The Triangle was only a couple of blocks wide, but that night it seemed somehow expanded, filled with secrets and possibilities. They walked slowly, as though neither was in a hurry for their journey together to end. A black cat followed them for a while, then slipped away into the shadows.

"So what were you doing back there?" Roe asked.

"Tryin' to warn my friends about the cops, but I was too late: they'd been busted already."

"We didn't think they'd show up so quickly," Roe said.

"You was lucky they got distracted."

"By the robbery."

"Uh-huh."

Roe glanced at him. "That was you?"

"Well, my friends." Cleve felt oddly embarrassed by the admission. "Once a shotgun came into it I was out, but that only happened real last minute. Why were you pulling the statue down?"

Roe pushed out his bottom jaw. "You know why."

"Do I?"

"You ought to."

"Maybe," Cleve said, and his bare shoulder bumped Roe's, and it was warm and smooth, somehow flawless, and a small charge shot through him. "Maybe you could school me."

"All those statues are racist propaganda," Roe said. "They're like, fake history."

"Fake?"

"They fold up like tinfoil because they were cheap and mass-produced by these rightwing assholes who wanted to, like, intimidate black people from claiming their rights after the civil war, and then later, during the nineteen-sixties."

Roe spoke fast, as if expecting interruption and contradiction, with a Valley Girlish undertone surely picked up off the TV, and even a hint of a sort of Englishness, and Cleve knew for sure no Pit Boy in the history of Claypit had ever talked like that. "I never knew all that," he said, when Roe paused for breath.

"Well, now you do. Thank the United Daughters of the Confederacy."

"What are they, dude, a Klan sorority or somethin'?"

"Pretty much, yeah."

"I reckon history class is way more interesting in your school than mine," Cleve said. "Where *do* you go to school?"

"Tyler A."

That was the fancy all boys' private school that Cleve cycled past daily, on his way to Welt. Hidden behind ivied brick walls and glimpsed through wrought iron gates, the kids at Welt High called it Hogwarts. Kids from the Tyler Academy never hung out on Main Street, and Cleve hadn't imagined it to have any black students. "I never talked to anyone from there," he said.

"Then we're both broadening our palates," Roe said. "I never talked to anyone from Milltown."

"Coleman East."

"My bad."

"How much longer you got?"

"Before parole? A year."

"You don't like it, then?"

"It's more like parole from here." Roe gestured extravagantly. "Claypit. The town named after mud and a hole in the ground."

"You goin' to college?"

"Somewhere decent, with any luck. I'm doing an accelerator, which means I have to read a ton of classics this summer so I can, like, try for a couple of scholarships. I'm weighing up HBU or not HBU." Seeing Cleve's blank expression, he added, "That's 'historically black' blah blah. You?"

"I don't reckon my folks can afford it. And I ain't really scholarship material."

Roe looked at Cleve but didn't comment, and Cleve liked that he hadn't offered false assurances.

In a little while they came to the river, which at that point sluiced through a wide, flat expanse of concrete, and the narrow footbridge that spanned it. On the far side Cleve's school and the serried rows of depressingly identical houses that made up Milltown waited silent and still. Above the light pollution from the streetlights the stars were visible, filling the sky more and more thickly the higher you lifted your gaze.

"Did you see something weird, just after the lightning hit?" Cleve asked as they reached the steps that led up to the bridge.

"What do you mean?"

"It looked like – I don't know, a light, or more like a door opening, like when it's dark and the lights are on inside. Then it closed."

"I thought maybe a power-line fell and hit the ground and caused a flash," Roe said. "Or a cable, like, broke and swung down and hit some metal or something." He shrugged. "Physics isn't my métier."

Though the bridge was wide enough for two to walk abreast, Cleve gestured for Roe to go up the zinc steps ahead of him. Roe went up quickly, his movements light, and Cleve got a look at his butt. It was neat, high and very present.

Cleve caught Roe up and they crossed the river side by side. "That's my school," he said, pointing at the set of featureless, bunker-like blocks that made up Welt County High. The fifteen foot chain-link fences surrounding the basketball courts, put up to stop balls from endlessly bouncing off into the river, made it look so much like a prison he felt compelled to add, "It's okay really," and then, clumsily, "It's pretty mixed."

Roe nodded.

In the middle of the bridge, which was surreally long because it had to arch over not only the actual river but also the wide banks of concrete that bordered it, Roe dawdled to a stop. Though he didn't really smoke, Cleve wished he had a cigarette to offer: it would have made this a moment instead of just random. "You don't need to be scared of Milltown," he said.

"No, I thought –" Roe looked back along the bridge and squinted as though trying to make something out. "I thought someone was behind us, like, following."

Cleve looked back, but he couldn't make anything out: just shadows. Certainly there was no one else on the bridge. He smacked the back of his neck, killing a mosquito. Then he gripped the metal handrail with both hands and lent back, stretching out his bare arms. Roe evidently noticed the bulge of Cleve's biceps when he pulled himself upright again because he said, "Maybe you could try for a sports scholarship."

"Nah," Cleve said, pleased. "I'm okay, but I don't excel."

"Maybe you haven't found what you're, like, good at."

"Maybe. D'you play any sports?"

"All jocks are my enemy."

"Oh."

"It's like why does throwing a ball about make them the übermensches?" Roe asked irritatedly. "Glorifying athletes leads to fascism. It's, like, the handmaid of eugenics. Superman stumping for US imperialism."

"Like in *The Dark Knight*," Cleve said.

"The film?"

"The comic."

"Frank Miller, right?"

"Yeah. In that, Superman stumps for Ronald Reagan."

"It's all bogus anyway," Roe said. "Hitler wasn't blond. None of the Nazi leadership were the Aryan ideal. They were mostly kind of trolls, actually."

"Not all jocks are blond," Cleve said. "Like, at my school about half of them are black. And not all blonds are jocks."

"True." Cleve became aware of Roe's eyes on his buzz-cut – his hair was what his mom called dirty blond – and found himself blushing again. "And are any of the black jocks blond?" Roe asked.

"One is sometimes. Like, in the vacations."

Roe smiled. "Some jocks are actually okay," he conceded. "Like, I know a couple who are cool."

"The ones who helped you pull the statue down?" Cleve asked. Roe nodded. "Are they all from Tyler A?"

"They're pretty much every black student there," Roe said. "In fact they *are* every black student there."

"You must've been pretty mad about it."

"It kind of started as a joke, then…" Roe shrugged.

Cleve thought of the robbery and how that had got started; and also that he had better get going. After seeing Roe through Milltown he would have to double back to Spider's house on foot, pick up his bicycle, then cycle the six miles home.

"Okay," he said reluctantly, "I guess we better get going." As an afterthought he asked, "Did you find out if the others got away?"

"My phone's dead," Roe said. "It was like the lightning did something to the battery." He wriggled it out of his pants pocket. "Huh, there's some charge now."

"You wanna call 'em?"

Roe scrolled and thumbed, listened, and hung up. "Straight to voicemail," he said. He tried two more numbers, each time ending the call without speaking.

He looked worried, and Cleve thought of footage of white cops killing black boys for nothing, for jokes, and felt afraid for Roe's friends, even if they were from Tyler A. He thought of the cop's hand on Spider's head, placed there to stop him from injuring himself on the doorframe as he slid into the cop car. Would Roe's friends be treated that way, with concern? He doubted it.

They crossed the Illitabi, descended the steps at the farther end, and went on, following the river along its eastern bank until it became a storm sewer, running underground. There, to get from one back alley to the next, they had to walk for several blocks along a wide and silent residential street. Cleve felt an unfamiliar, skin-crawly sense of being visible that it took him a while to realize was because he was with someone black.

In the morally ambivalent, mixed-up Triangle that hadn't mattered: both of them had been equally worried about being caught by the police, whatever their color. Here, though, ordinary people, ordinary white people –

Cleve was suddenly sharply aware of their, his, race – were the danger. Why would a black boy and a white boy walk together? It was abnormal, intrinsically suspicious, implicitly criminal. This familiar street was now hostile terrain, like in a video game, but real.

He and Roe walked fast, and in silence.

By the time they reached the old town square, which was at the east end of Main Street, two a.m. had come and gone. About a hundred yards along Main Street, in the direction of the intersection and on the farther side, was the entrance to Van Cleef Avenue. This, Cleve knew, led up into the Side.

Roe turned to Cleve and shook his hand again, prolonging the contact intriguingly, though in the low light his dark eyes were hard to read. "So, um, do you, like, have a cell phone?" he asked.

"Even Milltown boys have cell phones,' Cleve said.

"But you're not a Milltown boy," Roe teased.

"True."

"So do you want my digits?"

"Sure."

"Give me your phone." Cleve passed it to him, and Roe entered a number. "Maybe we could, like, go grab a soda or something."

"That'd be cool, dude. Definitely," Cleve said as Roe returned his phone to him. Cleve pressed "call" and Roe's phone buzzed once in his pocket. "Now you got mine," he added.

Roe smiled. They stood silent for a while.

"I hope your friends are okay, dude."

"Yeah."

Roe put his board down and pushed off, rolling away across the square on the diagonal. That late – or early – the sound of the wheels was jarringly loud, but there was no one to hear, and a minute later he had reached the turn into Van Cleef Avenue and was gone. Cleve sighed and turned back to face Milltown. It would be a long trudge to Spider's.

Now he was on his own the feeling of being hyper-visible left him, but a sense that he was being followed, possibly induced by Roe's fears earlier, grew on him to the extent that several times he stopped in the middle of the street and looked back. Maybe it was some animal – deer occasionally wandered down from the hills and got as far as Milltown, and there were always cats and stray dogs around – or maybe it was a paranoia that was natural after the arrest of the others. Either way, he saw and heard nothing.

It took him an hour to make his way to Spider's. The pickup truck stood in the driveway but the house was in darkness. He opened the screen door and tapped gently on the frame. No one answered, and he guessed Karen had dropped the truck and left immediately. He checked his phone as he hadn't thought to earlier. She hadn't tried to call him, but he didn't think she had his number anyway.

His bike lay where he had thrown it down that after-noon. He wheeled it to the street and pushed off. The chain needed oiling and the tires were kind of flabby, but once he built up a little speed it rolled along easily enough.

Avoiding Main Street he pedaled back through the middle of Milltown, heading diagonally northeast. His parents weren't expecting him back until the afternoon so he would have to be quiet going in, though coming home earlier than expected was better than coming home late.

Under the streetlights everything seemed artificial, even fake. When he had been with Roe it had all felt real, even hyperreal, but sinister. But then Roe giving Cleve his number had felt like a dream, and Cleve didn't know if he would have the courage to call him: to risk a daylit reality in which you found you had nothing in common; that you were, in fact, almost enemies.

He pedaled into the town square. The façades of its buildings looked as if they had been inspired by movies about Ancient Rome, and put up either back when Tanner's Cross was the center of what would later become Claypit, or just to seem like they had – like the statue of Colonel Tyler, as it turned out. The police station was a street back, and he thought momentarily of cycling past it but decided not to: it wasn't like there was anything he could do, and if he was seen it would look suspicious.

Fifteen minutes later he was passing the Tyler Academy, and its wrought iron gates and high brick walls set him thinking of Roe, and the intrigue and excitement of meeting someone like no one you had ever met before – someone who, despite everything, might share with you that one crucial thing that would make it you and him against the world.

Soon he was on Coleman East, and the road ran smooth and straight before him. A wall of hills rose steeply to his left, and to his right the woods spread dense and level. In the middle of those woods stood the ruins of the Tyler plantation house. The edges of the night sky were paling, and Cleve felt exhausted and spacey and free.

# *Chapter Seven*

O f the two hundred and seven students at Tyler A, precisely four were black. Apart from Roe, in his year there were Eriq Anthony and Will Williams Jr; and Mikey Fanning was in the year below. Other than excellent grades – all of them had had the "twice as good" mantra drummed into them in the womb – they had little in common. Roe was a punk-goth-geek, Eriq an easy-going jock, Will a wannabe revolutionary-slash-future dentist, and Mikey an aspirant rapper with a flair for astrophysics – but at certain key moments being black drew them all together.

Though none of them were present for it, the fight in the town hall over the statue of Colonel Tyler was one of those moments, and it turned out to be the most significant in any of their lives so far.

Each of them had experienced those particular moments of cultural cringe that afflict black students in majority white settings. Earlier that term Ms. Key, Roe's well-meaning Eng Lit. teacher, while setting up *Huckleberry Finn* for class discussion, seemingly noticing Roe's melanin for the first time, had blushingly stumbled her way around introducing Huck's runaway slave companion, managing to say, like oafish dad Peter Griffin in the cartoon *Family Guy*, "Er, um, er, N-word Jim" to derisive snorts from Roe's white classmates. She hadn't managed to get through a single sentence after that without a falter and a glance at her sole black student, and by the bell Roe was as exhausted as she was. Black History Month was always excruciating for all of them, and to add yet another level of awkwardness, this year *Othello* was a set text, and Eriq was mixed race.

Frustratingly, those sorts of psychological assaults – Roe, Eriq, Will and Mikey had quickly added "micro-aggressions" to their lexicons, and dropped the term into conversation at every opportunity – were mostly pretty much well-meaning, but there were others that weren't; that tipped over from, say, competitive putdowns into actual, blatant racism. Black was cool, it was athletic, it was authentic, it was courageous; but it was also ignorant, illiterate, tasteless, got unearned handouts and legs up, and got itself shot and choked by the police.

And so, despite their real-life presence, blackness at Tyler A was mostly a media-constructed white fantasy. As a consequence, though Roe, Eriq, Will and Mikey were all in their different ways well enough liked, they knew they were not exactly seen by the other students. Jokingly they were told they weren't "really" black precisely because they *were* really black, and not the fantasy the white boys had bought into. This was, of course, defeating. And then they were told by many of those same boys, meaning well and intending connection, that they didn't see color, just "people." That too was defeating. It was an odd pressure, like being a deep-sea diver, maybe, and mostly you barely noticed it because it was omnipresent.

Too, there was this: being at Tyler was a privilege, one their parents sacrificed for, for which they had to act grateful, and for which in some ways they *were* grateful.

It had high standards, both academic and athletic, great facilities, picturesque grounds, and was ambitious for its students.

The school had been founded in 1890 with an injection of cash from Randolph Tyler, son of Welt County's once-preeminent slaveholder and former colonel in the Confederate army, and Randolph Tyler wished his father honored. "Our illustrious founder," as the headmaster said on speech and prize days. No mention of the slaves he exploited, tormented, starved and, Roe supposed, raped, was ever made in Black History Month, which pretty much tended to begin and end with Martin Luther King, with a dry slice of George Washington Carver in the middle.

They had their different ways of coping with the cognitive dissonance.

Eriq mostly went full jock; Will quoted Malcolm X, Franz Fanon, Amiri Baraka and Huey P Newton like scripture. Mikey, despite never having left Claypit, punctuated his talk with the latest hip hop slang.

Roe, who had never left Claypit either, deracinated into goth and metal, and made a fetish of London punk, affecting John Lydon's snarky delivery (sometimes accidentally slithering over into Tim Curry's in *The Rocky Horror Picture Show*) – much to his parents' puzzlement and oftentimes extreme annoyance.

These different tribes at Tyler were Venn diagrams whose circles barely touched, never mind overlapped, but none of that mattered when they were together. Then, under the put-downs and one-upmanship, there was the relief of understanding without words.

On warm evenings, after classes and sports were done, once a week or so they would hang out on the old bandstand, legs dangling, chins resting on the low brass handrail, and talk the sun down. They called the bandstand Oz, after the notorious TV show about the men's prison – "See you at Oz" – and the other students were "Gen Pop," which in the TV show was short for "general population" – those inmates not admitted to the prison's privileged inner realm.

It was on a humid evening about a week before the end of term that they found themselves at Oz, discussing the Tyler statue. Roe's dad was a member of the town council, and he and other black elected officials had been calling for some time for the statue to be taken down.

"Eff the statue, he should try and get the school re-named," said Eriq, lighting a cheap cigar, both in hopes of looking like a sophisticate, and to deter the mosquitoes birthed by the billion in the ornamental fishponds nearby.

"I nominate Mumia Abu-Jamal Academy," Will said.

"We all know who Mumia is, Williams," Mikey said. "No crown for you."

"Eff you, Fanning," Will said, giving Mikey an amiable finger.

"Apparently Oglesby said he was, like, amazed my dad would, like, send his kid here if he hated Tyler that much," Roe said.

"That fat fascist pig," Will said.

Lee Hunter Oglesby, Claypit's Confederate-minded white mayor, was rumored to be in the Klan, and he didn't flat out deny it: the black votes he lost that way were outnumbered by the white votes he gained when election day came around.

"It's glandular," Mikey said.

"What, fascism?" said Eriq, blowing cigar smoke at the hovering mosquitoes.

"He could drop four hundred pounds and he'd still be a pig at heart." Will said.

Mikey turned to Roe, who'd heard the details of the meeting from his father at dinner the night before. "So then what happened?"

"My dad kept, like, pushing for it to be taken down and stuck in a museum, preferably next to the bathrooms."

"He actually said that?"

"Just the museum part."

"Don't embroider, Jones," Eriq said, then added, trying to sound like Basil Rathbone's Sherlock Holmes, "Just the *facts* if you please."

"My dad was like, really mad, which is like, really unusual for him," Roe said.

"How did it end up?"

"Like, super-lame," Roe said. "They agreed they'd put a, quote, historically contextualizing plaque on the base of the statue, so anyone who wanted to stand in the middle of the road could learn about how slavery was bad but white people had it bad too, or something even more lame."

"And that's it?" said Eriq.

"Literally."

"Eff that, man. We gotta do something," said Mikey.

"Fight the power," Will added.

"Do what, though?"

"What other towns are doing," Eriq said. "Take it down."

"By hook or by crook," Roe said.

"By hook or by crook," the others echoed.

They talked in much the same way that Cleve and his friends had talked about robbing the liquor store, and at around the same time; and, though their purpose was righteous, in very much the same way idle talk became a plan, speculative at first, then concrete, then committed to. Will floated involving the lumpenproletariat.

"Who?" said Mikey.

"Well, you know, man: the Pit Boys."

None of them knew any Pit Boys, however; and, though nobody would have admitted it, being good boys from the Side, they were scared of them. Eriq and Mikey had been to O'Flaherty's, the Main Street pool hall, a couple of times. Roe and Will had never been inside. Class in Claypit was nearly as much of a divide as race.

Unexpressed was the fear that the poor black citizens of Claypit, many of whom were struggling on welfare, not only wouldn't care much for quixotic gestures like pulling old statues down, they might be alarmed by, and even resent, any action that stirred up the racial hornets' nest. The town had recently lost a bid to build a private prison on its rundown southwestern side which would have brought hundreds of construction jobs to the area for both black and white workers. Instead there was little work, opioid abuse was worsening, tensions were high, and the Confederate flag still hung largely unchallenged on its pole in front of the town hall.

"Okay," Roe said, "I'm gonna say it. White students?"

"You're such a pawn of the integrationist agenda, Jones," Will said.

"Reverend Roe-L-K," Mikey said. "And *he* got shot."

"So did Malcolm," Eriq said. "No crown."

"There are only four of us," Roe said. "Is that even enough to, like, pull down a seven foot statue? Blah blah fulcrums, mass, leverage, whatever."

"They don't give an eff, Jones," Mikey said, meaning the white students.

"Some of 'em talk the talk," Eriq said.

"Maybe. So?"

"They get it. Or they act like they do."

It was true some of the white Tyler students could be vociferous: they'd seen *Django Unchained* if not *Harriet*. They knew the past was full of poison. It might have been just to annoy their financially stretched parents, and the establishmentarian teachers who were attempting to instill in them a patriotic pride in white Southern history, but they did speak up. In a way it was easier for them, because it was more a game than a reality – a TV show, and they could change channels any time. In another way, though, they risked ostracism, even getting beaten up, by the whitely prouder and more sociopathic.

For instance Andrew Mellon, Tyler's star quarterback, had stood up in a history lesson and said, "We deserved to lose the war because we wanted to keep owning people and that was pretty sick." He had been applauded by many of the other white students as their teacher blustered and threatened. And Eriq reckoned Andrew would have done the same even if his black friend on the football team hadn't been there to impress, though you could never quite be sure.

They discussed the issue at length, assessing who was at least somewhat woke; who was just attention seeking; and who would be able to accept that it would be the black students calling the shots. In the end it felt like too serious an action to take a chance on the unproven commitment of anyone who could at any moment just bail and fade into the background, so eventually they decided not to involve any white students.

Deciding to go it alone made them feel more heroic, more revolutionary.

They watched footage online of other takedowns, both legal and illegal, and considered how best to get the job done, settling on a Sunday night at around one a.m., when the streets of central Claypit would be at their quietest and emptiest.

Only Will had ever been arrested before. Though that was for nothing worse than stealing sweets when he was twelve, he called the others "virgins," which was irritating.

They divided up their tasks. Will would bring the ropes, Eriq the balaclavas, and all of them would bring their phones, in order to commemorate and disseminate news of the takedown, which would have to be done fast.

*

Roe lay on his bed in the dark, fully dressed, waiting for midnight to come around. At least he didn't have to sneak out of the house with anything incriminating on him.

But what if his parents caught him?

He guessed he could text the others, providing his mom didn't confiscate his phone. Of course any of them might get busted trying to sneak out too.

Dread grew in him as the minutes crawled by: the transition from mouthing off to actually doing something was an alarming one. Usually Roe thought what his dad did was boring, even futile, but now he worried how getting caught might damage his dad's standing, and therefore the family generally. He thought about the line Marilyn Manson sang about being a rebel from the waist down, and wondered what kind of rebel, if any, he really was.

"I am not a number, I am a free man!"

That was a statement of defiance from the opening credits of a sixties British TV show he had become obsessed with recently called *The Prisoner*. In it an unnamed secret agent is knocked out with gas, brought unconscious to a picturesque yet sinister village on a mysterious island, and tortured psychologically to extract information from him. Sentient giant balloons rolled along the twisty, Italianate streets, smothering anyone who tried to escape.

Roe had become fascinated with the show because of its anti-authoritarian premise, and also because the blazers and boaters the characters wore so exactly matched the Tyler Academy uniforms that it must have been someone's idea of an in-joke; and the gothic architecture of the school was as fake as that of The Village. He and the other geekier students would imitate the okay-finger-to-the-eye sign off the characters did in the show, and say "Be seeing you" to each other in wayward British accents, to the annoyance of the jocks, who didn't get it and knew they didn't.

This was different, though. This was real life. This was a town where the police smashed in the heads of young black men, even of black boys. Where twelve year old Will was arrested for stealing sweets, not just scolded as a white boy would have been. Where the Klan wasn't a joke like in *Django Unchained*, where they forgot to cut eyeholes in their hoods.

He was really afraid now.

Downstairs, the grandmother clock chimed twelve silvery strikes. As if released from some spell, Roe got up and crossed to the window, which he had opened fully earlier on because it squeaked noisily when you pushed it up in the frame. Checking his skateboard was strapped firmly in place he pulled his backpack on and climbed out through the window, feeling like Spiderman or (if he was honest) Catwoman as he crept along the garage roof on all fours, then dropped down noiselessly onto a strip of adjoining lawn. The parched grass was crisp underfoot. Claypit spread out in front of him, glittering; behind him was the black crown of the hill.

Where Cedar Close, the street he lived on, joined the top of Van Cleef Avenue he set his board down and stepped on, keen now to get there, get it done, get away. In the stillness of the night the new wheels he had blown a month's allowance on, and which were so much quieter than the old, sounded alarmingly loud as he hair-pinned his way down to Main Street.

At Mikey's suggestion they met one street north of O'Flaherty's, in the lot of a closed-down truck dealership they all knew how to find. Roe arrived ahead of the others, so had the unnerving experience of having to creep about and check every possible hiding place to make sure no one else had got there before him.

"No BPT," Eriq had said, and by 12:45 they were all there, crouched behind a dumpster, nerving themselves up for the task ahead. No one seemed to be around, there was no traffic on the streets, and there was nothing to do but do it.

Eriq handed out the balaclavas; Will kept hold of the ropes. Romantic as the idea of lassoing the statue was, none of them were cowboys and everything would be about speed, so they had agreed ahead of time that Mikey, the nimblest of the four, would climb up and lob the nooses over its head.

As one they rolled down their balaclavas. Roe's heart was hammering. He had never been so afraid in his life, and he wanted to vomit. Led by Eriq, he and the others left the lot at a purposive jog.

It had all gone well up until that weird lightning strike, though even that hadn't mattered much: no one had been electrocuted, and they'd already pulled the statue down and filmed it lying split open on the ground, as hollow as Lost Cause vanity; and Roe had put his foot on its cracked chest in triumph as the stoplight exploded overhead and sent sparks cascading down like a firework display, and that had been a sort of glory.

Then the sirens had sounded and the cop cars had come hurtling towards them, faster, probably, than anyone had ever driven down Main Street before, and Roe and the others had run in panic, a compass exploding, and by chance he'd at first headed southwest, into streets he didn't know, rundown streets scheduled to be replaced, now not to be replaced, by a private penitentiary.

He'd had sense enough to double back to Paper Street, ducking down behind a parked car when a pick-up truck filled with white youths trailing a Confederate flag came roaring up it in the direction of the intersection.

Until then he had only been thinking of getting caught by the cops.

Once the truck was out of sight, his skin crawling and his heart thudding, Roe ran across the street and made his way into the Triangle. There, wanting to keep well away from cop-infested Main Street and at the same time not accidentally find himself in blue collar, all-white Milltown, he'd lost his way. That was where he ran into Cleve, and they had their unexpected conversation, and Cleve escorted him safely through one of the scariest parts of town, if you were black.

Roe had never had an actual conversation with a boy like that. A Milltown Boy but not, tall, with pale, muscled arms, a blond buzz-cut, well constructed shoulders, one of which he habitually dropped, narrow hips, a lopsided smile and a snub nose, a strong, almost lantern jaw, and eyes Roe thought were greeny-blue. A boy who was almost an armed robber, but not. He looked like trouble – he probably *was* trouble – but Roe didn't think he cared.

Roe had had crushes on white boys at Tyler but this was different, and not just because it was happening outside the social bubble of a single sex school, where kind-of-gay romances were tolerated because they were better than no romances at all. Those had never felt real to Roe: they existed to be grown out of, and so were really heterosexual. Whereas Roe was actually gay, because he couldn't see how desiring a guy because he was a guy could be a prelude to the opposite and not its contradiction.

He thought how appalled his parents would be if he brought Cleve home. Though they encouraged their son to make friends who might become useful social and business contacts – part of the point of sending him to a private school – they were visibly uncomfortable with the few white classmates he had had over. Being seen by his white friends with his black parents in their black home, and therefore as black himself in a way he wasn't quite at school, had made Roe uncomfortable too. His friends' efforts to be polite had somehow jarred, even though weren't good manners good manners everywhere? He hadn't been able to work out what was wrong.

"Be seeing you," he had said at the door when he saw them out, making the OK sign, but the whole thing had been awkward, even embarrassing, and he hadn't repeated it.

Going to their houses was easier. Their parents would studiously pretend not to see race, which at least didn't require Roe to actually do anything. They would smile indulgently at any reference he made to classic literature, mainstream "white" TV and films, or classical music, and he would pretend their strained facial expressions were normal. Possibly they even were – though the way his friends rolled their eyes implied otherwise. He did his best to make believe he was in one of those zillion white teen shows he'd watched growing up, and adjusted his performance accordingly. And then sometimes he was Patrick McGoohan, the imprisoned secret agent known only as Number Six in *The Prisoner*, trying not to let them break him, playing along as Number Six did while fooling them all and escaping.

*One more year.*

Getting back up onto the garage roof without making a noise was harder than he had expected. Wrenching the statue down had strained his arms, the outflow of adrenaline had left him weak, and he had to avoid accidentally yanking the rose trellis away from the wall.

Clambering onto the water butt, he managed to pull himself up without getting tangled in the trellis or caught on the guttering, though he had to stifle a grunt as he hauled his ribcage onto the edge of the roof. Then he swung his right leg round and up, using his knee for purchase. Once on the roof, he crawled along on his hands and knees and in careful slow motion climbed through his bedroom window. It was just after 3 a.m.

Plugging his phone in to charge, he texted *U OK?* to Eriq, Will and Mikey, which he hoped wasn't too potentially incriminating, and waited.

No replies came.

Maybe their phones had totally shorted out.

Hopefully they'd all managed to get away.

*Or...*

He brought up and looked at Cleve's number, contemplating sending him some sort of a message – *Home OK?* – but didn't.

Putting the phone face down on the side-table, he squirmed out of his jeans, pulled off his tank top and socks, and lay back on his bed just in his briefs. It was too hot for covers. He closed his eyes and tried to go to sleep. Already the events of the night felt like a hallucination, a fever dream.

# Chapter Eight

Around an hour after Roe closed his eyes, Cleve was sneaking his bike along the side of his family's home and quietly laying it down on the parched back lawn. The house was one of about forty scattered along one side of Coleman Avenue East. Facing them were the woods.

At the far end of the long backyard, beyond a waist-high chain-link fence, scrub-covered hillside rose steeply. The back – kitchen – door was as usual unlocked, and Cleve opened it and went inside. All was quiet and breath-warm. He went over to the sink, ran the tap a while, filled a glass, and drank. He refilled it and drank again, and immediately felt stronger and more resilient. Somewhere overhead a pipe juddered, squawking as he turned the tap back off and making him tense up.

Coming home early wasn't a crime, he reminded himself.

But planning a robbery was a crime. Even failing to report such a plan probably was. Or at least it was the sort of thing the cops could use as leverage when they showed up at your door. He wished he had Karen's number: Spider might have managed to call her before the cops took his phone off him.

From the lounge off the hallway came a gasping sound that built up to a whooping that was almost a laugh. Then came choking. In a short while the choking subsided into gasps again, then mumbling. If you weren't used to it you would have freaked out, but Cleve barely reacted as he went down the hall to look in on his sleeping mom.

Myrtle was propped up Buddha style on the sagging couch, with pillows at her back. She made these noises every night, over and over – sleep apnea, it was called – never seeming to really wake up, though often in the morning she complained she was tired. But was that from sleeping badly, or some other problem amidst the many that constantly assailed her health, both physical and psychological?

It was hard to be sympathetic about the same thing, over and over.

Myrtle slept sitting up because she was now so heavy that if she lay back her throat would collapse under its own weight and might actually kill her. She could still move about the lower floor of the house, but could no longer get upstairs, and had to shower standing up, in the utility room.

For this she now needed Cleve's dad's help. They tried to keep things light, and his mom would joke about her weight: "Time to hose the elephant," she would say. But she was visibly getting heavier, and in a slow motion car-wreck way it was frightening to witness as well as intensely frustrating. She talked of "gaining" the way other people talked about aging, as though it were unavoidable.

Myrtle's weight affected them all. Chubby at twelve, his little sister Terri fretted over calories and sugar content, and looked up diets online. Several times this year Cleve had smelt vomit in the bathroom after Terri had used it.

Cleve didn't know what to do about any of that. "Don't be boring, sis," he would say when she asked him if he thought she looked fat, but her intensity creeped him out, and he knew he over-thought what he ate too.

As a consequence, he spent more and more time out of the house, and that was how come he met Spider and Karen. His father Kenneth was tolerant of the friendship: he had been wild in his youth. Myrtle, however, loathed them, calling them "Bad News Bears." The recently-discovered tattoo on Cleve's hip had confirmed her in her view.

"That's child abuse, that's endangering a minor, I'm gonna call the cops on that tramp," she had fumed.

"How's it endangering a minor?" Kenneth had asked, gently rubbing her broad back as Cleve wheeled her oxygen cylinder over.

"It's endangerin' his future prospects," Myrtle said, batting Kenneth's hand away irritably and rummaging in a bucket of salted buttered caramel popcorn the size of a wastebasket.

"It's not on his face, Myrt."

"Not yet!" she cried. "It's an addiction!"

"Can't argue with that," his dad said, trying to lighten things by rolling up first his right sleeve to reveal a blurry, sword-pierced heart, then his left to display a skull surrounded by clumsily-inked roses. "Don't get any more," he said to Cleve. "Your mom's right."

"Thank you!" Myrtle exclaimed breathlessly.

"'Sides, everyone's gettin' 'em now," Kenneth went on. "Queers are getting 'em. You don't wanna look like a queer."

Cleve had flinched at his dad's words. Both his parents sort of knew he wasn't into girls, but they never said anything about it, maybe thinking he'd grow out of it. This was an idea he found deeply weird. Like, would fancying Megan Fox be a pit stop on the way to fancying Chadwick Boseman? If so, how? If not, why would the reverse be true?

He didn't think they'd kick him out of the house when they knew for sure, but you could never tell about things like that, so he wasn't rushing to bring it up with them. Leaving his mom asleep on the couch, touching the newel post for luck, he quietly made his way upstairs.

In hopes of a breeze his sister had left her door open. It was opposite the bathroom, and though he didn't put the light on, and closed the lid rather than flushed, when he came back out she called softly, "Cleve, that you?"

"Naw, it's an axe murderer."

"Kill Cleve first please, axe murderer."

"Will do."

"Night, axe murderer."

"Night, victim number two."

Cleve's bedroom was up three steps and at the side of the house. Being under the eaves, it was stifling. He opened the dormer but there was no shift in the air. Cleve quickly stripped to his briefs and lay back on the bed, resting the water-glass on his breastbone and staring up at the ceiling. His mind turned to Roe, to his full lips, to the curves of his butt as he climbed the steps up to the bridge. Cleve's nipples prickled and he stirred sweatily on the mattress, setting the bed-frame creaking. Through the dormer window the paling sky was dulling the starlight. He closed his aching eyes.

Cleve woke just before 8 a.m. He could hear his father and sister banging about, following his mom's directions for fixing breakfast. His eyes ached from lack of sleep, but he knew he wouldn't be allowed to lie in on a Monday morning.

"Cleve!" Myrtle called. "It's on the table!"

Cleve rolled out of bed, rummaged in his dirty laundry bag and dragged out a pair of shorts and a singlet that didn't smell too obnoxious. Barefoot he went and washed his face, ran his wet hands briskly over his buzzed scalp, then went downstairs.

"Didn't hear you come in," his dad said as Cleve took his place at the table. Scrambled eggs and hash browns waited on his plate. Terri was eating dry toast and flicking her hair between bites.

"It was kinda late so I was tryin' to be quiet," Cleve mumbled as Myrtle set a glass of orange juice in front of him, then heavily took her seat.

After they had eaten in silence for a while Kenneth pushed his plate forward. "We need to talk," he said.

Cleve groaned inwardly. He wondered if somehow they had already learned about the robbery. Though the TV and radio were off, maybe a friend or relative of one of the others had called the house phone with the news. Myrtle was the kind of mom who might turn him in to the cops, while wailing how it was "for his own good."

No, she wouldn't do that, she wasn't *that* dumb, but –

Now his thoughts were scattering. What if one of the others, and it only needed to be one – probably Patty, she could be kind of a moron – had mentioned his name to the arresting officers? What if he'd left something incriminating at Spider's that he'd forgotten about and the cops had found it? What if –?

"Son, I need you to step up to the plate," his dad said. Sports metaphors were always worrying, though not quite as bad as military ones.

"Okay."

"The facility called this morning." Kenneth meant the Cleaver County Rehab Facility. It specialized in people struggling with prescription medication addiction who couldn't afford to pay for treatment, and Myrtle had been on the waiting list for more than two years. "They got a place for your mom."

"When?"

"Tomorrow."

"Wow."

"Yeah."

"Um, that's great, right?"

His dad nodded, grinding his stubbly jaw – he usually shaved after breakfast, when he shaved at all. "Yeah," he said, reaching out and taking his wife's hand. "So I have to drive her there, and it's pretty much four hours each way. Owing to your mom's weight and Terri bein' only twelve they can give us family accommodation up there for a week."

*Family accommodation.* Cleve imagined the three of them sharing a grim, thin-walled motel room for a week. It would, he didn't doubt, be the kind of room where you had to feed the TV with quarters, and in between brief visits to his mom they would sit in a row on the vibrating bed watching crappy reruns of crappy network TV shows. When they did see her, Myrtle would be in some sort of nightmare locked ward, tearfully begging for food and pills.

So much for his summer break.

Soon he would have to go pack. He reached out and took his mom's hand and tried not to act pissy. "That's great," he said.

"I think you're old enough," Kenneth said, "mature enough, to stay home alone. Do you agree?"

Cleve's heart leapt. "Yessir," he said.

"There's a bunch of chores'll need doing: I'll leave you a list, and I expect you to get through it without any chasing up."

"Cool. Thanks, Dad, I will."

It was exciting to be trusted, and strange and exciting to think that his mom was actually going to be helped by someone. In Cleve's head "the facility" had become a perpetual alibi, something that was always going to happen in some never-never future that permanently excused you from doing anything now.

He looked at his mom, who seemed distracted. She started to move her head back and forth as if to a beat only she could hear. "Don't have that bitch here," she said.

"Mom swore!" Terri said.

"Promise," Myrtle said.

"I promise," Cleve said. It felt like saying so out loud might keep harm from their door.

"Okay," she said, not looking at him. "Okay."

The rest of the morning passed slowly, and Cleve stuck close to the house. Any time a vehicle went by he tensed and listened for it turning in, worried it might be the cops. He checked his phone repeatedly but no calls or texts came. Patty and Tag were minors, so would presumably have been released into adult care in the morning, but even if they had thought to try and get in touch with him, neither had his number. The others, Spider, Choc, Rob and Rick, were probably still being held, Spider and Choc for sure. Fearing self-incrimination, Cleve didn't risk calling them.

As time dribbled by with nothing happening Cleve's thoughts increasingly turned to Roe, and how for the first time in his life he, Cleve, would be in the house on his own for more than a couple of hours. He could have someone over with no nosy kid sister to tattle on him, no housebound mom to listen in, no dad wandering in randomly between one mechanic's job and another. The prospect was intoxicating, and overwhelmed any guilt he might have felt that it was the result of his mom's bad health. Sprawling on his bed, he pushed a hand down the front of his shorts and gripped himself.

At 5 p.m. Myrtle called excitedly from the lounge –

"Cleve! Cleve!" – and he came hurrying down to see what she wanted. Usually it was to cope with spiders, of which she had a horror, or occasionally mice.

The TV was on as it always was in the afternoon, though untypically it was turned to the local news channel. Cleve's stomach lurched in anticipation of a report on the liquor store robbery – if it included pictures of Spider and the others his mom would immediately remember his unexpected early return – but the lead story was the pulling down of the Tyler statue.

Of course it was.

Perhaps because last night had been so strange, he had half-forgotten that that had really happened, and that it would be a big deal. A liquor store robbery was small potatoes, but the statue thing might even go national.

Myrtle looked round at him. A carnival dish of caramels rested on her outspread stomach. "That wasn't you, was it?" she asked.

"Naw, Mom, of course not."

"Okay," she said. "Because it's bad."

Cleve wanted to text Roe, to warn him, or alert him, or just to say something, he wasn't sure what. That he was on Roe's side, maybe, because he found that he was. The faces of three black teens came onscreen. The contrast had been jacked up to make their features look harsh. Their names were Eriq Anthony, Will Williams Jr. and Michael "Mikey" Fanning.

No Roe. Cleve exhaled.

"...students at the prestigious Tyler Academy," the newscaster was saying.

"A practical joke, I guess," Myrtle said.

"More like a protest," Cleve said.

"Against an old statue?"

"Against an old slave-owner."

"Honey, that was forever ago." Myrtle sighed, unwrapping a caramel and popping it in her mouth.

"They've got to let go of it. Let bygones be bygones and stop being so mad about everything. I mean, we're struggling and they're at a private academy. Likely owing to that affirmative racism. Or sports."

"Yeah, but having slave owners as our heroes," Cleve said. "Maybe it's us who have to let go of stuff."

"You got to be proud of who you are," his mom said. "You can't just throw it all in the trash, or who are you? Nothin'."

"We was never upper class, though. We never owned slaves, did we? Tyler ain't us."

Myrtle sighed. "Honey, could you fetch momma a soda?"

"Sure, Mom. Diet or regular?"

"Regular, honey. My sugar's crashin'."

Cleve went and fetched Myrtle her soda. By the time he got back she had switched channels, so had missed the robbery story for now. If he was lucky she wouldn't hear about it before she went away.

He wondered if the clinic could really do anything for her. To him the weight was the problem, more than the painkillers and antidepressants. If she lost weight she'd be in less pain; if she was in less pain she'd be more mobile and less depressed. His mom used to like people, but over the last two years had drifted into being a recluse. Now she was often moody and snappy, and rarely smiled.

Watching her life grow smaller and smaller sent the need to expand his own rampaging through Cleve, and recently he'd started picking fights with her, and with his dad and sister, because of it. Why couldn't she just eat less? And why did the rest of them conspire and feed her so much crap? Sometimes he tried refusing her, but what was the point? Terri wouldn't, or if not her, then Kenneth – and hunger made her turn nasty real fast. So you fed her and the volcano subsided.

He wondered what his dad would make of the statue being pulled down. It was an attack on white people, sort of, or white culture, whatever that was, really, and his dad had no black friends or even acquaintances so far as Cleve knew, but still he didn't know how Kenneth would react. His parents had never championed the Confederate flag, and didn't use racist language, but his dad had voted for Trump, for "change," and he remembered a sense of unease in the house back when Obama won – the only other president Cleve had consciously lived under, as he had been six years old when that happened. He remembered his mom tutting when Obama threw himself behind gay marriage – no, marriage *equality*.

Maybe it was because Obama was black – well, mixed race – Cleve had grown up with a sense that racism and homophobia were basically the same thing: the laser of prejudice turned this way or that, though no doubt some white gay people were racist, and some straight black people were homophobic.

Terri seemed like she would be cool about her big brother being gay, with a black boyfriend. She had a poster of Jaden Smith above her bed, looking dreamy-eyed and androgynous, surrounded by pictures cut from magazines of him in dresses and skirts. Cleve liked him most in the black Lycra bodysuit he wore in *After Earth*. The movie sucked, but Jaden was cute as he fled CGI baboons and condors, and clambered about tomboyishly in trees on a quest to save his injured father.

He imagined Roe in such a bodysuit and, feeling a giveaway flush of excitement, went up to his room to text him.

*RU OK? U seen news? It was great 2 meet. Meet again soon?*

Send.

# Chapter Nine

R oe's family's home was near the top of the Side, two thirds of the way along Cedar Close. As a general rule the higher up you were, the better off you were; or at least (as in the Jones's case) the longer your family had lived there. The shingle-roofed, clapboard houses were mostly built in a nineteenth century style, well-maintained and quaint, with verandas and porches, and carefully tended front yards ablaze with flowers. The summer air was fresher up there than it was down below, and there were few, if any, mosquitoes.

From the breakfast room at the back of the Jones home you had a view across north Claypit all the way to the glinting line of the freeway that demarcated its dusty, far-off western boundary. Beyond that was a further line of low, purple-brown hills. These curved round to the north, where they subsided into the worked-out china clay mines of the Pits. At dusk, as the lights came on, the town looked beautiful; by day it was bleached out, run-down and rust-pocked.

Over the top of Pine Bluff, the hill up which Cedar Close slanted, and to the east was Black Bear Gulch, down which the Illitabi River cascaded. The residents of the Side – the first community of black homeowners in Welt County – had not been permitted to build their houses on the summit of the Bluff, because then they would have committed the offence of overlooking prosperous, all-white Tanner's Cross residences on the opposite side of the gully. Consequently Pine Bluff remained crowned by ancient woodland, among which Roe and his two older sisters had rambled freely as children. His great grandmother lived independently in a small house at the upper end of the close.

Roe's life had been spent in attractive places – the Side; Tyler Academy – yet he knew the price was a conformity so smothering it at times left him literally breathless. If you lived on the Side, you not only acted like you were supposed to, it was your duty to think what you were supposed to think too.

"I am not a number, I am a free man!" he would mutter to himself as he dressed for school in the mornings, echoing the embattled Number Six, hero of *The Prisoner*, and affirming his determination to resist another day's social programming at home; another eight hours' brainwashing at Tyler A.

Having worked hard their entire lives to achieve comparative prosperity and social standing, his parents couldn't understand his resentments, his need to resist.

Or actually, maybe they did – or at least had done in the past. The row of vinyl LPs under the record player, through which Roe had flipped idly many times, included Funkadelic albums with surprisingly pornographic, even queer lyrics and titles like "Jimmy's Got a Little Bit of Bitch in Him"; and the by turns abrasive, and conscious, Public Enemy, Tupac Shakur, NWA and Ice T, never played now – or not in Roe's hearing – let Roe know there was a time when his father bopped his head to "Fuck Tha Police" and *Pimpin' Ain't Easy*, in amongst more melodic, romantic and partying albums by Boys II Men, Blackstreet, D'Angelo, Nelly and others. Those his dad and mom still played, especially when they had friends over. The songs on them were part of Roe's mental furniture to the point where he never really thought about whether he liked them or not, but he did construct his own musical tastes in opposition to them.

*I am a free man.*

But of course reaction wasn't really freedom.

Like Cleve, and for much the same reasons, Roe slept brokenly that night, and like Cleve he had to be called down to breakfast by his mother. Neither having a summer job, both resented being dragged from their beds just to eat at the same time as the rest of the family, who didn't have a choice about it.

On top of that, Roe's summer break looked set to be ruined by the lowering presence of his sister Phyllis, back from her freshman year at university and, to the chagrin of all, including herself, pregnant. She had arrived with the announcement that, though she had broken up with the (unnamed) father, she was going to keep it. The unlucky fetus exerted a baleful influence on the household from the moment of its revelation.

Roe pulled on jeans shorts and a tank-top and wriggled his feet into his sneakers – his parents forbade bare feet or thongs at the table – pricked through his Mohican, and clumped downstairs. His mom, dad and sister were waiting. Though he was by now a self-proclaimed atheist, he hadn't the strength this morning to refuse to take his mom's and Phyllis's hands and bow his head for his dad's brief prayer.

More than ever he felt himself filled with secret knowledge they had no understanding of.

That morning the feeling was literally true: the news of the statue coming down couldn't have reached them yet, as they didn't have the radio on, the TV was for evenings only, and the local paper didn't come out until Thursday.

His sister gave him a sharp look when he came in, though, and he worried she might have seen something on her multiple, constantly-updated social media feeds. Equally she might just have resented him for being the last to come down. She wore a white vest, gray track pants and pink trainers, no make-up, and her braids were pulled back so tightly she looked face-lifted.

It was impossible for Roe to remember the fun person she used to be. Their older sister Kathleen, eight years ahead of Phyllis and now married and living in Seattle, had never been close to either of them, but Roe and Phyllis had been a team. Today she just looked sour, a stranger.

His dad was smartly dressed as always, in well-cut navy pants and a crisply ironed white shirt, the conservatism of which was offset by French cuffs, gold-and-jade cufflinks, and a yellow silk tie. Nowadays Earl's stomach overspilt his belt when he sat down, and his hair was thinning, but he was still a handsome man, and solid, not flabby.

Roe's mom, Angela, wore a smart, pale blue skirt suit and a flame orange silk blouse. Her figure was trim, she was simply made up, and her hair was carefully coiffed – straightened enough to be "professional" while still being visibly Afro in texture. The blue of her nails matched the blue of her suit, but the attention she paid to that kind of detail was somehow efficient rather than self-conscious or overdone. She worked as an administrator for the Claypit Education Commission, quite high up. It was the sort of job where Roe never understood what she actually did, though to be fair he never really asked her. Committees were a part of it, and policy statements, and meetings that, like his father's, often ran on into the evening.

Slanting through the side window, the morning sunlight sparkled on the china, and on the glassware in the display cabinet, hurting Roe's sleep-deprived eyes. He thought of Klaus Kinski's vampire count in *Nosferatu* murmuring wearily, "I vont to be alone in ze shadows viz my thoughts" as his mom set the cafetière down on its cork coaster. All the windows were open, and a pleasant breeze stirred the curtains. This was the side of the house air and light were allowed to penetrate freely; the front room had to be saved from the bleaching powers of the sun as determinedly as if it were papered with antique watercolors.

"So what are your plans today?" his mom asked, pouring his dad's coffee.

"Mostly reading," he said, both of them taking for granted that she meant "other than the numerous chores you will of course do first."

"What are you reading?" his dad asked, glancing at Roe over his half-moon spectacles, and wincing only slightly as his eyes landed on his son's Mohican in the bright, hard-edged morning. A report on something municipal lay open next to his plate.

"It's only hair, Daad," Roe had said, dragging out the "Dad" Englishly when he first revealed his new look to his parents the day after term ended. He had done it himself, using two mirrors, with clippers his mom had bought as an economy measure, a pointed offset against his school fees. "It'll grow back by the time school starts again, and also it's, like, a statement in support of my genocidally massacred American Indian brothers."

Actually it was a homage to British punk, but Roe knew that wouldn't play so well with his father.

"It's your head," Earl had said with a grunt of displeasure, before turning back to the TV, adding, "And stop saying 'like' every other word."

Handily, Roe's hair crime paled by comparison with Phyllis's transgression. He toyed with dying it blond while he could get away with it.

"*Moby Dick*," he said.

His father nodded. It was a classic, reputable and lengthy. Nothing more needed to be said.

Roe's mind went to his phone, which was upstairs in his room: no phones at the table was another Jones family rule. No texts had been waiting when he woke in the morning; no calls had been missed in the night.

His father would find out about the statue the instant he reached the office, and Roe thought maybe he should say something about it to him. He hated the idea of his dad looking foolish.

Yes, he should definitely say something.

His heart rate began to accelerate, and the cereal he was spooning into his mouth became so tasteless he could hardly swallow it.

"Are you alright, son?" his mother asked.

"Sure, Mom," he mumbled. "Sorry."

The unexpected, disconnected word of apology evidently puzzled her, and she was about to say something more when, from the front of the house, there came the single whoop of a police siren.

Roe's hand jerked so violently he knocked his orange juice over. His mom went for some kitchen roll to mop up the spill. Roe and his father stood together, and Earl shot his son a penetrating look as a heavy knock came at the front door.

Adjusting his belt, Earl went down the hall and opened the door. A uniformed police officer was standing there. He was young and white, solidly built, clean shaven, and wore mirrored shades.

"Councilor Jones."

"Officer Peel. Good morning."

Roe, his mom and Phyllis hung back in the kitchen doorway, looking on. Behind Officer Peel they could see two police cars parked in the street, blocking their drive.

Several officers were in each. All the officers were white.

The brief sounding of the siren had brought all their immediate neighbors out onto their porches or into their yards, to watch. To witness.

"You've heard about the statue?" Flush-faced, Officer Peel thought to remove his sunglasses as he asked this. He was standing awkwardly on the porch as if he hoped to be invited in.

"What about the statue? You mean the Tyler statue, I presume?"

"I need to speak to your son, councilor."

"Do you? Why?"

"See, we caught three of the boys who pulled it down, but a fourth got away."

"The statue got pulled down?"

"Yes, sir. Last night, just a little after one a.m."

"And was there any description of the young man who got away?"

"Well, they all wore balaclavas over their faces, so not facially. But they was all – black."

"Were they?"

"They had bare arms, so..."

"So that's your description? Out of the thousands of young black men in Claypit, that's your grounds for coming here to interrogate my son?" Roe's dad's voice was level, but there was anger in it.

"Thing is, councilor, the boys we caught, they all go to the Tyler Academy and..."

"And?"

"The principal told me they only got four black students there. Four black boys pulled down the statue, them three was from there, and then one got away. And your son, well he's the fourth black boy at Tyler A."

Earl rolled his neck bullishly: Roe heard the vertebrae crackle. Then he sighed. Roe wanted to vomit. Now his dad would have to let them take him away. Trapped in an interrogation room, how many times would he be able to say he knew nothing before cracking? Fuck, the balaclava was sitting on his chest of drawers!

Roe began to hyperventilate. Why had he done it? What had been the point? This? He'd have a criminal record and –

His mom's hand found his and squeezed it so tight the pain broke his panic. Her face was taut.

"Our son was home all night," Earl said.

"I'm obliged to ask you, are you sure, sir?"

"I'm quite sure, officer."

"Youngsters do sometimes sneak out without their parents knowing."

"My son had food poisoning last night. My wife sat up with him until after one, then came to bed. He was making regular trips to the bathroom after that."

"That's right." Roe's mom came forward now, screening Roe and Phyllis from the officer's gaze. "You know how the hot weather can be. Curdled mayonnaise, we think."

"Maybe I could step inside," the officer said.

"Maybe if you hadn't sounded your siren," Earl replied, blocking the door, giving no ground.

"And you're sure your son was home all night?" the officer said. "I mean, it's something you could swear to, councilor? If it came to it?"

"Yes."

Officer Peel looked round at the respectable black folks of Cedar Close. Several had their phones out and were filming the situation from a distance that could not, he knew they knew, be deemed interference with his ability to discharge his duty, and they were on their own property. "It's pretty bad, what those boys did," he said. "Pretty much pure vandalism."

"You can rest assured I'll be contacting their parents directly," Roe's dad said meaningly. "To get to the bottom of it."

The officer nodded, then gave up. "Well, then, I thank you for your assistance, sir," he said.

"And as an elected representative and concerned parent I thank you for your diligence," Earl replied.

Putting his shades back on, the officer returned to his car. Roe's dad stood in the doorway and watched until both police cars had turned and driven away. He waved a hand to his neighbors to indicate all was okay and came back inside.

In silence the four of them returned to the kitchen and sat down at the table. Roe couldn't meet any of their eyes, and he was trembling as he waited for his father's inevitable explosion over his lying, sneaking out and general foolishness; for the waving and possibly even use of the belt.

It didn't come. Instead Earl put his hand on Roe's hunched shoulder, squeezed it and shook it, and then, for perhaps the first time in a decade, pulled his son into a tight hug, and Roe burst into tears.

Earl got Roe to give him the numbers of Eriq's, Will's and Mikey's parents, and made a series of fast calls – to them; to lawyers; to someone at Tyler A, maybe the vice-principal; to someone who might have been a journalist. As he was doing this Roe's mom left for work; Phyllis went upstairs to shower.

Roe sat slumped in the breakfast room, feeling pigeon-chested, tiny and fragile, only half-listening to his dad's conversations as Earl strode from room to room. Lawyers were discussed, along with possible charges, issues around civil disobedience, vandalism and activism; possibilities of suspension, expulsion.

"Well, there's the whole summer for things to cool down," Earl was saying, and for the first time, maybe, Roe understood what his father did, what his job meant. He had been so unafraid, dealing with the cop – or maybe afraid, but defiant – and he was unafraid now.

*My dad's my hero,* Roe thought. *Who knew?*

It was irritating and touching at the same time.

He looked up timidly as Earl came into the breakfast room. "Okay," his father said. "So it looks like we may be able to get most of the charges reduced from criminal damage to misdemeanors. With luck nothing on the boys' permanent records. Thank God no 'resisting arrest' charges got in there or we'd be in a whole other situation."

"Cool. Yeah."

"No footage has got online so far. I'll make a statement in session later today. That'll give reporters a constructive narrative to follow. We don't need white hotheads getting fired up and attacking people."

"Will it be on the news?" Roe asked, thinking of what they had filmed on their phones, and how it could be used against them.

"It will be and it should be," Earl said. "Stay in the house today. Don't answer the door, don't answer the phone. In particular don't speak to anyone from law enforcement or the school or journalists."

"Can I call my friends?"

"I doubt they'll be answering, but yeah, that's okay. They were all allowed home. But don't admit to anything. Not even casually or as a joke. Don't ask anything that could make it worse for them, or you. Just in case someone's listening in or reading texts or emails, or any social media – Twitter, Snapchat, whatever the hell else you kids use these days."

"Yes, sir."

"Okay, right," his dad said abstractedly, as though running through a list in his head. "I'm going to work now."

Roe went and got his father's jacket for him. Earl repeated his instructions as he slipped his arms into it, gathered up his papers and left the house. From the front door Roe watched him get in his car, back out, turn and head down the hill.

Overhead, the shower stopped running. Having no desire to hear his sister's opinions on the drama – she knew she was now well ahead in the respectability stakes, for the foreseeable future, anyhow – Roe wandered out onto the back porch. The sky was cloudless, the air already baking hot, and the charcoal streets and ash- and bone-colored low-rise buildings of Claypit looked even bleaker than usual. The few public parks were parched a urine yellow.

He wondered if his great grandmother would visit. As a kid he had been in and out of her house all summer long, sometimes with his sisters, more often on his own. Nowadays she seemed to dislike people coming over, apparently wanting social interaction only on her own terms. She had grown more overtly religious recently, and Roe's declarations of atheism had scandalized her.

"That school," she said. "It's making that boy a heathen."

"You mean secular, Grandma," Angela said. She and Earl were churchgoers by convention more than deep conviction, and had raised Roe and his sisters to be intellectually inquiring. His oldest sister currently identified as a Buddhist.

Roe's great grand had grunted and shaken her head, repeating "Heathen," not troubling to add the obvious "white." She considered black people had lost a lot since segregation ended, and it was true that integration had long ago done for almost all the black-owned small businesses that had originally financed the Side.

Roe's parents had struggled ideologically as well as financially with sending him to the Tyler Academy, which they knew couldn't root him in their notion of African

American cultural values, but was the best school in the district. It was either that or the brawling, disorderly Welt County High, which wouldn't champion black uplift either, and got poor exam results.

At home Earl and Angela worked hard to inculcate what the school failed to, making sure Roe knew who Shirley Chisholm was, and A. Philip Randolph – the sorts of activists they never got round to during Tyler A's sparsely observed Black History Month. Roe partway resented this – his championing of punk and heavy metal and gothic pallor was an assertion that he wouldn't be reduced to his parents' notion of blackness – but the names stuck anyway, as did the general impression that you could be black and do things.

You could change things.

As far as his great grand was concerned his atheism was something so taboo – more taboo, probably, than his as-yet-undisclosed-to-anyone gayness – that Phyllis's "accident" wouldn't boost his standing with her. What would his great grand think about the statue coming down?

He thought she would probably be more bothered by his Mohican.

He went up to his room, closed the door, sprawled face-down on the bed, and called his friends, Eriq first. All went to voicemail. He left no messages. At least he knew from his dad that they were all home and safe for now, unbeaten, unshot. But what would happen to them? Would Tyler A dare to expel 75% of its black students all at once? What they did was a political protest, not drunken vandalism, but maybe in the eyes of the authorities that made it worse.

What if they did all get expelled, and he was the single black student remaining? He really would be The Prisoner then.

He wondered what had already been put up on social

media. Would it be good or bad? Would it go viral? Become national news on regular TV? He had been filmed putting his foot on the statue. At least he didn't have any giveaway scars or tattoos on his arms. Maybe later on he'd want to claim it. Maybe...

He closed his eyes.

He woke with a jolt from jumbled dreams. *The balaclava*, he thought. *I've got to –*

He checked his phone: a message had just come through, and the buzz had probably been what had woken him. The time was 6:20 p.m. The message was from Cleve: *RU OK? U seen news? It was great 2 meet U. Meet again soon?*

Groggy but pleased, Roe messaged back. *Great 2 meet U 2. Yes. When?*

*2moro?*

Roe answered: *Cool.*

Actually he wasn't at all sure it would be cool for him to leave the house then, but the thought of Cleve's lips, his lopsided smile, overrode any hesitation. *So I am a rebel from the waist down*, he thought, though he'd done nothing sexual yet beyond jacking off. But he wanted to, and his heart, his crotch, his spirit and his DNA ached as he waited for the reply.

It came:

*Where?*

# Chapter Ten

*W here?*

It wasn't a tease: Cleve genuinely didn't have any ideas. He had $20 saved, which would be enough to go somewhere cheap; also his dad would give him housekeeping money for the week he and Myrtle and Terri were away. But where could a black boy and a white boy not from the same school or neighborhood go and hang out and not be challenged? Especially two boys who might be on a date.

Not Barney's Balls, that was for sure.

A park? All the public parks were baked into dust, and were in parts of town either almost wholly white or almost wholly black. Older men on welfare loafed in those parks, drinking alcohol or cough syrup hidden in paper bags as they slid into scary dereliction, while younger men played sports in the blaze, stoking each other up into ever more aggressive feats of machismo.

A wander in the woods, maybe? A ramble in the hills? Nah. Too vague, too hot, too bury-the-body-in-an-unmarked-grave. He and Roe didn't really know each other, after all.

Roe's reply came: *Violets Place*

*?*

*Diner on Crow Street*

Cleve knew that was a short street in the Triangle, and the Triangle was the one part of town where people mixed in, and you saw interracial couples sometimes. *OK I can find. 2moro, right?*

*Y. What time?*

*I got family biz in morning*, Cleve thumbed. *2pm?*

No reply.

A drip of sweat itched its way down Cleve's forearm, then reversed itself, seeming to trickle upwards. He looked down and saw a bee, clambering its way through the golden hairs. Moving carefully so he didn't scare it, he got to his feet and brought his forearm up so it was level with the open dormer window. With a puff of breath he blew it out of the window, and it swooped off into the deepening sky.

On the opposite side of the road the woods stretched away into the dusk. A small movement caught his eye nearer to, and he had the impression that someone standing on the other side of the road directly opposite his house had just stepped back under the cover of the trees. Spider, on the run? A cop staking him out? Cleve watched some more but saw nothing. His phone buzzed. *2pm. Be seeing U*, followed by a brown-fingered OK emoji.

Cleve replied with a generic yellow thumbs up and set his phone aside.

Anticipation thrilled through him. He had exchanged messages with guys online before, but nothing had come of it. He had been fifteen (claiming to be eighteen) when he first did it, and hadn't actually wanted anything to happen. He thought the men he messaged hadn't wanted anything to happen either, not really. Judging by what little they said they hadn't been interesting, and they sure hadn't taken any interest in him. Mostly a lot older, some of them had asked for photos, which he didn't send. He hadn't found any of them attractive, and even if he *had* wanted to meet up, how did you know that cute boy you liked the look of online wasn't really some grotesque troglodyte, the creepy school janitor using a ganked photo of Jaden Smith or whoever, or a girl stalker pretending to be a guy to get nude pix of a gay boy she fancied – or worse, some school bully who had hacked his way in somehow and wanted to control you?

Online was fantasy. This – him and Roe – was real. Like the robbery had been real, the statue coming down, the cop cars racing up Main Street, the arrests. And because he hadn't been arrested, and Roe hadn't either, Cleve could now allow himself to feel excited by the wildness of what had happened that night, by the improbable way it had led him to Roe; and excited about tomorrow.

He stayed in his room until the pizzas were delivered for dinner. Nowadays his mom mostly found cooking too much effort. Terri was too young to help out much, and it didn't occur to Myrtle to ask her son to help any more than it occurred to him to offer; and so a lot of the time they ate takeout. Usually it felt like a treat, and there were no plates or silverware to wash up afterwards, but there was something depressing about it too. It was a decline, and Cleve knew from his dad's occasional grumbles that it didn't help their finances any.

As always, two of the four boxes were for Myrtle.

Afterwards, while their parents watched *Judge Judy* reruns, shouting out opinions as the messy cases unfolded, Cleve and Terri sat on the stairs and talked. She had spent the meal surreptitiously picking the toppings off her pizza slices and balling them up in her serviette while everyone else pretended not to notice. Cleve put his arm around her shoulders and she leaned into him. Her body was hot, and her straight, shoulder length, dirty blonde hair smelt of strawberries.

"Do you think Mom'll get better?" she asked.

"Sure," he said too quickly. "I mean yeah, I think so. If she does what they say."

"What if she doesn't?"

"They probably have ways to get you to do what you're supposed to. I mean, like, they're supposed to be experts."

"I think she'll stay like she is. Just get bigger an' meaner."

Terri had never known their mom not on pills, not hugely overweight and volatile. Cleve, five years older than his sister, could remember Myrtle before she really lost control, but the memories were fading. There were photographs on the hall wall of him and his mom and dad at a theme park and she was only big, and was smiling; and other, happier ones from before Cleve was born.

"It's not our fault," he said. "It's something inside her."

"A hole," Terri said.

"Yeah."

"Why aren't we enough to fill her up?"

"You know she loves us, right?"

"I guess." Terri looked down, frowning.

"You get to spend a whole week with Dad, that's pretty cool."

"I guess." She sounded a little brighter.

"Dad'll take you places while Mom's getting treated."

"I wish you were coming too."

"Me too," Cleve said. "But Dad says I got to mind the house."

Right then he wasn't lying: he did want to be there for his mom and dad and sister. He knew, though, that "being there" would soon enough degenerate into bickering with Terri and arguing with his dad.

"Time for bed, Terri, honey," Myrtle called.

"Yes, Mom." Terri sighed, gave Cleve a hug and a peck on the cheek, and stomped her way to the bathroom, deliberately being noisy to prove to her listening mother that she was doing as she was told.

Cleve went to his room and looked up the Tyler statue story on his tediously-slow-to-start, semi-hobbled-by-parental-locks laptop. By then loads of pictures had been posted on Facebook, Twitter and Insta of it lying broken on the ground. Most of the comments were negative, some angry and some outright racist, replacing the "gg" of the n-word with swastikas so the social media algorithms wouldn't pick up on it and block them. Roe's arrested friends were there with red Xs Photoshopped over their faces, or bullet-holes.

A few posts were supportive, even combative, and Cleve felt he should post too, but he couldn't express his thoughts clearly or punchily enough to argue with so much anger and opposition. Instead he gave the pro-protest messages thumbs ups or hearts. Then, feeling gutless, he closed the laptop. Dissatisfied with himself, and disquieted by the hate, he tried to sleep.

The next morning he was up before the rest of the family and nervily laying the breakfast table – the one meal Myrtle moved from the lounge for. He heard his dad moving about upstairs, then heard him humping bags and cases down to the truck, and belatedly thought to help out.

Terri came down with her pink unicorn backpack on, dragging a bulging sausage bag. Cleve carried it out for her and stowed it on the flatbed with the others. Myrtle heaved herself through to the kitchen.

Unusually they said grace before eating, his dad leading the prayer. As he echoed the amen, Cleve felt a dreadful sense of futility. How could this work? How could his mom change?

Then again, she'd given him the gift of a week to himself, and there was Roe. There could be a change for Cleve even if Myrtle came back exactly the same. Just with another hope amputated, like the little toe she'd lost last year to diabetes.

As they'd all anticipated without discussing it, getting his mom into the truck was the hardest part of the whole thing. Their attempts to lift the ominously sagging, mysterious parts of her onto the backseat and shove them round without hurting her, failed. She repeatedly wailed in pain – or possibly, Cleve suspected, from hysteria about the hunger that lay ahead. "She could go on the flatbed," he suggested eventually, sweaty and breathless and frustrated after what felt like the hundredth panicked "I can't I can't I can't I can't I can't!"

"Your mom's not riding on the flatbed like a God-damn freak," his father snapped, surely frustrated himself, red-faced and humiliated on his wife's behalf. "Have some Goddamn respect and help her out here."

His face burning, Cleve did as he was told, and eventually all of Myrtle was pushed in, and she could lift and pull enough of her thigh round for Kenneth to close the door on her. He then pressed a roll of dollar bills into Cleve's hand. Cleve taking it from him became a sort of goodbye handshake. Kenneth met his son's eyes, nodded, then went round and climbed in behind the steering wheel.

Cleve lent in through the wound-down rear window and kissed his mom's flushed cheek as Terri clambered into the front passenger seat, pleased to be riding shotgun with her dad, a position normally reserved for her older brother.

The pickup backed slowly out of the drive, and Cleve waved as they drove away. And then, for the first time in his life, he was on his own, though he didn't feel the excitement of it yet. Any time in the next hour or two they could return for some forgotten thing, and of course they would call to remind him of some chore not on his list, or to exert some other form of parental control.

He went upstairs and showered. Then he had to decide what to wear. He'd never dressed for a date before, and all his clothes dissatisfied him. Did gay men dress for dates like straight men? Kind of, he supposed. But what girls wanted a boy to look like wasn't what boys wanted boys to look like. And too dressed up was also too noticeable. Anyhow, it was way too hot for a jacket.

Eventually he decided on a red satin basketball vest that fitted close around his torso, matching knee length shorts, white socks, red hi-tops, and a red wristband.

Fishing about in a dish on his bedside table, he rooted out a necklace of white pebbles he'd never worn and fastened it round his neck. It was quite tight, and one of the pebbles sat in the indentation just below his Adam's apple. It moved each time he swallowed, and the movement seemed somehow provocative.

He took it off. He'd put it back on when he left the house. He didn't want to feel too sensual yet, and there were still hours to go.

He turned his laptop on and looked at the posts on the Tyler statue story. There were about a zillion more since last night. He scrolled down, took a breath, and typed, *I'm white and those statues make people who fought to keep slavery look like heroes, so I agree with what happened.* He clicked on "post" and closed the laptop, fear surging through him.

It was ten a.m.

The fan inside the laptop rushed noisily.

# Chapter Eleven

T hough he had his driving license, and their neighbor, Dale Rippell, occasionally let him borrow his old, rust-holed pickup, Cleve decided to cycle to the diner. He didn't want to be tied to getting back when Dale said: for once he wanted to revel in there being no one to sweat him about mealtimes or curfews.

He set off at one, to give himself time to reach the Triangle and find Crow Street without having to rush. He knew it was a backstreet a few along from the one Discretions was on, but wasn't sure exactly where.

It was strange to arrange to meet someone at a diner – or anyplace where you had to commit to spending money just to be there; part of being a real adult, maybe. Lacking financial independence, Cleve mostly felt like a fake one.

He thought about Spider and Karen and the others as he pedaled along under a cloudless sky. That was all over now: the Bohemians, the Defibrillators. Would they even want to see him again? For sure they'd resent him for having been right to walk away. They didn't know he'd gone back to try and warn them.

He tried to imagine an integrated life, with Roe hanging out at Spider's, but couldn't get anywhere with it. All he saw was Roe sitting there, ill at ease, while Karen made borderline racist remarks.

Main Street when he eventually reached it was its usual dead self. The cypresses were dusty, and the whitewashed breezeblock storefronts glared in the brash sunlight. The few benches were unoccupied. Mister Cole's Rascal was parked outside the gun store, its pennants flaccid. A tanker truck rumbled past Cleve scarily close, heading for the freeway, raising a fine, chalky dust that made him choke and sneeze. On its side was a hazchem warning.

Cleve turned into the Triangle, crossed two quiet intersections, dismounted, and wheeled his bicycle down an alley. Emerging at its far end he found that somehow he had taken a wrong turn and was slightly lost. No street ran straight here; no block was at right angles to any other. It was a queer, mixed up place, and coming here made him seem somehow queer too.

But then he was, wasn't he?

He went on. A glance at the next street sign he came to told him that, to his relief, he had found Crow Street.

It was narrow and mostly made up of clapboard houses. Once family homes, stacked doorbells revealed that they had long ago been subdivided into apartments, the curtains of which were permanently drawn against the intrusive eyes of the neighbors directly opposite. There were also a couple of stores partway along, including a small drugstore and a place that sold beat-up-looking furniture. Opposite the furniture store was Violet's Place, an eatery hardly wider than a typical row house. Its front windows were folded back shutter-style, so patrons could catch any breeze that might happen along, which at the moment was no breeze at all, and a candy-stripe awning leant out to offer a slab of shade.

Roe was sitting at a table center front, scrolling on his phone. Cleve now saw he had a Mohican. Something about the shaved sides of his scalp was provocative. He was wearing visor-like sci-fi shades and a tank top that showed off his shoulders and arms and the flatness of his torso. On his wrists were studded leather bands. The vest was red with a black lightning bolt on it that made Cleve think of some heavy metal band or other. Roe looked up, saw Cleve, and smiled.

Cleve leant his bike against the storefront window-frame carefully and went in. Bigger than it looked from the outside, the dimly lit diner extended back through the house; the kitchen, which was maybe in a rear lean-to, was reached through a swing door. An elderly black man sat in a booth by the swing door, absorbed in his newspaper, a bottle of beer in front of him on red and white check oilcloth, a pen behind his ear. There was no one at the counter where the cash register sat. Behind the counter, rows of bottles glinted on a display shelf.

Roe stood as Cleve came over to his table, and he was wearing close fitting black jeans that showed off the lozenges of his thighs, and, despite the heat, chunky black bike boots. They fumbled through a handshake that slipped untidily between soul and regular, at least managing to prolong the warm contact as they took their seats in the window, facing each other.

Disconcerted by Roe's mirror shades, Cleve looked away from him, taking in the diner's décor. It was old fashioned and dark, all Christmassy reds and greens. Underpowered lamps were dotted here and there. Most had fringed fabric shades ruched up in a bordello style, and orange bulbs.

The pictures on the walls were mostly folk art prints – Cleve recognized Frieda Kahlo and Grandma Moses from books his mom had. Some were real paintings, done by the owner, maybe. They had stickers on them saying prices, but these had faded to illegibility: only the dollar signs could still be read. "It's kind of a time warp in here," he said, quickly adding, "It's cool, though."

"It's Eriq's mom's place. She's been running it, like, forever."

"So his mom's Violet?"

"Yeah. Her husband's white, so I thought... Have you heard from any of your friends yet?"

Cleve shook his head. "You?"

"No, but my dad's a councilor. He got involved when the police showed up at our house –"

"Shit."

"– so I know they're pretty much okay. They might get expelled though."

"That's still really bad."

"It's better than jail." Roe caught himself. "Sorry."

Cleve shrugged. "Tag and Patty are probably young enough to get off on being minors. The others, I don't know. Spider's a veteran, so maybe he'll get a pass. Choc..." He shrugged again as a waitress came through the swing-door. She was a middle aged, heavyset, light-skinned black woman wearing a loose African print top and slacks, with an elaborate hairdo and a face framed by lacquered curls. Looking dour, perhaps from the heat, or more likely from worry about her son, she handed them menus.

"Miz Anthony, this is my friend Cleve," Roe said.

The woman softened very slightly. "What can I get you, Cleve?"

Cleve saw Roe had a Coke in front of him, in one of those old fashioned curvy bottles. "Just a Coke for now, please, ma'am."

Miz Anthony nodded and went and fetched one from a chiller cabinet behind the counter, popped the lid, slid in a straw, and set it before him.

Having made his impression, Roe now removed his

sunglasses. His brown eyes were dark and warm and bright and vulnerable.

Cleve sucked on his straw. "How does she keep this place going?" he asked, murmuring the question as Miz Anthony took a seat on a stool behind the counter and got her phone out.

"How do any of the stores round here stay open?" Roe asked in return. "I mean, look at that couch." In the window of the used furniture store across the way sat an outsize brown leatherette couch with arms that were scratched up to the point of being worn through to the frame. "*And* it's not even cheap: I checked."

"I reckon all the stores in Claypit are fronts for something else," Cleve said.

"Like what? Drugs?"

"I'd say Satanic covens."

"Satanism's passé," Roe said. "I'd say aliens."

"Or doppelgängers."

"*Ja, mein herr.*"

"Like, you go in totally innocently to buy a hideous plastic couch with rips in the arms. And then you get lured into a backroom and replaced with a lookalike."

"But with a couple of giveaway signs," Roe said.

"There are always signs," Cleve agreed.

"Like maybe you can't unscramble the images when you look at a TV; you just see a bunch of lines or pixels."

"Or you don't blink when you look at the sun."

Roe smiled like he got Cleve's reference, which was to *It Came From Outer Space*, a B movie Cleve had loved ever since being allowed to stay up to watch it one Halloween when he was around eight years old. He leaned in. "Maybe it's the Illuminati," he said. "It usually is."

Roe bent forward and sucked on his candy-stripe straw and Cleve noted the shape and fullness of his lips, the dive and swoop and softness of them. Hints of a moustache framed the edges of Roe's mouth, and Cleve was suddenly aware of his own hairiness. Pornstars mostly waxed. Would it turn Roe off? Cleve had never had a thought like that before. Shaving your pubes off felt like it would be a real chore.

Roe's knee bumped his under the table. Cleve's heart lurched and electricity surged up between his legs. "What?" Roe asked mock innocently, twiddling his straw and smiling.

"You," Cleve said.

Now it was Roe's turn to blush. He glanced round at the diner's only other patron, who seemed to be marking up sporting fixtures and was certainly paying them no attention, and cleared his throat. "Um, I've never been on an actual date before," he said. "I mean, if this is, you know, a date."

"Me either. And I reckon it is a date. I mean, it is to me. You ever um, done stuff?"

"Some," Roe said. "But just, um, fooling around, though. Like, what – second base?" The corny reference made Cleve smile. "I mean, it's different when it's two guys, though. What about you?"

"Pretty much nothin'," Cleve said. "Second base with a girl, but that don't count, does it?"

"Not if you're gay."

"It don't count, then." It was exciting to Cleve just to say that out loud.

"Does anyone know? Like, your family?"

"They kinda do, I reckon, and they don't ask, cos they don't know if they can handle it. What about yours?"

"The same. I used to be really close to my great grand, but she's kind of hardcore religious now so I can't face telling her," Roe said. "She'd say I was possessed, white people did it, I should pray it away even though I'm an atheist, which actually pisses her off a lot more, probably. I think my parents would be cool eventually. I mean we've got a whole shelf of Baldwin."

He glanced at Cleve to check the white boy at least knew that Baldwin was "James."

Cleve did. He'd seen videos on YouTube, and been intrigued by the fey, urbane, big eyed, black gay political activist with the odd citizen-of-the-world voice you could listen to forever. He nodded, looking serious to show he got the reference.

"Sometimes you think they've guessed, but then last month my mom was talking to me about college," Roe went on, "and she said, 'Just don't go getting some girl pregnant.' I rolled my eyes and almost came out to her right then. But I didn't." He sighed. "It's weird, isn't it?"

"What?"

"If you're gay, it doesn't matter what your family's like, what color you are, if you're rich, poor, urban, rural, suburban, whatever, you have to, like, go through the whole crazy 'Will my entire family disown me if I tell them? Will they throw me out for being me?' Straight people don't have to deal with that."

"Does it ever make you wish you were straight?"

"It makes me wish straight people weren't jerks."

Cleve nodded. "I think my mom and dad'll get past it when it happens," he said. "I mean, they're not too religious or anything. You got any brothers or sisters?"

"Two sisters, both older than me. You?"

"A kid sister."

"So we're both only sons, liable to get zapped by guilt-rays for murdering the family name. Not that Jones is about to be consigned to oblivion as a surname."

"Olsen either."

They sat quietly for a while, enjoying being in each others' presence, noting with pleasure the shapes of each others' hands, sharing glances and small smiles, and in that interval the Triangle became for Cleve a home, a place in which you could move towards becoming yourself, unlike the rest of Claypit. "We're both kinda floatin'," he said.

"How do you mean?"

"Cut adrift from our friends, and the whole summer's out there waiting."

"I thought you meant more like, stuck in a racially schizoid, opioid riddled, mostly homophobic southern town that's dying on its ass," Roe said.

"Well, that too, obviously." Cleve rubbed the mouth of his Coke bottle with the ball of his thumb. The curved glass was already warm. "Claypit's so dead end we can't even get a prison to come here."

"It's fucked up that we even want one."

"It's jobs, but yeah. Were your parents pissed about your hair?"

"Yeah, but then my sister came back from college pregnant, which pretty much gave me a Get Out Of Jail Free card." Roe looked away, and Cleve thought he probably hadn't meant to mention the pregnancy because he went on quickly, "You said your parents were going away."

"Yeah, for a week. They went this mornin'. My mom's – she's been through some stuff." Now Cleve was awkward in his turn. But then why not tell Roe? Wasn't the point of love that you could take off your masks and be yourself? Okay, love was pushing it: this was just a first date; but even so. "She's kinda big," he admitted.

"What, like *My 600-lb Life* big?" Roe grinned, then saw Cleve's expression. "Wow, really? I'm sorry."

"I don't know how heavy she is," Cleve said. "Barely standing big. And she can be mean too. It's partly pain, but..."

"Do you know if there's a reason why?" Roe asked. "Like, I don't want to say abuse, but you know. Abuse."

"She was always heavy, but it was pretty much normal. Then when Terri was born – my sister; she's twelve now – it was a mess and she had like, all these surgical problems afterwards. They had to give her a ton of steroids and she kinda exploded. Then she got this depression, um, they call it post partum. The pills they put her on to get her out of that are messing her up in a different way. I mean, I guess she loves us, but she loves pills and stuffing her face more."

Cleve fell silent. After a glance at Miz Anthony, who was still absorbed in her phone at the counter, Roe reached out and put his hand on Cleve's and squeezed it, and didn't let go for maybe a minute. "Addiction's, like, really tough," he said. "Does your dad work?"

"He used to work on tanker trucks – he's a mechanic – but they don't hardly come through anymore. Now it's mostly under the radar jobs. We do okay for money, but it's tight. I was supposed to get a summer job, but I didn't. Hey," he went on, changing the subject, "You ever been inside a haunted house?"

Roe raised an eyebrow. "Um…"

Cleve had wanted to invite Roe to his home, with its rapturous, brand new promise of privacy, but had realized as he'd never had reason to realize before that black people never visited Coleman East; that no black families lived there; that Roe – and therefore he and Roe – would be startlingly, alarmingly visible.

Maybe he would invite him there afterwards.

If there was an afterwards.

He tried to imagine introducing Roe to his parents, to Terri. Terri would be okay. Myrtle would get over it. And Kenneth? His dad voting for Trump seemed suddenly a whole lot less abstract to Cleve. "How about tomorrow afternoon?" he went on quickly. "We could meet at the truck stop at the top of Peach Street." Peach Street ran down to the Tanner Peach Farm, and was about halfway between Tanner's Cross and Cleve's house. "You know it, right?"

"I know where it is."

Cleve could see that Roe thought the idea of visiting a supposedly haunted house was kid's stuff, but also that the invitation might mean something else a lot more interesting. "So, you up for it?"

"Sure." Roe was doing his best to sound easy, but there was a small catch in his voice as he added, "Why not?"

"Say noon tomorrow?"

"Sure."

"Your folks won't mind?"

"They'll be at work."

"Won't your sister rat you out?"

"She'll be glad I'm out of the house, instead of lolling about pretending to read *Moby Dick* and listening in on her phone calls."

"Cool."

Somehow that brought their date to a conclusion. Awkwardly they got up and went to the counter. Each paid for his own drink and dropped a few coins in the tip jar by the cash register. Out in the street they shook hands, more deftly this time, the shake transitioning into a hand-to-forearm lock, then a shoulder bump that leant in more intimately than it would have done if they'd been two hetero jocks, but didn't give too much away.

Cleve watched as Roe set his board down and, pumping a couple of times with his booted left foot to build up speed, rumbled away down the street. With a tilt of his hips and a cheeky wiggle of his butt Roe swept around the corner and vanished from Cleve's sight.

Cleve looked after him for a minute. Then he got on his bike and began to pedal home, excitement for tomorrow already building in him.

## Chapter Twelve

Neither Roe nor Cleve slept well that night: both of them were looking forward to meeting up again way too much. Also, as dusk fell the air grew thunderstorm heavy and stayed that way, despite a cloudless sky. The full moon brought a weight and madness of its own, perhaps, because in the restless, mammalian small hours, loud barking broke out near both their homes, waking them repeatedly; and both had uneasy dreams in which a figure looked on, somehow from above, as though suspended, and the figure's face was in shadow.

Cleve, being unsupervised, lazed in bed until his dad called at 9:30 a.m. to check up on him, then lazed some more.

Roe rose as usual at 7:15, had breakfast with his parents and sister, cleared the table, then put out the trash. His dad had no further news of the charges against his classmates, and after his parents left for work Roe called Eriq's house phone and Eriq picked up. He and Will and

Mikey were all grounded, Eriq said, deprived of their phones and on social media lockdown, but nothing worse so far.

Roe went online as they talked, and searched about for news on The Tyler Takedown, as it was being called, for Eriq to relay to the others. Perhaps because (most of) the perpetrators had been caught straight away, all were middle class, and none of them had made any public statements claiming affiliation with some wider political group or movement, it felt like the story was already slipping down the newsfeeds, with some hours of community service for the "vandals" set to be the most likely outcome. It was a relief but also saddening: they had risked their necks, their futures, and what had they achieved?

"Are your folks mad at you?" Eriq asked.

"Kind of almost proud, actually," Roe said. "My dad literally alibied me when the cops showed up looking for the only black student at Tyler A they hadn't already busted. Racial profiling zero evidence blah blah. What about yours?"

"Dad always has to prove he's super woke 'cause he's white," Eriq said. "So he didn't say much, just kinda gripped my shoulder and looked intense. Mom was more Talented Tenth about it and says I let the race down by vandalizing. I can tell she's still glad the statue got trashed, though. Just if someone else's kid did it she could enjoy it uninhibitedly."

"Has the school called?"

"The vice principal did, pissed obviously. Being on the squad's gonna help me, though. Meanwhile I already read two hundred and thirty pages of *Wuthering Heights*. It's really good, actually. Maybe I'll get a Mohawk like yours," he added. "Give my mom something else to aerate over."

"I was thinking of going blond."

"It's not a competition, Jones."

They talked a while longer before hanging up. Roe was glad Eriq was cheerful, and that it looked like he, Will and Mikey might avoid even a suspension. He felt then the unclean and undeserved insulation he knew would have been absent if they'd been Pit Boys. Nothing a Pit Boy did would get dismissed as a prank: it would always be a flat-out crime.

Thinking of crime made him think of Cleve.

He went out to the back porch with a juice and sat on the swing seat, mixing failing to read *Moby Dick* with gazing out blankly over the town and remembering Cleve's blue-green eyes; their receptive black centers; his lips, full for a white boy's, and ruddy; the slight and somehow beguiling cobra-cocking of his head to one side; the accompanying drop of one shoulder; the curves of his collarbone, the bump of his Adam's apple; the blond cropped hair that looked like it would bristle under the palms of Roe's hands tinglingly.

He adjusted his crotch, swallowed his juice, and tried to focus on the rendering of a whale into dreck before the sharks consumed it from underneath.

Eventually it was time to set out. After checking his appearance in the wardrobe mirror, Roe took his skate-board and backpack and left without saying goodbye to his sister, who had retreated to her room and was playing Beyoncé at full blast. He reckoned he had about three miles to cover once he had bombed the Side down to Main Street, in order to reach the truck stop.

Out past the town square the eastern road ran wide and pretty much level, with a minimal camber. Roe kept his speed up with regular but not too frequent pumps of his bike-booted left foot. He often rode his board to school this way.

Past Tyler A's padlocked gates the cypresses and syc-amores crowded down to the road's edges, offering stretches of pleasant, dappled shade. Every so often and without stopping Roe pulled out his sport bottle and squeezed some water into his mouth. Music from his phone filled his earbuds. After a while he traded Bloc Party, a raucous British indie-punk band with a black gay lead singer named Kele Okerere, for Taylor Swift, his guilty pleasure.

He hadn't ever been out this way that he could remember, though he must have driven through it at some point with his family, surely. Or was the freeway always faster, even when it was three sides of a square? There was little traffic in either direction.

A couple of miles along, he came to the billboards.

There were three of them, and, disconcerted by what they showed, he stopped to take photos with his phone. To his left rose Squab Hill; to his right was scrub and then woodland. On that stretch of the road there were no houses.

The first billboard, which bore the curlicued slogan *Gracious Living is Returning to Tannerville*, displayed an illustration of an immaculately restored plantation house the size of the White House. It was surrounded by striped lawns, and in front of it were multi-tiered fountains, and plumed horses pulled fairytale carriages. Behind and on both sides were vast, oddly stylized, near-abstract cotton fields devoid of laborers. On the veranda that fronted the mansion white men and women in modern dress took their ease much as their Southern belle and beau counterparts might have done one hundred and seventy years earlier, back in slavery times. At the bottom was the legend *Gracious Lodge Living™*.

The second billboard announced in a less fancy font, over a pastel-hued aerial map of a large cotton plantation, *A Mint Julep Heritage Endeavor. With the support of Welt County Citizens Council, Bringing jobs to communities, Celebrating Our History, Together. Over 80 De*

*Luxe suites planned. Extensive Hunting and Fishing tariffs. Rifle Ranges for Sport Shooting. Follow us @mintjulepheritage.*

Other than the black on white Mint Julep Heritage logo, which to Roe's eyes had a definite hint of the swastika about it, the third billboard was plain and all business: *Reconstruction work beginning soon. Skilled + semi-skilled labor required. Excellent ongoing employment opportunities for male + female waitstaff, barstaff, housekeep, catering. We love to hire local!*

Below this were an out of state head office address, a website address, a couple of toll-free numbers for business and marketing inquiries, and the logos of various local concerns apparently endorsing the project.

As he squinted up at the billboards and took dramatically-angled photographs, Roe wondered if his dad knew about this. He vaguely remembered that there had been an "alternative" to the private prison bid that had mentioned tourism as a way of bringing jobs to Claypit. Was this that? Literally resurrecting a plantation? Would unemployed black people be dragooned into playing slaves for minimum wage or see their welfare payments docked? He thought he remembered reading about places where that had happened – plantation museums – and felt sick.

With nerveless fingers he uploaded the images to his Facebook and Insta, under the title "#FutureofClaypit: is slavery back in style? Is black the new black? @Iamnotanumber."

It was now a quarter of twelve. He put his board down and punted off again, though now the thought of meeting Cleve seemed somehow unpleasant. Here the road ran very slightly uphill, and offered no shade. The sun seemed in the last few minutes to have intensified, as if he was under some sort of racial magnifying glass that made everything harder and more painful.

Resentfully, he built up his speed. Keeping his balance while avoiding potholes and swerving round road-kill pulled his mind into the present and expelled some of his anger. But still when he reached the Peach Street truck stop his gut was twisted up inside.

He glanced at his phone: one minute past twelve. No Cleve waited on the dirt forecourt. Four Exxon pumps glinted in front of a long, low single-story building with a tatty awning, which seemed to once have been a diner as well as a convenience store/pay-station. After the billboards, the dust scurfed, old fashioned advertisement for Coca-Cola on the awning seemed latently menacing, the swirling 1950s lettering something persisting from segregation times.

*Old poison.*

Just past the gas station was the turn into Peach Street. A faded sign pointed the way to Tanner's Farms & Cannery.

An eight-wheeled tanker truck was pulled up next to the diner, the only vehicle on an otherwise empty lot. Beyond it a disused tractor rusted among straw-dry weeds, and back of that were some dilapidated trailers. He wondered if anyone lived in them. No one was around, and it didn't seem like a place you would choose to stop at and put down roots. More like you broke down there and gave up, and that became your life.

Roe flipped his board up and Velcro-strapped it to his backpack, trying to push *Jeepers Creepers*-style horror movie scenarios out of his head. He could feel the sweat bead on the shaved sides of his scalp.

The convenience store door opened, setting the bell above it jingling, and Cleve came out with a small pack slung over one shoulder. Today he wore a tight fitting blue vest that showed off his torso, and knee length jean shorts that hugged his thighs and crotch. His well shaped calves and forearms were dusted with gold, and his buzzed scalp was symmetrical and flawless.

Seeing Roe he broke into a smile and loped quickly over to him. He was wearing mirror shades, and he removed them as he moved in for a faux-macho Roman grip and chest bump that Roe matched, and for a hot moment their eyes met as their chests pressed together.

# Chapter Thirteen

Squinting in the glare, Cleve slipped his shades back on. "C'mon," he said, leading Roe across the forecourt in the direction of Peach Street. "The trail ain't far."

Putting the gas station behind them, they started down a wide dirt side road that was dusty underfoot. Unseen cicadas chirruped in the dense, vibrating heat, a screen of sound. To the right the peach trees grew wild, though further along Roe could see things became more orderly. The underbrush, dense here, was cleared away; and the trees were increasingly rigorously pruned as they segued into the few fruit farms that remained economically viable. The cannery was down there too, on the bank of the Nooseneck.

In the dry, yellow scrub grass at the trees' roots fallen peaches rotted in piles. Around these wasps buzzed dozily, intoxicated by the fermenting fruit, and there was a sweetness in the dust-mote-heavy air that was halfway between mouthwatering and putrid.

On the left side of the road were sycamores, cedars and oaks, along with a handful of peach trees that were escapees from the Tanner orchards. A fence ran along for a while, then gave up. A hundred yards or so past it, next to a faded "Private Property – No Trespassing" sign, Cleve turned aside and led Roe under the cover of the trees.

Roe was relieved to be out of the sun and away from the dust they had been kicking up, though clouds of tiny insects hung gauzily beneath the canopy of leaves, and whenever they touched his skin the sweat glued them there itchily.

"So, like, where are we going?" he asked.

"The old Tyler place," Cleve said.

"Literally the plantation house? I thought it totally fell down like a century ago."

"Nah, it's still there. Well, the ruins of it. It's gonna be torn down this fall, apparently, so it's kinda the last chance to see the real deal."

"I thought it was going to be, like, restored back to what it was," Roe said, thinking of the billboards.

"Nah, it'll be some plastic B.S.," Cleve said. "Probably actual, literal plastic, like fake marble spraycanned with, um, marbling and shit. It's gonna be propaganda, I guess." He glanced round at Roe. "I mean, don't you think?"

"I do."

"Like a Disneyland palace."

"Did you know Mickey Mouse was based on black-face?"

"Yeah?" Cleve said. "I didn't, but it figures. Some of the stuff my mom collects, like old signs an' labels from junk stores, they've got faces on 'em kinda like that. Like say for Tanner Peach Jam, round black faces all white round the mouths. Red lips. They creeped me out as a kid."

"Why?"

"I dunno. The smiles were so fake. Clowny, kinda.

And the eyes were too stare-y. I never thought they were people, though. Or not exactly. They were these kinda manic creatures that always thought everything was 'yummy' – that was the slogan, right? I always preferred Daffy Duck to Mickey Mouse," he added.

"He was manic too, though," Roe said. "I mean, like, clinically. I think what they want to do here is way worse than Disneyland."

"How do you mean?"

To try to speak honestly about anything to do with race with a white boy was immediately tiring, but liking Cleve gave Roe a reason to make the effort. And Cleve was trying too.

"Fairytales are made up," Roe said. "So prettying them up doesn't matter. What they want to do here is, it's, like, erasing real suffering that happened to real people. Making it over as cutesie, nostalgic. It's like a machine where the purpose is to let white people off the hook for slavery."

"I hear that," Cleve said. "So what do you reckon they oughtta do?"

"Bulldoze it. Concrete it over."

"Forget it?"

"Well, no. Leave true information; erase romance. Like they did at Auschwitz," Roe said, not a hundred percent sure he had remembered rightly how the death camps of the Holocaust were actually commemorated.

"I guess it's easier to see some stuff from a distance, ain't it?" Cleve said, pausing to hold a branch back so it wouldn't smack Roe in the face. "More than if you're a part of it, I mean. My folks have lived round here for like forever; like, my granddad was a farmer and so was his dad. We don't have a farm now, but that's our land... But if I go backwards with that it's gonna get to some bad places pretty fast. It's gonna get to stuff I..." He shrugged awkwardly. "You can go back now if you want. I mean, I'd get it," he said, gesturing with his big hands.

"Not everything that is faced can be changed," Roe said, and Cleve could tell he was quoting someone, "but nothing can be changed until it's faced."

"Deep. Who said it?"

"James Baldwin." Roe brought out his water bottle, took a suck, then offered it to Cleve, who squirted some into his mouth then returned it.

"Thanks."

"I guess some ghosts are more fun than others," Roe said, twitching a smile.

"Fun ghosts." Cleve considered. "Like...?"

"Contortionist Korean girls with hair over their faces who never heard of Alice bands."

"Oh, okay. Whey-faced Japanese boys with black eyes, pudding bowl haircuts an' halitosis."

"Found footage flicks where you never see anything that costs money."

"Dude, who says 'flicks'?"

"I'm bringing it back," Roe said. "The flickering image, spools of film clattering round on old projection reels blah blah. Plus also: alliteration."

"Like moronic Marvel movies?"

"Exactly. Though I did kinda like –"

The trees grew denser as they ambled along, and the trail narrower, more winding, and busier with stickers. They were in no hurry, however, and neither being keen to work up more of a sweat than was strictly necessary, they took their time.

Scents of jasmine and honeysuckle replaced the smell of rotting peaches. Small animals rustled in the undergrowth, and somewhere nearby a large bird took to the air and clattered away, unseen. The rest of the world felt very far away, and it seemed to Roe they were winding their way down into some sort of spinney.

"You could've got a summer job picking peaches," he

said, apropos of nothing in particular.

"Only Hispanics do that stuff," Cleve said. Then, flushing, he added, "That sounds dumb, don't it?"

Roe shrugged.

"My dad used to pick fruit for old man Tanner as a kid," Cleve went on, "but that was way back in the eighties, and he never said for me to do it, not even when he was ragging on me for not gettin' a job this summer."

"You could, though," Roe said.

"I'd feel weird going down there."

"Do you feel weird with me?"

"Naw. And you *are* weird."

"Yeah?" Roe found himself smiling as Cleve caught his hand in a way so natural Roe barely registered it.

"This is it."

Roe found himself looking out over a natural amphitheater where creepers – jasmine, clematis, bougainvillea and lilac – twined thickly over humps of – what? Slumped tombstones? Clogged fountains? The still air was cloyingly fragrant here.

Facing Roe and Cleve, on the far side of what was in effect a large, shallow dish, was what was left of the plantation house: three stories of gaping windows, their glass long since shattered, their shutters long since fallen. Ivy clawed at the lower story as if hoping to pull itself up, or pull the building down. Its many gables were sagging, and parts had wholly collapsed. Bared beams jutted through gaps in the roof like set spears.

Some chimney stacks still stood; others had tumbled down through the building's interior, part-collapsing the floors inside. Evidently the back wall had partly fallen too: chinks of daylight showed through gaps in the façade like leopard spots in negative. By the pilastered and still impressive main entrance a red-lettered sign read *Danger Keep Out*. The steps leading up to the front door were of stone, and root- and weather-split. One of a pair of tall, dark wood doors stood half-open, as if in invitation.

"We better skirt the edge," Cleve said. "There's an old well somewhere in the middle. It's kinda deep, and the sides have fallen in."

They struggled round under the enclosing circle of trees, forcing their way with their thighs through twining tendrils. There was no path, though every now and again Roe's foot would strike a paving stone adrift and buried in the tangle. *There must be a slave's graveyard too*, he thought, wondering where it was. Somewhere way back, he supposed. Would they have put up stones? It seemed unlikely.

"What sort of ghosts are they meant to be?" he asked, stumbling over a knot of low lying honeysuckle and shaking some butterflies loose from its flowers. They fluttered off limply, barely able to drag up the energy to keep in the air. The croaking of toads told him there were ponds nearby, or at least boggy ground.

"I don't know," Cleve said, adding sheepishly, "It was just a line really. I never heard of any for real. I just thought there had to be some, you know? I mean if there even are ghosts."

"Restless spirits."

"Yeah."

"If ghosts were real, if you went to Auschwitz your head would, like, literally explode," Roe said. "I mean if you, like, held a séance or a summoning or something."

"You know how to do any of that stuff?"

"If you count 'ability to Google' as knowing about stuff then I'm Aleister Crowley."

"Who's that?"

"A big deal English Satanist who summoned up a de-mon and everyone there went mad."

"For real?"

"Supposedly. He said 'Let Do What Thou Wilt Be The Whole Of The Law'. Which works, but only if no one else does."

With a final thrusting rip they reached the bottom of the steps, and both of them were breathless in the close air. Spiny seeds and hook-haired pods dotted the fronts of Cleve's shorts and Roe's jeans, and were resistant to being brushed away.

The house's interior waited. Cleve and Roe exchanged a look, and nodded.

So far they were only playing at fear.

The air within was neither cooler nor warmer than that outside, but the smell of soil and rotten brick and plaster clung unpleasantly to the linings of their nostrils. Here and there shafts of sunlight fell as if upon a stage, revealing a large, gloomy room disappointingly devoid of furnishings. Cleve and Roe wandered about, treading with care on spongy, yielding boards, poking into corners with the toes of their shoes in hopes of turning over something interesting.

No luck.

Several doorways opened onto dim passages. A staircase to the upper floors had wholly collapsed, rendering them inaccessible.

"I kind of thought it'd be spookier," Cleve said. He and Roe were now standing side by side in the middle of the room, wondering whether it was worth exploring further.

"Did you never go inside before?"

"We used to sneak in the grounds when we were small, me and some of the neighbors' kids."

"Cute." Roe thought of the woods above his house. There would probably be a breeze up there, and certainly no smell of decay, of rotting history.

"We'd tell scary stories an' dare each other to go in," Cleve said, "but I don't remember anyone actually did it. Now I'm thinking maybe we all did and it was a letdown so I forgot."

"What do you want to do now?"

"Um... This, I guess."

Cleve leant in and darted a kiss on Roe's cheek.

At the brief hummingbird contact Roe's heart heaved into his mouth. He turned to Cleve and kissed him softly on the lips, closing his eyes as he did so. The contact was warm and soft, a yielding and then an assertion that grew rapidly in firmness. Above all it was so natural as to be beyond thought, and he tasted Spearmint on Cleve's tongue. Cleve's hands found Roe's hips with a confidence that was a different order of knowledge from any other; and Roe slid his hands around Cleve's broad, hot upper back, and under the smooth muscle he felt the bone blades spread and rise.

Their bodies sealed together in an embrace that was for both of them the first true embrace of adult life, and it was strange that it should happen here, in a place so saturated with such a particular, pernicious history.

Cleve tasted a faint orange sweetness on Roe's lips, a slickness of cocoa lip balm; and beneath the shafts of daylight he and Roe were, it seemed to him then, like dancers on one of those TV shows where they snap to a climactic clustering of spotlights for the final clinch. The performers freeze and hold, and all is still but their chests, heaving uncontrollably in the breathless air.

And they were breathless.

From one of the neighboring rooms there came a sound then, a creaking exhalation like the rheumatic groan of some creature made of rotten wood and plaster, followed by what seemed like something heavy – a roof-beam, maybe – falling with a thud and rustle that possibly presaged some further internal structural collapse.

Cleve and Roe broke off their kiss and, their bodies still pressed together, looked in the direction of the sound. It was followed by a stirring closer to that seemed purposive. An animal? A person?

Hands still linked they moved slightly apart. It was impossible to ignore what might be the presence of someone else, someone who might well not find a first kiss romantic and innocent when it was between two boys, the more so one being black, one white. Someone filled with visceral, incontinent hatred, to whom the past was never dead. Both their minds went to derelicts, to illicit or actually criminal endeavors, to meth labs, klavens and other, murkier conspiracies, Claypit's sinister underbelly manifesting itself in the wreck of a plantation house. The real world.

Holding their breaths, they listened some more.

Nothing. Still:

"Let's go see," Cleve said quietly.

Roe exhaled. "Okay."

# Chapter Fourteen

T hey crossed to the doorway from which they thought the sound of movement had come and peered through. Beyond was blackness, and the air seemed cooler, and clammy.

"You reckon the floor'll be okay in there?" Cleve asked in a low voice.

"We'd better be careful," Roe said quietly. "We don't want to end up in the vaults with busted ankles." He wrinkled his brow. "*Are* there vaults?"

"Cellars, maybe. I dunno."

Cleve went first, partly because he felt responsible for the whole situation, partly because he wanted to impress Roe; and after all a tramp was only a tramp, even if tweaking, and he, Cleve, was fit and strong, and Roe was at least fit.

The floorboards proved to be solid underfoot, and their trailing fingertips told them they were in a window-less passageway. They passed several doors that, when they tried the handles, were locked, which seemed odd, and turned a corner. Up ahead an oblong of dim light showed, and surprisingly quickly they found themselves outside again.

The rear of the house was in far worse shape than the front. Here bricks lay in tumbled heaps, walls had entirely collapsed, and creepers covered everything in a leafy, flowery, cushioned carpet. Roe and Cleve stood back and looked up at the exposed rear rooms. It was like staring into a giant, decaying dolls' house. Overhead the sun blazed, and the air was as solid as glass. The foliage, scattered with white and yellow blossoms, made the sight almost pretty, and yet –

"My hackles are rising," Cleve said.

"Mine too," Roe said. "It's like there's a buildup of static somewhere."

"Don't you need metal for that?"

"I flunked physics," Roe said. "Stuff like nylon can do it too, right? Like, sliding on rugs, or chubby girls walking in slacks and making sparks..."

Gazing up at what remained of the top floor, Roe started and touched Cleve's arm.

"What?"

"Did you see –?"

"Don't shit me, dude."

"No, I thought..." Roe squinted. "It was like a fin, or a black sail, billowing..."

"There's no wind, dude."

"I'm literally spooking myself." Roe half smiled. Then: "No, something *did* move."

"Where? I don't see –"

"There."

Roe was pointing out an upper room that was almost a separate turret, though perhaps that was only because the other parts of the building around it had fallen away. Cleve could see it had a small window with enough structure at back of it for the interior to be an enclosed block of black.

And then it wasn't: it was a brick frame with cloudless

blue sky behind it.

"Weird," Cleve said. "Maybe it's..." He trailed off, rubbing a hand firmly up and down the back of his neck, which was prickling and crawling more intensely now. "Some kind of, I dunno, optical illusion?"

"My neck's cramping up," Roe said through oddly gritted teeth. He rolled his head and the bones clicked with a hollow sound, as though they were in a large empty room, not outside. Then from somewhere high up within the building there came a rustling sound, like dry leaves rushing in a rising wind.

Something was coming.

The real leaves on the real trees that surrounded them hung limp and still.

Roe's hand found Cleve's, and gripped it. It was as moist and sweaty as his own.

Something was coming, but what? The static, if that was what it was, began to penetrate their bodies like a fine, persistent rain.

*Muscles work on electric current*, Cleve thought as Roe's fingers tightened painfully and apparently involuntarily around his own. He remembered an experiment at school that had involved attaching a battery to severed frog's legs, and the legs twitching as though alive. Roe thought of electric eels, those nearly blind fish whose muscles are stacked in series, not parallel. They could amplify enough charge through those muscles to kill a horse. Torpid and near sightless, they floated in slow river-currents, sensing the electrical fields of their oblivious prey.

A hunting creature, then: they knew this as mice know the nature of the serpent. It had been up there, and now it was coming down. A black fin, Roe had said.

His muscles cramping as though he had run ten miles then slumped in front of the TV without stretching, Cleve struggled to lift one of his feet. It seemed barely possible.

Whatever it was, it was gaining in influence over them.

The tangle of creepers was so dense here, extending up the surrounding tree trunks like canopied camouflage netting, that their best chance of escape seemed to be –

"Back the way we came." Cleve spoke with difficulty, his tongue gluing to the roof of his mouth. "We gotta –"

"Go now," Roe agreed throatily.

Dragging their feet up as if from sucking mud, hand in hand they staggered back into the house. The darkness within was block-solid after the bright sunlight, but the instant they were inside some influence was cut off and they could move more normally.

They hurried through, not realizing they had missed the turning that led back to the main hall until they found themselves in a small side room. It offered no way out other than the way they had come in. Empty bottles and cans were strewn about on the floor, and leaves and soil had been tracked in by animals. The walls were looped with unskilled spray-can graffiti, and there was a large, shutterless, glassless window.

"We can climb out," Roe said, crossing to the window. Lilac twined prettily around its central mullion.

"Hold up."

"What?" Roe looked round. "Let's go!"

"Look."

In a corner, on an old, stained mattress, were stacked some items of clothing. They were folded with incongruous neatness, and on top of them sat a small, well cared for brown leather satchel with a brass clasp and leather strap.

"Some tramp's junk," Roe said, taking hold of the mullion to pull himself up as Cleve knelt to examine the clothes. "Not interesting."

"No, come and look, dude."

Exasperated, and casting an uneasy glance back along the passageway, Roe got down and went over, squatted next to Cleve and quickly checked through the clothes. They were all men's, and included a dull green formal-type army jacket, several old-fashioned white shirts, a pair of pleated, high-waisted gray pants, a gray vest and some navy socks. "Okay, so, yeah, weird," he conceded. "They're all, like, 1940s or '50s. Like these –" He held up what could only be called drawers.

"But new, dude."

"So a tramp got cast-offs from a film studio that went bust, or a fancy dress hire store or something. Don't go in his bag."

"Too late," Cleve said, taking hold of the satchel.

From deeper inside the house, in a sweeping rush like chill air, the static poured over them again, as if it were an occult fluidium presaging the arrival of something frightful.

Hackles stiffening, Roe jumped up and crossed to the window. This time Cleve was hard on his heels, and side by side they clambered up onto the sill and jumped down into the matted undergrowth below. Without delay they began to force their way through the tangle in front of the house, taking a direct line across the semi-circle, not thinking of the hidden well now, or falling into vaults, barking their shins on buried debris as they went, and only narrowly avoiding twisted ankles as their feet ripped through the carpets of creeper into the sunken corpses of flowerbeds beneath.

They didn't stop until they had floundered free of the undergrowth and were once more under the cover of the trees across from the house. There, gasping for breath, they dared to stop and look back.

Everything looked the same, but there was a sense of watchfulness in the blank windows that hadn't been present before. Or was that – was it all – somehow just a product of their imaginations? Roe offered Cleve his water, and this time Cleve sucked greedily on the plastic teat. His pale, peach-tinted skin was speckled with tiny brown bark fragments. He returned the bottle to Roe, who finished it and put it back in his pack.

They turned away from the house. To be anywhere near it was unpleasant now. In silence they took the first trail they came to, wanting without discussing it to put some distance between themselves and – what?

Nothing?

Kids scaring each other?

But they weren't kids, and there definitely *had* been something, even if it was the sort of something you couldn't put into words.

Not what you could call a ghost.

Did any of it actually matter, though, Roe asked himself as they left the ruin behind them, and his first flush of alarm fell away. He had always suspected that if you saw a ghost – or a UFO, or Bigfoot – it would probably bug you for a limited period. Then you'd get on with your life as if it had never happened, because it didn't add any meaning to anything: it was an experience *over there*. A story to tell at parties. Not real life.

But if you decided it meant that ghosts – or aliens or Bigfoot – were real, and you followed the logic of that decision through, what then?

So far as he could see, your life got boringly consumed with online conspiracy theories, and if you totally lost your grip you ended up having stays galore in mental hospitals. Your life fell down one or another basically depressing rabbit hole, and he had things he wanted to do: move to New York; be an experimental artist of some sort; be out and proud; make his mark. Live his reality, not become an obsessive I-was-abducted-by-a-UFO-slept-with-a-ghost type bore.

That would be almost as tedious as getting religion.

Coming upon a fallen log in a clearing, they sat to catch their breaths. It was then Roe noticed with irritation that Cleve had brought the tramp's bag with him. "That might have important stuff in it," he said.

"So?"

"We'd have to take it back."

"Such a good boy," Cleve said, smiling and reaching up to touch Roe's cheek.

Roe let him. "Armed robber," he murmured.

"Vandal."

"Purse snatcher."

"It ain't a purse."

Roe sighed. "So what's in it, then?"

"Let's see." Cleve popped the clasp and reached inside. The first thing he brought out was an age-spotted, unsealed A5 manila envelope, inside which was a stack of what appeared to be postcards, as the backs had a vertical line to divide message from address, and printed along the bottom of each was the same small legend: *Jack Bean – photographic services: weddings, funerals &c, 122 Coleman Avenue West.*

Perhaps a job lot from a junk store, they were clearly old. Most had stamps on them, and the stamps, which had all been franked, meaning the cards had gone through the postal system, were priced at two cents. The writing, though in varied hands, was all old fashioned, the blue-black ink here and there faded almost wholly away, and the edges were stained sepia. Yet when Cleve turned them over and shuffled through them, all the fronts were devoid of images.

"Who mails blank postcards?" he asked, handing them to Roe.

Roe looked at a card which was unstamped and unaddressed, but had been written on. "I am sending this in an envelope as it would not do for the kids to see it," he read aloud. "As you can see, we had a real party this night." There was no salutation and no sign off. "I don't get it," he said, turning the card over. The slightly shiny front had no suggestion that anything had ever been printed on it.

"Are there any dates?" Cleve asked.

Roe checked. "Some have days of the week. Oh, yeah, the franking here says something July 1947. The others, it's smudged."

They divided up the rest of the cards and glanced over what was written on them. Several correspondents referred to "a memorable evening" and "a surprise party." One mentioned "real Claypit hospitality!" ending with, "Amazed I made it to church the next morning." One said vaguely, "Known locally, apparently. Some homecoming."

The mailing addresses were mostly towns in the south, a couple in New York, one somewhere in Chicago. Several were Welt County addresses. "You know any of these names?" Roe asked.

Cleve shook his head. Roe returned the postcards to the envelope. "What else is in there?" he asked.

Cleve tipped out the rest of the contents of the bag: an old fashioned pen-knife, a few dollar bills and some change, a small brass compass with odd symbols marking the cardinals rather than the usual letters, and something the size of a large iPod in a black velvet bag with its string drawn closed. "Aha. Treasure."

"Shit."

Cleve pulled the mouth of the bag open, and slid out what was inside.

# *Chapter Fifteen*

The thing was a flattish rectangular block. It appeared to be made of quartz or onyx, or some other pale, translucent mineral, and its edges, like an iPod's, were slightly rounded. It had the symmetricality of something manufactured, and seemed at once to both Cleve and Roe to be some sort of device, but there were no buttons or holes around its edges for a charger or headphones, and neither of the flat sides appeared to be a screen or touch-pad.

Cleve weighed it in his hand. "It's kinda heavy." He passed the device to Roe.

"Heavier than lead," Roe said as he took it from him. Sensing some sort of energy within, he lifted it to his ear to see if he could hear anything like a hard drive whirring away inside – his old iPod had got quite noisy before the battery eventually burnt out – but it was as silent as a stone. He put it down on the velvet bag on the log between them. "It must, like, *do* something," he said.

"Maybe it's just a carving."

"Maybe..." By idle chance Roe and Cleve reached out for it together, and the simultaneous contact of their fingertips with the crystalline surface seemed to create a sudden surge of energy. Though their bodies did not move, both boys felt a curious sense of tipping backwards and plummeting down through icy blackness. They snatched their hands away. Cleve stood but staggered sideways, as if on a ship's deck in a pitching sea. He reached out blindly and Roe caught his hand, and the warmth of Roe's touch drove out the icy dark. Cleve sat back down as awkwardly as a doddery senior.

"Wow. That was, um..." He tailed off.

Still holding hands, they looked back in the direction of the ruin, now hidden from view by the intervening trees. There could be no doubt that this was connected with that, whatever *that* had been; whatever *this* was; and therefore that what had happened there was real.

"You better come back to mine," Cleve said. That had been his plan all along, of course, but now the invitation came from a place of fear. And not fear of being beaten up by drug dealers or meth heads in the backwoods; it was something connected to what couldn't be seen in the dark – primal sources of unease that persisted even in a world you were repeatedly told was safe.

Cleve's phone rang loudly, making him and Roe start.

"My old man," Cleve said apologetically. If this day had gone differently he would have let the call go to voicemail, but in the odd vulnerability of the moment he felt compelled to answer it. "Hey, Dad – oh, hey, Terri. How's Mom? Yeah? Cool..."

Roe looked at the crystal block, resting like a gemstone on the plush black velvet. He had forgotten Cleve's family were away, though that had been part of the lure in meeting up with him today: the possibility of privacy later.

The surface of the box was flawless and yet somehow he knew it was old. It was hard to tell in the bright daylight, but he had the impression that it was now glowing softly from within, possibly even very faintly pulsing. He thought of the hypnotic chromatophores of cuttlefish, the way they radiated along the creature's outspread arms to mesmerize unwary shrimp. Once again he had the impression he was beginning to fall, only this time he was tipping forward not back.

He closed his eyes and the sensation left him. "So from now she's only gonna drink diet soda?" Cleve was saying. "That's cool. Naw, it don't cause cancer... Because if it did a zillion people would be dead already."

Keeping his eyes closed, Roe turned his head so when he opened them again he was staring not at the box but at the trees that lined the clearing.

He drew a sharp breath. Was someone standing there? He squinted. No, nobody. But had someone maybe stepped behind one of the trees? Uneasily he touched the still-chattering Cleve on the arm and indicated they should move on.

Cleve nodded and, without thinking, reached for the device to put it away. "Shit," he said as he took hold of it.

"What?"

"My phone just died. It was on, like, 80% five seconds ago. Huh." He slipped it into his shorts' back pocket. "My mom's doin' fine," he added as he dropped the crystal box into its velvet bag. After tightening the drawstring he returned it to the leather satchel, which he put in his backpack. "Let's go," he said.

They went on in silence, bumping shoulders now and again, oppressed by a feeling of being watched. After a while their glances back grew less frequent, however, and their disquiet left them. Soon they were just two friends ambling homewards on a summer's afternoon as the sun sank westwards.

After a while they reached and clambered over a section of collapsed chain-link fencing they assumed marked the northern boundary of the Tyler Estate. It had been pulled down by masses of honeysuckle, and as they crossed it their steps were as bouncy as if the rusted mesh was a trampoline. They steadied each other with held hands, and on the farther side began to share smiles and small talk again.

Cleve now found himself thinking about the childish aspects of his bedroom – the outsize Harry Potter poster over the bed; the Batman duvet cover; a row of superhero figurines on a shelf; some Disney DVDs and board games. Normally that stuff was invisible to him: only he ever saw it, after all – oh, and Terri, but she wouldn't know what was childish and what wasn't. What would Roe think? Likely he had his own embarrassing mementoes, but they weren't going to Roe's house.

At least he could have picked up his dirty clothes and put them in the laundry bag.

Maybe we can just make out on the couch, he thought, though tipping into the indentation caused by his mom's supermorbid obesity didn't seem a huge improvement on being shamed by the kid crap in his bedroom. He wondered what Roe might want to do beyond kissing.

Looking round, he found that Roe was watching him. Maybe he was wondering the exact same thing about Cleve.

The trees petered out into scrub interspersed with bushes, some low, others head height.

Now he and Roe had left the woods behind, uneasiness of a more everyday sort began to well up in Cleve's mind. Though the black youth didn't know it, Cleve was leading them on the slant, aiming to come out as near his house as was possible without being visible from the road.

Though most people in Coleman East would angrily deny being racist, the fact was no black people had ever lived there or even came to visit, and if that wasn't racist, what was it? Simple choice, with each preferring his or her own, or something more pernicious? Whatever it was, it meant that to be seen bringing Roe in seemed – what? Not shameful: Cleve was in no way ashamed. Dangerous? Not exactly – it wasn't like anyone he knew was going to do anything, or he didn't think so, and anyway, do what? Be actually violent? Naw – but even so...

Cleve pushed his feelings down. He didn't want Roe to know he was having them; didn't want Roe to change his mind, though surely as a black person he must be having thoughts of his own about going to an unfamiliar, poor white area with someone white who he hardly knew really, and who he had, after all, met in the sketchiest of circumstances.

Cleve would have to try to borrow Dale Rippel's truck tomorrow so he could drive Roe home – Dale usually didn't mind when he didn't need to use it himself. Then again, would Roe want to be seen on the Side with Cleve, in a rust-pocked pickup with an outsize Confederate flag decal blazoned on its grill?

*I'll get him safely outta the area, anyway.*

It was close on 6 p.m., and the shadows were stretching their fingers eastward. Ahead, Squab Hill rose steeply. The worst heat of the day had departed, though in its wake it left a dense humidity, and so they walked slowly. Roe's water and the two bottles of soda Cleve had bought at the truck stop had long ago vanished down their throats and were now pressing on their bladders, and their mouths were sticky and dry.

Scattered along the far side of the road, at the hill's feet, Roe could make out a line of houses.

'That's where we're headed,' Cleve said, pointing, but the sight was somehow unfamiliar to him that evening. Perhaps it was because he was coming home as someone else, and with another someone whose appearance told the tale entire.

*I'm outside of my old life.*

And then there were the things that had happened in the Tyler house that, being formless, he had begun to push from his mind. Despite the weight of the leather satchel in his pack, the whole thing now felt like some TV show he'd got caught up in at the time, but didn't matter now the credits had rolled.

Cleve glanced back one last time as they neared the road. He saw no sinister figure silhouetted there; nothing following on, just the darkening tree line. By now he was more worried about his neighbors noticing Roe, but their front yards were unoccupied, and no one was sitting out on any of the porches or staring from a window. No kids were playing, and for a moment he had that feeling you get when you wonder if everyone else on the planet has suddenly vanished – that mixture of anxiety and relief.

They crossed the road. "This is it," Cleve said as he led Roe up the drive.

It was strange to know no one would be inside. Terri had sounded cheerful when they talked earlier. She had said their mom was doing good, though had been cut off before Cleve could ask what that actually meant. He didn't think Myrtle's problems were the sort you could fix just like that.

Stepping up onto the porch, he opened the screen door for Roe to go in ahead of him, then had to awkwardly squeeze past to unlock the front door.

"Mi casa," he said. "I apologize for everything in advance."

# Chapter Sixteen

Roe smiled as Cleve pushed the door open then stood aside to let him enter first, reaching alongside him to click on a light as Roe stepped over the threshold. The hall was narrow, the walls were paneled floor to ceiling with varnished pine, and the ceiling was swirled with stucco like yellowed cake frosting. The carpet, faded to grayness at its center, was at its edges sage green, and, as Roe was to discover, it spread throughout the house. There was the lemony smell of household cleaning spray, and behind that, along with other odors, a trace of burnt pizza crust.

"Aw, dude," Cleve grumbled as Roe paused to study a cluster of framed family photographs that hung on the wall above a spindly-legged side table on which a pink plastic rose stood in a white china vase, inevitably zooming in on the one where Cleve looked goofiest and most sun-dazzled. "Go on through."

Passing stairs to the upper floor and doorways to right and left – one Roe supposed a bathroom; the other the lounge, its thick green velveteen drapes closed against the incursion of sunlight – he found himself in a kitchen-diner that ran the width of the back of the house, its halves nominally divided by a stuccoed arch. The dining room side had sliding glass doors. In the backyard Roe could see a kids' blow-up paddling pool that needed re-inflating and had just a slick of water in it. Beyond the fence at the far end of the backyard was the steep, darkening rise of Squab Hill.

Framed watercolors, A5 and A4 size, dotted the walls in both parts of the room, several of them views through the sliding doors, all signed "Myrtle". Roe thought them quite skillful. Numerous old tin signs and labels were also hung on the walls, mostly in the kitchen half, some of them featuring the bug-eyed "yummy" black grotesques with their red lips and rictus grins. Roe imagined Cleve's mom sitting there with a small paint-box and a jar of water, breathing heavily as she bent over her work, making careful strokes with a tiny brush as they looked down on her. Did they give her pleasure? If so, why?

"You want something to drink?" Cleve asked, pulling out a dining chair for Roe. Nodding yes, Roe wriggled off his backpack and sat.

The placemats on the wood-veneered table illustrated different types of ducks. One had a pan-burn on it that obscured the image. Everything was clean, but worn; scrubbed rather than polished. This was the poorest home Roe had ever been in, he realized as he watched Cleve open the fridge to get out a carton of juice. Kids' drawings were attached to the door by magnets.

Roe looked away. A small whatnot stood in the corner to the left of the sliding doors, and he was surprised to see books on its shelves by Nabokov, Hemingway, Steinbeck, Fitzgerald and Carson McCullers, as well as Jackie Collins, Robert Ludlum and Stephen King.

"My mom used to love to read," Cleve said, handing Roe a glass of orange juice. "She says the pills stop her concentrating."

"Have you read any of them?"

"Some. *Carrie*, *The Great Gatsby*, *Reflections in a Golden Eye*."

"I had to read *Ballad of the Sad Café* for my accelerator."

"Ain't that the best title ever?"

"There's *The Heart is a Lonely Hunter* too. Did you know her husband was gay?"

"Carson McCullers?"

"Yeah."

"TBH, I didn't even know she was a she."

Suddenly shy, they both looked down, then looked up again and met each others' eyes. "You wanna go in the lounge?" Cleve asked.

"Sure."

Roe let Cleve take his hand and lead him through. His heart began to race. Life was happening to him at last. All the TV shows, the comic books, the fantasy sense of himself, fell away in the eight feet between the kitchen and the lounge.

Leaving the curtains closed, Cleve snapped on some lamps. With the ease of habit he stepped up onto a small side table. It creaked uneasily under his weight as, balancing briefly on one foot, he switched on the ceiling fan, the hanging cord of which had evidently broken off some time ago, then quickly stepped back down. The fan began to turn lazily, then picked up speed, lightening the air. The walls of the lounge were paneled with the same varnished pine as the hall.

The couch was covered in brushed brown draylon and looked broken down. In front of it was a low glass coffee-table on which stood a large glass vase of white and pink silk roses, and it was flanked by a matching armchair and a leatherette recliner. Of course Roe took the couch. It was immediately uncomfortable: the springs had given up and the foam cushions had been pressed down into the unyielding frame. Cleve sat down beside him, grunt-ing as his coccyx struck some poorly-padded cross-strut, but he slid his arm around Roe's shoulders and turned into him.

The two of them kissed, then kissed again. Cleve's breath was orange-sweetened, and warm and wet. The kiss deepened. Roe was aware of the smooth bulge of Cleve's bare bicep cushioning his neck, of Cleve's other hand touching him on his side. Craning forward so he wouldn't break the lip-lock, Roe pushed Cleve back, swung round and straddled his hips. Cleve gasped into Roe's mouth and his chest lurched.

At that moment a loud knocking came at the front door, bang bang bang assertive.

Roe jumped up as though he'd been given an electric shock, stumbled backwards into the coffee table and knocked over the vase. Cleve wiped a hand across his mouth, gave Roe a worried look, and stood up too.

Bang bang bang.

Going over to the window, Cleve pulled back a corner of one of the drapes and peeked out.

"Shit."

"What?"

"Cops."

Roe blenched. If the police had come to arrest Cleve for the armed robbery, how on earth could he account for his own presence here? He would be assumed to be a fence or a dealer, and "We were on a date, officer" didn't seem like a winning explanation, given how they'd met. He could try to hide or run, but to hide and be caught, or to run and be caught would make everything worse.

Only now did he wonder what other criminal activi-ties Cleve had been involved in. Maybe he had done genuinely nasty things with his friends. Roe didn't think so. But then wasn't that the bleat of anyone whose partner turned out to be violent? "He wouldn't do anything like that."

Giving him a look that was probably meant to be reassuring but just seemed scared, Cleve gestured to Roe to stay in the lounge while he went and answered the door. Roe listened tensely.

"Hey, officer."

"We've had reports of a break-in here."

"From who?"

"Do you live here?"

"Sure I do. Look." Roe heard the soft click of Cleve unhooking one of the family photos from the wall. "See?"

Roe could hear the officer's slightly open-mouthed breathing. "What's your name, son?"

"Cleve Olsen. My dad's Ken Olsen."

"Where are your folks?"

"Off visiting."

"Home alone, huh?"

"Yeah. My dad reckons I'm old enough."

"A neighbor said a black male was seen entering this domicile."

"Yeah, he came in with me."

"Yeah?"

"He's my study buddy."

"Is that so?"

"He's doin' some tutoring. He's on some scholarship at Tyler A."

"I'll need to see this marvel."

"Sure. Roe!" Cleve called.

With a mouth full of cotton wool, Roe came out into the hall. At least it wasn't the same officer as had come to his house the morning before.

"What's your name?"

"Monroe Jones, sir."

"You got ID?"

"Yes, sir."

With a carefulness that seemed odd to Cleve – almost

a mime – Roe produced his wallet from his jeans' back pocket and from it a student ID and a Tyler Academy library card. The officer looked at them incuriously. "You got something else?"

Cleve started to rise to what was clearly a provocation, but a flash of Roe's eyes stopped him. Roe fished out a public library card. The officer looked it over too, then returned the three pieces without remark.

"We've had reports of an African American male loitering in the area," he said.

"We haven't noticed anyone," Cleve said.

The officer grunted. "Your folks know you're being – tutored?"

"Sure, it was my mom's idea."

"Is that right?"

"You can call her if you like."

"Huh." Dragging the moment out to prove he was in charge, the cop eventually said, "I'll be keeping an eye out. We know there's a meth lab round here."

Roe and Cleve watched him go back to his car, his fingers drumming on the holster at his hip. Roe made the "be seeing you" sign-off from *The Prisoner* and ended up giving the cop's broad back the finger, but didn't say anything. The police car backed out of the drive and left.

"Fuckin' neighbors," Cleve said, leaning out and looking up and down the road. There was still no one around so far as he could see. He closed the door and turned the lock, and he and Roe returned to the lounge, disquieted.

"I should go," Roe said.

"I can drive you out in the morning," Cleve said. "The guy next door lets me use his truck when he's not working and doesn't need it."

"He might've been the one who made the call."

"Naw, the pickup and car are both gone: they're out. Anyway, he'da seen you was with me, so –"

Roe gave him a look that said, *Being with me makes*

*you different from who you were before; they may treat
you differently now.*

"Please stay."

Roe wavered. To get away from Coleman East under
his own steam he would have to ride his board. Even if he
left right now he wouldn't get home before it was fully
dark. Skateboarding dressed in black on an unlit country
road was dangerous, and boarding through a poor white
part of town while being black would be doubly so, at
least.

"Okay," he said. "I'd better call my mom, though."

"Cool. You got charge?"

Roe checked. "Yeah." He scrolled to his mom's number and pressed "call." It went to voicemail. "Hey, Mom,
I'm staying over at Eriq's. His mom said it was cool. Sorry
I'm leaving it so late." He then texted Eriq: *Say I'm with
you if my mom calls.*

Eriq replied, *What's the story, Jones?*

Roe felt a sudden urge to come out to him, but instead
typed, *It's complicated.*

*That sounds like a relationship update.*

*Could be. Be seeing you.*

Roe put his phone away. "When the knock came, I
thought it was going to be about the robbery."

"Me too, dude."

Cleve looked at Roe and wondered again how far his
parents, like his neighbors and the cops, were racist. It
had never mattered to him before, whether it had been
his dad planting a "Make America Great Again" flag on
the front lawn, or his mom griping about the zoners
changing the name Squaw Hill to Squab Hill for reasons
of cultural sensitivity. Now, with Roe standing in front of
him, nervy, coltish and tremulously vulnerable, it suddenly mattered a great deal.

# Chapter Seventeen

A n awkward silence fell between them. "You wanna eat something?" Cleve offered.

"What do you have?"

"There's a stack of pizzas in the freezer."

"Sure, whatever."

Roe went and looked out the kitchen window. Squab Hill's lower parts were in darkness now, though the tail-end of the setting sun threw tiger-stripe tree shadows across its upper half. Tones of gold and pink in the softening light made the room feel cozy and welcoming. The hostile world of adults was shut outside – for now, anyway.

Cleve disappeared into a utility room and returned with two rigid, frost coated pizzas. Roe watched his butt as he moved about the kitchen, putting on the oven, peeling off the plastic covering, rooting out baking trays, slipping the discs of dough off their polystyrene bases. It was nice to admire another boy's butt without worrying about being caught and having to have a line ready to head off homophobic B.S. – wit, or denial. He imagined this was how straight boys felt all the time.

"What do you want to do?" he asked, more to get the conversation going again than out of any particular curiosity. "I mean, like, after high school, or college. Like, would you stay here?"

"That'd be kinda like committing to being dead in advance," Cleve said, but he didn't say he would leave. "What about you?"

"I'll go to New York. Well, or somewhere you can be yourself, anyway."

"You can't do that here?"

"What do you think?"

Cleve thought of Discretions: no, he couldn't be himself here either. But did he have the strength to leave it all behind? To stop drifting like a jellyfish on the tide, as he felt he was doing now, say goodbye to his mom and dad and sister, and head on out to – what?

To Roe, leaving seemed a settled thing. For Cleve to go with Roe, that might mean something. But alone?

"What?"

"Just thinkin'."

Cleve joined Roe at the window. Outside the dusk was deepening fast.

"If we leave all the lights off we can open the slidin' doors an' let some heat out without a zillion moths home invadin'."

"Cool."

Roe watched as Cleve pulled one of the glass doors along its aluminum groove, grunting when it reached a familiar sticking point, taking in the way his biceps flexed. No fresh air came in, but to sit in the low light together was pleasingly intimate.

"You wanna take another look at that thing we found?" Cleve asked.

"Okay." Roe was surprised to realize that actually he wasn't especially keen to. It seemed like bringing trouble in; like inviting some spirit or entity over the threshold.

But Cleve was already squatting down and unzipping his pack and pulling out the satchel. He popped the catch, lifted out the black velvet bag and loosened the drawstring. Then, careful not to touch the crystalline block inside, he tipped it out onto a placemat depicting a mallard duck. It sat there just as cryptic as before, despite its new domestic setting.

"It made me feel like I was falling," Roe said.

"Me too."

A breeze stirred the leaves on the trees, and the rustling sound made them look round, but it was a normal breeze and they could see the leaves shiver.

"You still wanna try an' give it back?" Cleve asked. Roe didn't answer. He thought of curses; of the occult retributions exacted on tomb- and grave-robbers, even casual ones who knew no better; of the lack of forgiveness even when restitution was made.

The ping of the oven made them both start. Cleve got up and, using oven gloves the shape of lobster claws, put the pizzas in, closing the door with a sharp slam to get the catch to click, and turned the timer dial. Then he sat back down next to Roe.

"I'm sure there's, like, something inside it," Roe said.

"You mean like electronic parts?"

"I guess."

"Do you wanna try an' open it up?"

"There are no seams or hinges to get a knife blade or screwdriver into."

"It's kinda like trying to open one of them IUDs."

"IUDs?"

"Like in Fallujah."

"That's an IED. An IUD's like what my sister should have been using."

"Whatever: a bomb."

Roe had been half reaching for the milky crystal block. At the word *bomb* he withdrew his hand. "It makes me think how I don't know how so much stuff works," he said. "I mean, like say I use my Wi-Fi to download a bunch of MP3 files to my phone then synch my cordless headphones to listen to them, how does any of that, like, actually happen? Or say I'm playing a real-time multi-player game with someone in Tokyo, someone else in London – how does any of that really work? It might as well be a bunch of spells."

"Motors I get," Cleve said, nodding in agreement. "You can see what does what an' how. But you open up a phone and there's a bunch of tiny metal blobs on a circuit board printed with microscopic – I dunno – nano this an' that..." He shrugged.

"This is a manufactured thing," Roe said. "I mean, it's not a piece of art, is it?"

"I felt like it was a machine too."

Cleve reached for Roe's hand and took it, looking down and enjoying the contrast of peach-vanilla and mocha, or, as he saw it now, the complement. He moved his thumb gently over the veins on the back of Roe's hand.

An orange glow radiated from the oven, the only source of light in a house now sunk in shadow. A large brown moth came fluttering in. It looped across the room and began to bump futilely against the toughened glass of the oven door. Cleve got up, went over to it, and after a couple of tries – he was touchingly careful, Roe thought, not to harm it – caught the moth in his cupped hands, and went to put it outside.

The moth's wings vibrated against Cleve's skin with surprising power. It was as he released it that he saw the man standing in the backyard.

# Chapter Eighteen

"Roe," Cleve said, and Roe, seeing the stranger, got to his feet.

The man was standing facing the house, about twenty feet away. He was black, maybe in his late twenties, around six feet tall and solidly built, clean-shaven, with a sharp, low fade into which a side part had been razored. His skin was even, mid-brown, and his features were handsome, and would have if anything seemed friendly had he not been wearing a jazzman's sunglasses – the sort with leather surrounds that wholly conceal the eyes – despite the oncoming night. He had on a dull green, military style shirt and pants, and black army boots. His hands hung loose at his sides, and he stood as immobile as a stone. His head was tilted oddly to one side.

Cleve's mind flashed back to the figure he thought he had glimpsed from his bedroom window the night before: had it been this man? And the cop had mentioned a black prowler being seen in the area. Maybe that hadn't been racist lies to get at Roe.

"Hey, dude," he said, uneasily aware the man would

have seen him and Roe holding hands. "So, um, how come you're in my backyard?"

"You took something that belongs to me."

The man turned his head to indicate the crystal block sitting in plain sight on the dining table. The gristle in his neck crackled oddly as he did so. In the dimness of the room the box seemed very faintly to pulse from within.

"I need it back." His voice was strained and flat.

"How'd we know it's yours?" Cleve said. Roe jogged his elbow, but Cleve pressed on. "You mighta looked in just now and –"

"I know what it is. What it does. Do you?"

"Uh, well..."

"I need it. I –" The man looked away, and his brow furrowed as if he was listening for something. "See, you got to be real careful: once they're out, once they're *through* they can..." He cut himself off. "I don't have time for this."

Abruptly he strode forward. Afraid to block him, but more afraid to let him in, neither boy stepped back, and as the man tried to push past them, though he was taller and more heavily built than either of them, his strength seemed suddenly to go; and rather than shoving through he was instead taking hold of Cleve's shoulder and Roe's upper arm as if to stop himself collapsing.

The two young men turned with him and steered him backwards into a dining chair that Cleve hooked out from the table with one foot as they swung round. Though the man's grip was strong, he was dead-weight heavy. Backs straining, they lowered him onto the chair, placing their hands on his chest so he wouldn't slump forwards and tip face-first onto the floor.

"You can let go of us now, dude," Cleve said.

Reluctantly the man did so. With an effort he sat up. His face was sheened with sweat. Roe watched him warily as Cleve went and filled a glass of water at the tap, brought it over and set it down by him on the table. He didn't have the caved in look of a meth head, but apart from the blatant total casualties Roe had occasionally seen around Main Street, he didn't really know how meth heads looked or acted. Certainly the man was in some way seriously unwell.

He took a sip of water, then put the glass back down.

"Dude, what's going on?" Cleve asked him. "You can't just come shoving into people's houses. I mean, we've already had the cops here once this evening," he added, to seed the idea in the man's head that the authorities might show up at any moment.

"The farther you go," the man said, "the more fuel gets used up. That's true there as well as here. And the farther you go, the harder it is to keep moving. Everything runs down."

"Dude –"

"The spiral uses you up. Uses *it* up. The box. The nearer you get to the center. You go off course near the end, you're screwed. No energy, you dig? At the center of the spiral it's all down to you, and by then you could be crawling. That's where I am now."

Cleve and Roe exchanged glances. What were you supposed to do when someone with what appeared to be serious mental health problems staggered into your home? Humor them? Try and get them to talk sense and get a name and address out of them?

At least the man didn't seem to be in any condition to be actually dangerous, just potentially horribly socially awkward.

Cleve wondered what his parents would do if they were here, if Terri was here, a kid, vulnerable. Call the cops, probably. Or maybe the state mental hospital. Maybe that was what he should do.

"So, um," Roe said.

"Call me Hark," the man said, stretching out a hand.

Roe shook it briefly and a shade reluctantly. It was warm and smooth, only slightly clammy with sweat. "I'm Roe," he said. "This is Cleve." Hark nodded, not offering Cleve his hand. "He's my, um, friend. This is, like, his house."

"So what's with the sunglasses, Hark?" Cleve asked, slightly annoyed to witness a connection being forged from which he was excluded.

"The cheaters? They're to –" Hark moved his head sharply, tilting an ear toward the ceiling. "You hear that? Upstairs?"

Roe and Cleve listened intently. "I don't hear anything," Roe said. "Cleve?"

"No."

"It's easier for them in the dark," Hark said. "More like what they're used to. Out there, where there's less of everything."

"'Them'?" Cleve asked.

"They don't have a name." Hark abruptly drained the rest of the glass of water. "You ever seen them ugly fish pulled up in nets sometimes, from the deepwater places no light ever gets to?"

Cleve and Roe nodded.

"They don't look like that, they don't look like anything you can put words to, but that's the spirit of 'em," Hark said. "Mouth and teeth. Appetite and no mind, you dig? And you make a crack. You have to, that's how it works. You pass through where they float, waiting. It's an in between place you got to go through, dig, to get from A to B. They sense you in there – they got *other* senses – and they come rushin'. Sometimes you don't move fast enough, don't zip it up quick enough, and one gets through. Then there's nothin' you can do but keep moving. Or if there is, I haven't figured it out. I didn't oughtta be talking 'bout this, though: they find out, they'll bust my chops."

This second "they" seemed to be different from the first.

"Keep movin', keep ahead of 'em and maybe they'll starve. There's a formulation to it, a calculation. Like, a cheetah'll run so far then give up. But I'm so damn tired."

Roe indicated the crystal block. "So what is it?"

"That's an ancestor box, brother."

"What's an ancestor box?"

"You never seen one before?" Hark said. "I guess not. You shouldn't be seeing it now. Either of you. If they find out I let you..."

"So what's it *for*?" Roe interrupted. All he could think to do was keep talking to Hark as if what he was saying was real and made sense. Sometimes being with his great grand was like this: her alluding to things hidden, things unseen, bibliomancy and cryptic prophecy, none of which he believed in. But that was at least within a framework he understood: the Bible.

"You can use it to move," Hark said. "Up and down. Backwards and forwards. On the diagonal." He spoke as though those directions were unusual and significant. "It opens doors in and doors out."

"Is it a machine?"

Hark turned his blind man's glasses towards it. "Well, it's a device. Yeah, I'll say that. Some dope they don't never give you."

"But it's yours, right?"

"It was assigned to me."

"By who?"

"First off I thought I was inside it," Hark said. "I thought it was a coffin. My coffin, you dig?" He smiled teeth-baringly, as if such a mistake were easily made and understandable. "Then I thought it was what them pharaohs used when they hoped for resurrection of the body. A what you call it, canopic jar. Yeah. That. They store the brains and guts inside, seal it up with wax against the worm and time. Put a head on top like say, Anubis or Bast. But that was wrong too. It's just a box."

"So, um, what's really inside it, then?" Roe asked.

"Rage and pain and terror."

"Whose?"

Hark bared his teeth again. "Mine."

"But how –"

"That's what powers it. But it's dying now."

"I saw you," Cleve said suddenly. "*We* saw you." He turned to Roe. "When you was pullin' down the statue and the stoplight exploded: the lightning bolt. I told you I saw –"

"A door opening," Roe said.

"An' someone coming through –"

"The statue." Hark swiveled his blind man's shades onto Roe. "That was you?"

"Uh, yeah. Me and some friends. We felt like we had to –"

"Goddamn it, that's why I – See, how it is, there are systems of navigation, points of orientation. Moon maps. Slave graveyards. Confederate statues. Needles in the skin of a suffering world. Ley lines, you heard of them?"

"Theoretical points of connection between circles of Neolithic standing stones," Roe said. Off Cleve's look he added, "So I'm a geek."

"See, there's an architecture to it. I mean, spirit physics. Triangulations." Hark was talking to himself now, it seemed. "I gotta figure this. Get back on the beam." He looked up at Cleve. "You got some joe, bro?"

"Joe?"

"Mocha loca, java, joe. Coffee." A violent shudder passed through Hark. "I'm freezing."

Cleve and Roe exchanged a look: the night was humid and, despite what he had just said, Hark was sweating heavily.

"I'll fix us some," Cleve said.

"Swell."

Not wanting to just sit there next to Hark, Roe went to help Cleve, opening unfamiliar cupboards at random in search of mugs as Cleve filled the percolator at the sink. Glancing back, he saw Hark reach out and take hold of the crystal block. If Roe was expecting something to happen, he was disappointed: Hark slipped the box into the breast pocket of his shirt with all the drama of someone putting away a pack of cigarettes.

Gripping the edges of the table, Hark tried to pull himself upright and stand, but he didn't have the strength. With a pained grunt that made Cleve look round he sank back down, tilting the dining table as he did so. Its far-side feet lifted then came back down with a thud, and several placemats slid and clacked together.

"Dude," Cleve said, "being real with you: do we need to call an ambulance?"

"The dead don't need ambulances."

"So, um, you're dead?"

Cocking his head to one side, Hark smiled tightly. "It's – complicated."

# Chapter Nineteen

"**I** guess it would be," Cleve said amiably. "You want cream in that, or sugar? Or, um, sweetener?"

"Just black, strong and hot."

"If you're dead," Roe said, "how did you die?"

The blind man's smoked lenses swiveled his way. "That's personal."

"Oh, right."

Roe and Cleve stood awkwardly in the middle of the room, waiting for the pot to perk, wishing they could talk privately but not prepared to leave Hark unwatched.

Eventually the coffee was ready. Cleve poured a steaming mug and brought it over to Hark, and he and Roe watched as Hark drank the scalding liquid straight down. Thinking of the damage to his gullet it must have caused, both their minds once more went to thoughts of mental illness; to the impulse to self harm, and the possibility that such an impulse might get turned outwards, against them.

Hark wiped the back of his hand across his mouth. "There's just one more to get cleared off," he said. He sounded revitalized.

"One more what?" Cleve asked.

"Postcard."

"Why do you collect blank postcards?" Roe asked.

"They're not blank."

"There's nothing on them, dude," Cleve said, tired of what was starting to feel like an endless circle of random statements that never got anywhere.

"But there *was*, buddy," Hark said. "And I had to take it off, see?" He held the mug out for a refill.

Reluctantly Cleve took it from him and went back to the pot. "Don't burn your mouth, dude," he said as he brought the mug back brimming.

"It's cold out there in the lightless places," Hark said. "It gets deep in your bones. What I need is – do you have a thermometer?"

"What?" Cleve said. "Why?"

"For the mercury."

"I don't know. Maybe somewhere. But I don't feel like you're making a whole lot of sense, and I gotta be honest, it's gettin' kinda difficult to keep going with it."

Cleve wanted to ask – tell – Hark to go, but somehow his being black was intertwined with Roe being black; and though Cleve was white, his being with Roe now meant there was a connection to this man he wouldn't previously have felt. Even if it was a connection Roe might himself repudiate, still Cleve couldn't just tell Hark to leave.

Hark took another swallow of the near-boiling coffee. "I gotta find it first, though, and your horns interfere."

"Horns?" Roe said. Hark pointed to where Cleve's phone sat charging by the toaster. "You mean cell phones?"

"Cell?" Hark turned the word over in his mind. "Beehives. Penitentiaries... Huh. Something about 'em pulls the alignment off, just a little. It was easier in the past. Then it was just radio waves you had to navigate."

"You're not that old," Roe said.

Hark shrugged. "So you guys, you in a, ah, a – situation?"

Roe glanced at Cleve. "Uh, yeah," he said, forcing definiteness, even defiance into his voice. "Is that a problem?"

"Ah, naw, it's copa," Hark said, waving a hand dismissively.

"What?"

"Chill, little brother. When I was over there in Europe I saw – *everything*, you dig? I saw comrades in arms. Yeah. And boys who smiled to see you. French, Belgian, all that. It wasn't nothin' to me."

"Okay."

"And since then I've gotten me a – wider perspective."

"So, um, Hark," Cleve said carefully, "what are you planning on doing next?"

"Track the last card. Dismantle it. That's what the mercury's for. Then I'm done. I'm at the center of the spiral, and I'm free." He turned to Roe. "It's kinda like we met before, someplace."

"Not likely."

"There's somethin'..."

"How do you track a postcard?" Cleve asked, once again moving the conversation in the direction of Hark leaving.

"It's near, real near. I know that. But I had my last ride. The box is done. Now I have to find it on foot. Quarter the area like a Choctaw. When I'm close by, the compass'll help."

Cleve and Roe remembered the device with the curious cardinals they had found in Hark's bag and put aside without further interest.

"Ordinals," Hark said, pulling the satchel towards him by the strap.

"Um, I don't think," Roe began, vaguely remembering

that cardinal numbers had nothing to do with cardinal points, but cutting himself off because what did it matter what weird word Hark chose for the points of his whacky compass? Ordinals, whatever.

Hark rummaged in the bag, found the compass and set it on the table. It was brass, about three inches across. The needle rotated lazily, refusing to settle. Roe looked more closely at the letters that marked the points. They were of black enamel and looked like runes, sigils, or possibly First Nations letters, and were inlaid in a disc of bone or maybe ivory. Something old, anyway.

Roe sighed. Like Cleve, he could see the pair of them getting caught up in trailing around after some crazy person just to be polite, looking for an old postcard with nothing on it, (which apparently meant there was really some big deal something on it), eventually guiltily getting shot of him somewhere, with no guarantee Hark wouldn't show up at the house again now he'd found someplace where someone had let him in. And Roe just wanted to be on his own with Cleve: their window of privacy was brief and unlikely to be repeated.

Hark's head tipped forward. Had he fallen asleep? Roe exchanged a look with Cleve, and quietly said, "Hark?"

No reply came. Cleve waved a hand in front of the man's hidden eyes. No response. He reached for the sunglasses, then decided against it. What, after all, could there be to be revealed? Quietly he said to Roe, "Let's go in the lounge."

Keeping their eyes on Hark they went through, leaving the door open so they could watch him where he sat. Beyond the open patio doors the night and the hillside were now blue-black.

"What d'you think?" Cleve asked, taking Roe's hand in his. The connection was reassuring, and reminded them both that there was a real, solid world to keep hold of. "I mean, he's got a screw loose, right?"

"I wish he'd just, like, go," Roe said. "He's like some dreaded uncle or something." He slipped a forefinger through a loop on the front of Cleve's jeans shorts and pulled their hips together. It was like activating an electromagnet. They kissed deeply, excitedly, then broke off self-consciously and looked round at Hark. He still seemed asleep. Roe kissed Cleve again, reaching up and cupping the base of Cleve's buzz-cut skull in his hands, the sharkskin feel thrilling against his palms, and Cleve exhaled warmth into Roe's mouth and slid his tongue in.

It was then that they heard the sound from upstairs.

A heavy thud, and then rustling, like an old silk hoop-skirt being dragged along.

Hand in hand, they went over to the lounge doorway, leant out and looked up the stairs that led from the hall to the second floor. No lights were on up there. Roe became aware that his skin was prickling and goosebumping, as if with cold, or fear, or – static.

*Shit.*

Keeping his eyes on the staircase, Cleve slipped along to the kitchen, opened a drawer, and returned with a carving knife. Together he and Roe looked up the stairs into the dark.

Roe thought of the predatory fish of the deep oceans that never see the light; that hang silently waiting, mouths a-gape. He wondered if coldblooded creatures longed for the warmth of the warmly living, and were drawn towards it. Would light help deter whatever was up there? He reached for the wall switch and flicked it. Up above there was the soft plink of a bulb blowing, and the darkness, if anything, deepened.

Cleve put his foot on the bottom step. It creaked: a dead giveaway.

# Chapter Twenty

"**D**on't."

Roe and Cleve looked round to see Hark standing in the kitchen doorway. He was holding the ancestor box cupped in both hands, looking down at it as though it was an offering, a lit candle to be carried carefully. Slowly he came forward.

"Stand back."

Cleve and Roe moved away from the foot of the stairs. The static field intensified with each step Hark took towards them, and the backs of their necks crawled as they had in the ruins of the plantation house, except now it was ten times worse, and was accompanied by a rapidly expanding, formless fear that was physically sickening.

Up above, something heavy was dragging itself effortfully along. Roe wanted to shout aloud to release the tension, but his jaws were locked; Cleve wanted to vomit and his mouth was watering grotesquely.

Hark bent forward, murmured some words over the little box and breathed on it. It glowed from within, like an ember reviving, but only very faintly.

"You can do it," Hark murmured, and he exhaled on it

again. "C'mon now. Please..."

A blue spark flashed from the box up into the dark. The cloying static vanished as abruptly and totally as if it had never existed, and a moment later a smell came drifting down like burning hair or horn that caught unpleasantly in their nostrils and clung to the roofs of their mouths.

Hark drew a shuddering breath and looked down at his cupped hands. "Dead now," he said sadly.

Cleve and Roe looked. What rested there was no longer a crystal block but the skeleton of some small and unfamiliar animal, near to a mouse or vole in size and general outline, but with an unusually high-domed skull and queerly elongated paws. They saw it only briefly, and would later argue over whether Hark had managed some sleight-of-hand substitution in the seconds when they looked away. The thought didn't occur to them then, however; and at the sight of the small skeleton both young men experienced an inexplicable sense of loss.

Roe rubbed his goose-bumped upper arms briskly: the prickly sensation still coated his skin. "You want to go see what's up there?" he asked Cleve.

Cleve looked up the stairs and said, "Dude, I do not." Then, to qualify what might be seen as a lack of courage, he added, "Well, yeah, sure, in the morning. When it's light and we can see properly and –"

A pinging sound from the direction of the kitchen made the three of them look round. It was the oven. The pizza was ready.

Roe half-laughed, surprised to realize that only twenty minutes had passed since he and Cleve first saw Hark in the backyard, and disconcerted by the irruption of the banal into what had become so quickly deeply weird.

A glance at Hark's hands showed Roe the little skeleton was gone.

"Let's eat," Cleve said.

They trooped through to the kitchen, Cleve took the pair of pizzas from the oven and split them three ways, and they ate in silence round the dining table. At first Cleve and Roe, due to the after-effects of the static build up on their guts, took only tiny bites, but after a while their stomachs settled and their appetites returned. Soon they felt less cowed by what had happened.

"Do you reckon there are any more of those things around?" Cleve asked. At that moment, though unseen, the shadowy hunting creatures were as real to him as mountain lions or bears.

"Not close by," Hark said, setting a crust down on the baking tray and blotting his mouth with kitchen roll. He seemed almost cheerful.

"How do you know?" Roe asked.

Hark tapped the compass with a knuckle. "Letters'd change. It's got two faces, see."

"Right. Um –"

"Moon letters and sun letters."

"Right."

Roe finished his slice, set down a sliver of crust next to Hark's, wiped his fingers and blotted his lips too. *He sacrificed his ancestor box, his magical traveling box for us*, he thought. *Maybe saved our lives.* He realized they were talking as if everything Hark had told them was true; as if it explained what had happened in the Tyler house, and now in Cleve's house.

He was sure at that moment that Cleve believed too, but as in the ruins of the plantation house, what had they actually *seen*? A spark jump into shadows. Some little bones, of a harvest mouse or something. Roe despised stories where the characters were perversely resistant to plain proof of the supernatural, but what he found himself confronted by now was too messy and vague to be solidly convincing. And even if it was convincing, of what did it convince? That some psychic – parapsychic –

poison had poured out of an old plantation house, perhaps out of history itself?

Okay, yeah. That, somehow. But what more?

Maybe, whatever Hark babbled on about, it was something – an emanation – revived or even created by two boys, one black, one white, on a date in the wrong place, and wouldn't it always be the wrong time?

The thought arrived with the force of a conviction: *We were the catalysts.*

He shuddered. "Home alone with a cute boy" had turned into not daring to go upstairs because of something gross up there that was possibly – or impossibly – of a supernatural nature, combined with having to play nice with a home invader, all the while desperate to get passionate but not being able to because said home invader was mentally ill or (let's face it, considerably less likely) genuinely possessed of supernatural powers.

Roe imagined a counter-factual: himself and Cleve sitting on the couch in his own front room, his sister Phyllis giving them the hairy eyeball as they waited for her to go to bed so they could cozy up together. Of course she would sit on and on, flicking idly and noisily through *O* magazine while the grandmother clock clunked and whirred and chimed one then another, then another, quarter hour.

Stuffed with not-very-special pizza, in the warmth of the kitchen Roe found himself yawning and stretching his arms as though, rather than 9 p.m., it was two in the morning.

Cleve cleared the debris away, and out of some desire to mark a transition, the three of them trailed through to the lounge. Hark took the sofa, sinking down onto it with a grunt and preventing Roe and Cleve from sitting together, though this didn't seem intentional. He made no attempts at conversation, and soon enough seemed to doze off again.

Wordlessly Cleve caught Roe's hand and led him through to the backyard. The sky was clear, the moon was full, and beyond its bright corona the stars were dense.

"Okay, so, um," Cleve said, sotto voce, "first up. Do you – believe any of it?"

"It's certainly weird," Roe said. "Like, extremely."

"Yeah, but *and*?"

"You mean, is he crazy?"

"Yeah."

"Probably. But don't forget the law of the excluded middle."

"What's that?"

"He could be, like, certifiable *and* it could all still be true. Well, not the bit about being dead, obviously – I mean, he ate pizza. But some of it."

A bat swooped by, nearly invisible in the dark, and vanished against the black backdrop of the trees. "Yeah, but the thing is," Cleve said, "back in the house, that all happened *first*, right? Before we looked in the bag. It wasn't like – I mean, no one said you're gonna see, I dunno, a creature."

"But we didn't, though, did we? I mean, like, actually see anything."

"Aw, Roe, yeah, but we felt it, though."

Roe smiled. "I like you saying my name."

Cleve smiled too, and his hand found Roe's again and took it lightly. "Till you spoke with that cop I thought it was 'row' like in rowboat. Do we – is there anything we actually need to do? I mean, he's gonna go in the morning, I guess, and then that's kind of it."

"I guess so."

"Do you wanna – help him?"

Roe shrugged. "I don't know. I kind of feel something..." He tailed off.

"Is it to do with, um – I mean, with you both being, you know, black?" Cleve asked.

"Us 'being, you know, black'?" Roe echoed, gently mocking but not withdrawing his hand. "It's more because he's blaming me for throwing him off course. So I feel like if I – if we – hadn't pulled the statue down he'd be okay."

"Doing whatever he's doing."

"Whatever that is. If any of it's real."

"I'd say come to bed but it's all turned out too weird."

"Yeah."

"Hang on, dude," Cleve said, struck by some sudden thought. "Stay there."

Roe waited as Cleve went back inside, disappearing round an L at the far end of the dining room, returning bent over and ass first, dragging an outsize denim beanbag. "We call it the Big Ass," he said as Roe helped him pull it out into the yard.

Roe surveyed the giant pockets sewn onto the beanbag and smiled. After brushing away cobwebs and spider eggs he and Cleve sat down on it. Indented in the middle, it was like lying in a giant donut, and they were tipped into each other enjoyably. They squirmed about a bit, got comfortable, lay back and looked up at the stars.

"As a date I'd say this has been quite memorable," Roe said, as Cleve slid an arm around his shoulders.

"Yeah?" Cleve asked. "Yeah," he nodded in agreement with himself. And smiling and serious he lent in and kissed Roe gently on the lips.

# Chapter Twenty-One

S nuggling into each other, Cleve and Roe drifted into sleep, waking cramped and slightly chilled in the small hours of the morning. With achy backs they struggled up from the now dew-fringed Big Ass, dragged it back into the house, then went through to the lounge. There they found Hark sleeping stretched out on the couch. Cleve gestured for Roe to take the leatherette recliner, which you could lie back on more fully than the armchair, and they dozed some more.

Cleve woke again a little after six a.m. The sun was bright around the edges of the drapes and spilled in through the open doorway. He took a moment to lightly kiss Roe's bare, smooth shoulder, then wandered out into the hall.

The stairs and upper floor were waiting for him.

Cleve took a breath, put a hand on the newel post for luck, and quickly went up. More than anything he wanted there to be nothing to find. In a rising morning bright with birdsong he wanted to forget all the weirdness and get on with his new life with Roe. That was enough of a challenge, enough excitement for someone living in a small southern town; maybe more than enough.

Still, he anticipated discovering some spiny fishlike thing lying on the landing, something with blind white eyes and the serrated teeth of a piranha or a great white shark. Something disgusting he would need to scoop into a trash bag and bury in the yard before it stank the house out with its rapid, decompressed rotting.

All he found, however, was a large black mark on the carpet, as if someone had burnt a heap of paper and ground the ash into the nap. Going down on his hands and knees, Cleve bent forward and sniffed it. There was a smell like charcoal, but no hint of any accelerant like paraffin or lighter fluid. The mark was lozenge-shaped with a sort of short tail, and about four feet long and at its widest point two feet across.

Cleve sighed. He would have to try and scrub it away before his parents got back. Not that his mom could get upstairs, but his dad would, and what explanation could he offer that didn't sound like total B.S.?

He passed the black mark by and went and emptied his bladder, washed his face, splashed his armpits and deodorized, brushed his teeth and came back downstairs. Roe and Hark were still asleep so he went through to the kitchen and checked his phone. No calls, no messages. He pulled out the connector. The charge remained at 100%: no weird power drain. Everything about him looked and felt normal, Hark's leather satchel the only testament to the reality of last night.

"Hey."

Cleve turned and saw Roe leaning in the doorway, looking sleepy and slender and cute. "Hey, dude."

Roe mooched into the kitchen and they kissed briefly. "Can I shower?"

"Sure. It's upstairs."

"Is that, um, going to be okay?"

"What? Oh, yeah. There's nothing up there, just kind

of a weird burn mark on the carpet." It was like they were discussing the aftermath of a drunken party where some things got spilt and your parents would be mad. "The bathroom's first on the right. There's towels in the airing cupboard."

"Thanks."

Cleve smiled to himself as he listened to Roe climb the creaky stairs. In a jumbled-up way this was the domestic life he had imagined for himself: *my man in my home*. He wondered how Roe liked his eggs – if he even liked eggs. Maybe he preferred cereal.

That was when Cleve realized there were only a few slops left in the milk carton, and they'd likely turned sour. The nearest store wouldn't be open until 7:30 and was a twenty minute bike ride away. *I got bread*, he thought. So: toast, eggs, coffee, O.J., and there was leftover bacon in the fridge he could fry up. *Okay*.

He went through to the lounge and looked in on Hark, who still slept, apparently heavily. What if he didn't wake up naturally and then couldn't be woken? Psychiatric medication could be hardcore, Cleve had read.

The shower began to run overhead, and in a little while Cleve heard Roe singing fragments of songs rather more tuneful than you would expect from an avowed punk/death metal-head. Cleve broke eggs into a bowl, added black pepper and – after a wary sniff – a dash of the leftover milk, and whisked them up to scramble.

He had left the sliding doors open overnight, and now he noticed a few dry leaves had blown in over the threshold. If she had been here, that would have earned him a scolding from his mom. Trapped downstairs and in her own body, Myrtle was fearful of intruders, especially "meth heads" who would "just hack you up for the hell of it," and incursions by wild animals. "Raccoons look cute, but they can have rabies," she would lecture. "Even squirrels can have it. Mammals."

"What about deer?" He tried, but couldn't picture a deer in a frothing, frenzied rage.

"Just keep the doors shut, Cleve. Is that too much to ask?"

His carelessness gave him a thrill of guilt and pleasure.

Filling a plastic bowl with hot water and detergent, Cleve pulled on rubber gloves, dug out some dishcloths and went up to the landing to swab away the worst of the charcoal mess. At first he just spread it out alarmingly, but after a while he got a blotting technique together that worked better, helped by wringing the cloths out frequently as he worked. There was an odd red undertone to the ash, but otherwise it seemed normal. Non-spooky.

The bathroom door opened and Roe emerged, fully dressed, in a drift of steam. He had used Cleve's deodorant, making the familiar scent strange and exciting, and Cleve decided he should shower too.

Of course if he'd been quicker off the mark he could have suggested sharing the shower, though those moments when your butt bumped against the cold tiles or clammy shower curtain before the water warmed up weren't very sensually appealing.

After reducing the stain on the carpet to a pale, grayish swirl, he left it to see how visible it would be when it dried out, and went back downstairs. Roe had taken a seat at the dining table. Cleve emptied and washed out the bowl, hung the gloves over the taps to dry, and went back upstairs to shower. He found that Roe had placed his used towel neatly in the laundry basket.

The warm water felt good on his skin, and washed strangeness away.

Rinsing out the tub afterwards, Cleve noticed a few coiled hairs dotted about, intimate proofs of an unfamiliar presence, and it seemed almost a repudiation to sluice them away. Some of his sister Terri's long, straight hairs

latticed the plughole, slowing the outflow. Cleve deodorized, went through to his bedroom, put on a fresh tee and
briefs and his jeans shorts, and came downstairs. Roe was
still sitting at the table, now half reading a Jackie Collins.

Hark came ambling through from the lounge, yawning. He still wore his blind man's shades, and Roe
thought of people who wrapped tinfoil round their heads
to stop their thoughts being read, and other manifesta-
tions of mental problems.

"You wanna shower?" Cleve offered.

Hark nodded. "That'd be jake." Cleve led him upstairs
and showed him where the towels were, and left him to it.
By then it was nearly seven a.m. Soon it would be time to
try and borrow Dale's pickup.

The water ran for a long time and there was no sound
of movement. Cleve and Roe found themselves exchanging uneasy glances. Eventually Cleve cracked and went up
to find out what was going on. The stain on the carpet
was paler now, but still obvious. He tapped on the bathroom door. No response. The water kept running. "You
okay in there?" he called.

Silence.

"Hark? You okay?" he called again.

Still nothing. He reached for the knob.

"Dude, I'm worried. I'm coming in, okay?"

Despite his words he waited another thirty seconds
before going in. The door wasn't locked – the lock had
seized up years ago; Cleve and his dad and sister just
pushed the laundry basket up against it to stop others
from entering while they were in there.

Opening the door, Cleve saw Hark standing at the
sink, facing away from him, a towel round his waist. His
broad brown back was strongly muscled, and pocked with
small, shiny scars. The blind man's shades sat on the
shelf above the sink and Hark was staring at his reflection
in the mirror. As if he hadn't realized Cleve was there, he

wiped condensation from its surface.

Then Cleve saw Hark's eyes, and his world fell away.

In place of pupils and irises there was silver, or mercury, or shards of mirror. "I'm sorry," Cleve blurted.

Hark looked round, surprised, and there was no doubting it: his eyes were liquid metal – what was that old word? Cleve couldn't think. Hark reached for his shades quickly but Cleve was already pounding down the stairs and hurrying into the kitchen.

"What?" Roe asked, taking in Cleve's startled expression and half-rising from his chair.

"His eyes, dude," Cleve said. "They're" (yeah, that was the word) "quicksilver."

They were back in the trap. Everything Hark had told them, everything that had happened last night was real.

# Chapter Twenty-Two

There was nothing for Roe and Cleve to do but wait for Hark to come down. When eventually he did so, the blind man's glasses were firmly back in place. His appearance otherwise was normal, even smart.

"Cleve said your eyes..." Roe began.

"There's a price you got to pay to see where you're going," Hark said. "To see where *I'm* going. You need spirit eyes, little brother. You dig?"

The compass was where he had left it the night before, on the table next to the satchel. Hark slung the satchel over his shoulder and picked the compass up.

"I best be leavin' now. You said you could give me a ride."

"Yeah." Cleve looked up at the wall clock: 7:35. Most days the Rippels were up well before then, so he reckoned it would be okay to go ask them about borrowing the truck. If they wouldn't lend it to him he didn't know what he would do.

He tugged on his trainers and went out. The morning was bright and already hot.

As he crossed from his front yard to theirs, he had an

uneasy feeling he would be somehow revealed to the Rippels. Revealed as what, though? A white person who chose to be in the company of black people? But that was invisible when it was just him, wasn't it? Anyway, so what?

Velma smiled when she came to see who was rattling at her screen door, and welcomed him in. "How you managin', honey?" she asked. Big boned herself, she had watched Myrtle being shoveled into the family vehicle with genuine sympathy, and knew Cleve was home alone.

"Just fine, thank you," Cleve said, trying not to come across shifty as he asked, "I was wonderin' if Dale'd let me use his truck this mornin'. I promised my dad I'd go pick up some posts from the timber yard."

"I'm sure that'll be fine. Dale?" Velma called through. "Is it okay if Cleve borrows the pickup?"

"Long as it's back by four," her husband called back. "Keys are by the door."

Velma unhooked them and handed them to Cleve. "So long as it's back by four," she repeated. "I fixed pancakes for breakfast. Can I tempt you? They've turned out pretty good."

"Aw, I would, but I guess I'd better get on."

"Well, okay, then, hon." She smiled again. "Be seeing you."

"Be seeing you." The phrase was Roe's now, along with his funny hand-gesture. Velma went back inside. She hadn't mentioned hearing about the prowler, and seemed not to know the police had come to Cleve's house.

Now Cleve just had to sneak Roe and Hark into the truck. He decided the best way would be to park it briefly in his own driveway, where, owing to a high laurel hedge between their properties, it would be pretty much out of sight of the Rippels. The engine juddered even more than usual, and it took Cleve several goes to jam the stick into reverse, but he managed eventually.

"You got that thermometer, buddy?" Hark asked, the instant he came back in.

Cleve went upstairs, rummaged about in the bathroom medicine cabinet and came back with one from when Terri was a baby. "Is this okay?"

Hark examined it. "Yeah, I reckon that's enough to do the job."

"Okay," Cleve said, "let's go. I reckon – am I bein' paranoid? – once you're in, maybe kind of lean over so no one sees you."

Neither Roe nor Hark demurred. Somehow that morning everything had converged to make the presence of these two black men in the all-white community of Coleman East criminal, despite no crime having been committed; despite one of them being an invited and indeed welcome guest.

Roe slung his pack over one shoulder and they slipped from the house, Roe first, then Hark, then Cleve, hurrying across the lawn and clambering quickly into the rusty old pickup.

"So where to?" Cleve asked as he backed out onto the deserted highway.

Hark, who was looking down at his compass, shrugged. "Onwards, buddy."

"Not helpful, dude."

Cleve decided to head in the direction of Claypit. Roe and Hark slumped low in their seats, though Roe was quick to sit up again once they were past the houses. The sun was low and bright behind them, throwing long shadows forward.

They had been driving for about ten minutes when suddenly Hark said, "Stop here. Here!"

"Okay, okay," Cleve said. Without checking his rearview mirror he pulled over, bringing the truck to a jerky halt, and yanked up the handbrake. "Jeez."

He looked round, and found they were in front of the

padlocked gates of the Tyler Academy.

Ivy clung to its high, red brick walls, and on their tops shards of glass sparkled in the morning sunshine.

"Look," Hark said. He offered up the compass, keeping it level on the palm of his hand. The needle, which before had rotated constantly, never settling, now pointed steadily through the gates towards the gothic edifice beyond.

It seemed to Roe that the compass's cardinals, which Hark had called ordinals, were different from the ones he had seen the night before. This morning they seemed not so much runic but more kind of Arabic. "That's my school," he said. "It's closed for the summer."

"Good," Hark said. "That makes it easier."

"Easier for what?"

"Getting in."

"You're going to break into my school?"

"We are."

"Um, no."

"I have the need but not the strength."

The truck's idling engine juddered stomach-churningly. Cleve turned it off. Across the road birds twittered glintingly among the trees, and it was as if he had never noticed how loud birdsong was.

"They're, like, having a bunch of building stuff done," Roe said, as though he was continuing a conversation they hadn't actually quite been having. There had been a fundraiser to refurbish the science block, he said, and the principal had told the students the work would be carried out over the summer break. "I guess that means there'll be, like, people about, doing stuff."

"By night, then." Hark leant across Roe to study the gates and scope the high brick walls. "Get me in there and you'll never see me again."

"Is that a promise, dude?" Cleve asked.

"Oh, yeah."

To Cleve the conversation was disquietingly like the one he had had with Spider, Karen and Choc in Spider's lounge that had led to planning the robbery; and it reminded Roe of the debates he had had with Eriq, Will and Mikey on the bandstand, at Oz, which had led to their decision to take down the statue of Colonel Tyler. In both cases you found yourself agreeing to something rash, drawn on by the desire to make things happen, even things that were dangerous to the point of being self-destructive; and by a sense of invincibility you knew was misguided, but you felt it anyway. And wasn't that how come he and Roe had met, Cleve thought, and wouldn't more of it add to the thrill? A glance told him Roe felt the same. There was no question: they would do this.

"We could all meet back here later, like after mid-night," he said.

"I'm, like, expected home pretty much now," Roe said, glancing at the time on his phone. "If I don't show up, my mom'll call Eriq, he'll lie badly as usual and get busted, and I'll get grounded, especially after the other night."

It seemed almost stupid to Roe to be talking of such childish things as groundings; to be referring to that other, mundane, parental reality. Another sort of past clawing at his young man's heels.

Cleve restarted the truck. After a careful check of his mirrors, he pulled out. "I can drop you at the bottom of the Side. I mean, if that's okay?" He had noticed Roe notice the Confederate flag decal on Dale's truck when he got in.

"That'd be fine," Roe said.

"You live up on the Side?" Hark said. "I haven't been there in..." He laughed softly and shook his head. Roe and Cleve exchanged a look: this was the first time Hark had mentioned a personal connection to the area. "Do you know –" he began, then cut himself off. "No, you wouldn't. That was..." He shrugged.

"So you got people in Claypit, Hark?" Cleve asked.

"Not anymore."

Hark couldn't be more than thirty years old, and Cleve wondered if he had been in prison; had maybe ratted someone out to get a reduced sentence, and so was afraid to go back where he used to live. But Cleve knew people who'd done time, like Spider, or were doing time, like his cousin Vince, and Hark didn't have their particular erratic mix of boldness and unease in his dealings with the world.

"The Side," Hark said. "Yeah, I could see it again." He turned to Roe. "I reckon I'll walk up with you, young brother."

"Oh."

"If that's copa with you."

"Um, 'copa'?" Hark had used the unfamiliar word once before.

"Copa – copacetic. It means okay, you dig? Okay with you."

Roe shrugged a grudging assent. "It's a free country, kind of."

They reached the town square just before eight a.m. A handful of vehicles were already parked in designated spaces around its edges. Baseball-capped street sweepers in municipal overalls were unhurriedly brushing dead leaves from the gutters, and picking trash from low, trimly-boxed hedges with long-handled grabs.

A hundred yards or so along Main Street, just past the turn into Van Cleef Avenue, Cleve pulled over. No one was around. Hark got out first.

"See you at midnight," Roe said, finding the courage to shoot Cleve a kiss on the cheek despite Hark's presence, and Cleve smiled as Roe slid out of the truck and slammed the door behind him.

Cleve watched Roe and Hark in his wing mirror as they headed back into the dazzle, and the effect was almost magical. Soon they took the tree-framed turning up into the Side and passed from his sight. He sighed, forced the truck into gear, did an illegal u-turn and gunned the clattering engine. There would be nothing to do once he got home but wait for the night.

As he was passing back through the town square his phone rang. Roe? No: it was Karen. He answered guiltily and with forced brightness, "Hey, Karen."

"So you got new friends?" she said.

"Aw, Karen, what?" – cradling the phone awkwardly under his jaw as he changed up the gears.

"I saw you. Just now."

"I didn't see you."

"Yeah, well maybe you didn't want to. So?"

"So?"

"Who are they?"

"One's a friend, the other I was givin' a ride to. If that's okay with you."

She didn't reply.

"Karen? You there?"

"Yeah."

"Is Spider out yet?"

"He couldn't make bail. They sent him to Welt."

"Okay, well, my cousin's there, so I guess I can, I dunno, let him know or somethin'."

"How come the cops turned up so fast?"

"What?"

"You know what."

"Wow, I can't believe you're even –"

"You bailed on us, Cleve, and then thirty seconds later they –"

"Fuck, Karen," Cleve interrupted, forcing another gear-change. "It was nothin' to do with me. It was the statue. The cops were comin' to that an' they musta seen the robbery goin' on. I mean, they had to drive literally right past it. I'd gone to the intersection. By the time I got back to warn 'em they were already being busted."

"What were you doing there?"

"I heard a weird noise so I went to see."

"Okay," she said. "I guess."

"What about the others?" Cleve asked, but she had ended the call. He threw the phone down on the passenger seat, dissatisfied.

# Chapter Twenty-Three

The day was already oppressively hot as, slowly and in silence, Roe and Hark began to make their way up Van Cleef Avenue. Named for Claypit's first black council member, it zigzagged its way up the face of the steep hillside of Pine Bluff, and though it had enough turns to keep each slant fairly gentle, Roe still remembered how terrifying it had been the first time he rode his board all the way down without stopping, going so fast he had almost barreled under a passing truck on Main Street.

As well as small spur streets branching outwards, lanes ran inwards at each bend, layering in an extra row of homes above and below those that fronted onto the avenue itself. All were of a good size, old fashioned, and most were well maintained, with carefully tended gardens. Others were neglected, however, and here and there were "For Sale" signs that had been up for a long time.

Even so, after his visit to Coleman East, Roe was reminded of the comparative prosperity of his community. He was also properly respectful of what an achievement it had been to establish such a community back in segregation times.

Yet that achievement was also a burden. The effort everyone poured into maintaining their social standing, into respectability, into conformity, was enormous. Often it left Roe feeling stifled, and with the wild longing to become a stripper or some other thing no one called respectable, because that in some way set you free.

At the fifth bend a large lemon tree overhung the street. They paused in its shade to catch their breaths. There were no sidewalks along Van Cleef, just sprinkler-fed lawns that tumbled down to the smooth black asphalt. Lemons crowded the branches overhead, bright green and yellow.

Hark reached out and touched the trunk. "Huh," he said, as though surprised to find it there. Roe groped for a facetious remark about Hark liking lemons, but couldn't think of one and abandoned the effort. He felt burdened by Hark's presence, his declared lack of anywhere to go.

An immaculately maintained, sky blue Plymouth came winding down the hill towards them. Roe knew the driver, the extremely elderly Mrs. Oglesby. She was a church friend of his great grand's, and he raised a hand as at a funereal pace the vehicle drew near. It had been her husband the Reverend Oglesby's car, and in defiance of practicality she had kept it going the quarter century since he passed. "It's my faith," she said, when asked why she didn't trade it in for something with more easily obtainable spare parts.

Perhaps offended by his Mohican, she didn't respond to Roe's wave as the Plymouth crawled past. Her shoulders were hunched as she focused with furrowed brow on the trafficless road ahead.

The moment in its small way embodied everything Roe hated about the Side, everything he wanted to escape. *Imagine if I'd been walking up with Cleve*, he thought. *Her head would've spun round. Then exploded.*

Hark reached up and pulled a low-hanging lemon from a branch. That irritated Roe too. The tree probably belonged to someone who would be making a complaint sometime soon.

In New York, he thought, no one would notice, or care.

There wouldn't be any lemon trees in any case.

Other cars now began to descend the hill. It was the nearest the Side got to a rush hour. Roe knew all the faces and could have put names to most of them, and it made his life feel the size of a goldfish bowl. He thought of saying something about it to Hark, but doubted he would understand. Despite his age, he seemed more like Roe's parents in his attitudes, or even more old fashioned than that. Instead he asked, "Why do you use all that retro slang?"

"It's not retro to me."

"O-*kay*,"

Roe wondered how he could avoid inviting Hark in when they reached Cedar Close; and if he couldn't avoid it, how to explain who Hark was. The thought of the awkward conversation that would inevitably take place about Hark's perpetually worn sunglasses made him feel sick in advance.

Just then his mom's car turned the bend, coming down. As she drew level with them she stopped and lowered the driver side window.

"Hey, Mom," Roe said. "Sorry I missed breakfast. This is Hark. He's Eriq's family, visiting."

"Ma'am." Hark touched a finger politely to his forehead, an echo of a hat-tilt.

"Hark."

"I used to have family up here," Hark said. "Your son's being kind enough to give me the tour."

Angela looked at him intently, and Roe suddenly wondered if she was trying to figure out if he was a gay pickup. He was for sure at least ten years older than Roe, but...

His mom glanced at her wristwatch. "Well, good to meet you, Hark," she said. "Roe, remember to help your sister out and get your chores and reading done. You don't want to fall behind right at the start of the summer."

"Yes, Mom."

"I'll see you later." She angled her cheek for a kiss. Self-consciously Roe leant in and obliged.

The window slid up and the car rolled off down toward Main Street.

Roe and Hark ambled on. When they reached the turn to Roe's house near the top of the hill he felt obliged to ask Hark in, and of course Hark said yes.

They found Phyllis at the breakfast table, idly scrolling on her phone. The used plates, cups, glasses and silverware were still scattered about, and she was looking slobbish in a vest and sweat pants. She looked up when they came in, and Roe was secretly pleased by the way a good-looking male stranger's appearance made her instantly close her legs and sit up straighter.

"This is my sister Phyllis," he said. "Phyll, this is Hark, he's, like, Eriq's second cousin or something."

Phyllis pushed her hair up at the back to give it some body. "Hi, Hark," she said. "Cool shades." Then, suddenly aware she was exposing an as-yet-unshowered armpit, she quickly put her arm back down by her side.

Hark wandered over to the breakfast room window, with its view over Claypit.

"Yeah, well, I'm going to shower," Phyllis said, put out that Hark wasn't engaging with her. To Roe she added a graceless, "Clear up," as she left the room. He gave her retreating, increasingly fulsome backside the finger, but started loading up the dishwasher anyway. It was a chore more tedious than it had any right to be.

Now he was irrevocably lumbered with Hark, the day loomed before Roe interminably. Fifteen hours to get through till midnight. "Would you like a Coke?" he offered. Hark nodded, setting the lemon he had picked down on the table. "Diet or regular?"

Hark smiled oddly. "Regular."

Roe went into the fridge, got a can out, popped it and handed it to Hark. Then he got a diet one for himself. They went outside and sat on the swing seat on the back porch, which at that hour was pleasantly in the shade.

"So you and the white boy –"

"Cleve."

"You're an item, right?"

"I guess, yeah," Roe said, slightly resentfully. Yet while he didn't like being grilled about anything to do with his sexuality, he found that he did like it that for once someone was forcing him to break his habit of passing for straight. "I've never met anyone like him," he went on. "And I like him a lot. I mean, really a lot." The realization halfway surprised him.

Roe was also surprised by how his usual articulateness seemed to have deserted him. He sipped his Coke and avoided looking at Hark.

"So you're one of them checkerboard boys?"

"I guess."

It was true Roe saw his black schoolmates as brothers rather than romantic prospects. He had tended to consider this a matter of statistics. There were only three of them in the entire student body (along with himself.) If about 3% of people were gay, then by the law of averages at most one hand or one foot of one of them would be gay. Another hand or foot might be bi-curious, and the other two and eight tenths black students at Tyler A. would be irredeemably, unresponsively heterosexual. And that, he had tended to think, was that.

Maybe there was something more to it, though. Maybe it represented another escape from the constraints of respectability, in this case the respectability of defaulting to your own race in terms of romantic partners. Not that being gay could ever quite scrape in as respectable, marriage equality or no marriage equality.

"He likes you too," Hark said.

"Yeah?" Roe recalled his mom's appraising look, and wondered if Hark might himself be gay. "So um, do you have, like, a partner?"

"I had a wife."

"Did you like, break up?"

"She was widowed."

"You mean, like, before you and her got married?"

"Afterwards."

Roe looked out over the town, which in the blazing sunlight appeared glary and inhospitable. *I died*, Hark had said, back in Cleve's house.

Roe thought how he only had Cleve's word for it about Hark's eyes. Sipping a soda on the back porch of his family home, he found himself slipping back into the worldview normal people had, which was that he was sitting here with someone who was mostly lucid, but had a few crazy ideas that you did your best quickly to move on from whenever they brought them up.

From Phyllis's room Beyoncé began to play loudly, "Single Ladies."

Hark tilted his head and listened for a short while. "Is your sister a single lady?" he asked.

"Why? Do you like her?"

Hark shrugged and sipped his Coke. "This is a good place," he said.

"It's kind of going down, though," Roe said. "The whole town's been dying on its ass pretty much my entire life."

"The first to be fired," Hark said.

"Kinda."

Through the house Roe heard the light clack of the screen door opening, and then a rattle at the front door. Excusing himself, he went through to see who it was and found his great grandmother letting herself in.

"Praise the lord it's a fine day," she said.

"Amen," he replied, to avoid trouble. "Please come through to the kitchen, grand. Mom and Dad are at work already."

"And how is your reading program going?" she asked. "I imagine you're struggling, what with that devil's noise" – she pointed an arthritis-buckled forefinger in the direction of Phyllis's room.

"It's only Beyoncé, grand."

"Single ladies, hmph."

"She's married now, grand. To Jay-Z."

"Hmph. Wasn't he some kind of criminal?"

Roe smiled and let her lead the way into the kitchen. Without being asked, he got a can of Coke from the fridge for her, opened it and poured it into a tall glass she called her highball glass. Seeing Hark's lemon on the table, he brought out the chopping board, cut a slice and added it to his great grand's glass before handing it to her. He pulled out a chair at the breakfast table for her, but she headed out to the back porch. There she discovered Hark on the swing seat.

Hark stood as she stepped out onto the porch. "Ma'am," he said, and there was a suppressed tension in his voice that was perhaps because he was having to face a stranger, perhaps for another reason.

"This is my great grand, Miz Ellison," Roe said. "Grand, this is Hark."

Smiling oddly, Hark took her slanted hand delicately in his. "A pleasure to meet you, Miz Ellison."

Unusually, for she rarely took to strangers, Roe's grand joined him on the seat, and he kept hold of her hand, supporting her as she carefully lowered herself onto the floral print cushions, and there was something curious in his mirroring of her movements. She didn't hurry to take back her hand, but once she was settled he released it.

Roe brought out a kitchen chair for himself, set it by the door, and sat quietly. Normally grand was so shut in on herself that any attempt at conversation soon ground to a halt.

"You live close by, Miz Ellison?" Hark asked.

"Just up the hill a step, at the top of the close. Been there since I was, my goodness, we moved in when I was just twelve years old."

And oddly Hark said, "I recall."

# Chapter Twenty-Four

Roe sipped his Coke as his great grand asked Hark, "Can I see your eyes?"

Hark shook his head. "They were damaged, ma'am. In the war."

"I'm sorry to hear that." Once more she took Hark's hand in hers. "There's so much cruelty and suffering in this world."

"Amen," Hark said.

She looked away from him and out across the sprawl of the town. Today she was wearing a loose silk dress of yellow twined with large red roses, and had wooden bangles stacked on her wrists. Her hair, which was now totally white, was brushed back into a neat bun, and her cheeks were speckled with freckles.

She wore no scrap of makeup, and that morning seemed younger to Roe than she had for years, or maybe just less elderly and failing, though her head moved slightly all the time now. He wondered what that felt like, if it was tiring.

"Are the Thompsons still here?" Hark asked.

"Not for a long time," Miz Ellison said. "The son left

for – I believe it was Vancouver, someplace like that. The daughter didn't marry. Ernestine. She stayed on to look after them when they needed it, but she passed first. Cancer – of the uterus I believe. She was diagnosed late. Had a fear of doctors."

"I'm sorry to hear that."

Roe's grand shrugged. "There was a good turnout for the funeral. They kept on here till the finish: they didn't want to end up in that home out by the freeway. We heard they disrespected colored folks there something wicked. You wouldn't see me go there, even now. Black president or no black president, hearts that were bad before are still bad now he's gone. I watch the news. I'd rather die in my own bed."

Hark mentioned other names, bringing forth similar potted histories, and Roe watched and wondered. He thought of shows he'd seen about phony mediums: the technique of cold reading that enabled a con artist to extract intimate information from someone without them realizing, then feed it back to them as revelation. Was Hark doing that?

Yet he didn't try to insert himself into the stories, just nodded and every so often offered another name. Roe supposed you could get a list of old names and addresses from the local library or online, off the electoral roll or whatever. But why bother?

His grand was clearly enjoying the conversation, and was sharper-minded than she had been in a while.

Then Hark started to ask her about her children and grandchildren – Roe's maternal grandparents and mother. His grand's replies weren't anything you could call confidential, but he started to wish Phyllis would come down and interrupt the subtle, persistent inquisition. She seemed determined to stay in her room, however, Hark's handsomeness notwithstanding. Now Rihanna was playing. Roe disliked her even more than Beyoncé.

The endless romantic wrangling between straight men and women bored and repelled him.

"So you remarried?" Hark was asking. Roe didn't know his grand had married twice, or maybe he did and had tuned it out.

"Mister Ellison was a kind man," she replied. "He was a blessing to me. That was when my little girl was fifteen, going on sixteen, but she took to him and he was very loving towards her. In a properly Christian spirit," she added.

"I'm glad to hear it," Hark said, and his voice was oddly tremulous. Roe listened, half interested, half bored as he always was by any recital of family history, puzzled by the assertion that blood meant something ineradicable and couldn't simply be disavowed. Because what if you thought you were related to someone then found out you weren't? Did that make everything you felt before unreal? His phone toad-croaked. He turned it over to find a text from Cleve:

*R U OK?*

With a half eye on Hark and his grand, Roe thumbed a quick reply. *U Know Who + my g grandma getting on great guns.*

*Kool.*

*I think marriage may be in the air LOL. U OK?*

*Y. Weird being alone. Wish U were here. Can't wait 4 2nite. Esp after.*

Roe shifted in his seat, feeling a warmth spread out from between his thighs, and typed *Me 2.*

Roe's grand had now worked her way down to her granddaughter's wedding to Roe's father. He stifled a yawn. There were no exciting anecdotes in the Jones family history, and listening to a recital of aunts and uncles, many of whom he had never met, made it a challenge for him to keep his eyes open. He didn't want to think about breaking into the school tonight.

"Do you have any photographs?" Hark asked, and Roe's mind went to the blank postcards and Hark's curious fixation with them. Who in their right mind ever asked to see some old person's family photos when they weren't even related to them?

But then Hark wasn't in his right mind, was he? Or not quite, anyway. Roe would have to be watchful. He didn't want his great grand cheated or robbed.

He checked his phone: 9:27. Fourteen hours and thirty-three minutes until midnight. He yawned again and his jaw clicked.

"All in albums in the front parlor," his grand was saying. "Perhaps Monroe could bring you over to visit sometime."

"I'd like that, ma'am."

Phyllis came bouncing into the kitchen then, went to the fridge and got herself a Diet Coke. She was now wearing black, knee length leggings, pink trainers, a skinny rib vest with spaghetti-strap shoulders and just a little make up. Roe grudgingly admitted she looked pretty as she came out onto the porch with a cheerful expression on her face. She bent down and kissed her great grandmother on the cheek. "Hi, grand."

"A perfume that cloying is for the evening, Phyllis, not the daytime," the old lady stated.

"I'll remember that, grand," Phyllis said, rolling her eyes.

"Remind me what it's called again," Roe said.

"Red Sin."

"I thought it was, like, Cheap Whore," Roe snarked.

She gave him the finger behind their great grandmother's back. "Remind me who you're dating again," she said. Roe wasn't out to her, but she wasn't blind.

Grand turned in her seat expectantly.

Roe didn't say anything, just gave Phyllis a dirty look. Eventually he said, "I hope it's sextuplets," but the line landed wrong.

Phyllis's arrival had broken the mood, and grand started to fuss and get to her feet. Hark kept his feet planted on the ground to steady the swing seat as she rose, then stood himself. She seemed to no longer know him, but at the kitchen door she turned back. "I'll remember you in my prayers," she said.

"Thank you, ma'am."

Roe accompanied his grand through the house as she shuffled slowly to the front door, reaching past to pull it open for her, then came out with her onto the front porch, to make sure she got down the three steps okay. This small descent took all her concentration.

"Did you know him, grand?" he asked her, once she was safely on the little paved path.

"Who, Paul?"

"Hark."

"Paul," she repeated. "Saint Paul," she added. Then: "Saints and martyrs. Martyrs and holy ghosts. I haven't thought about all that for the longest time. I thought if I did, I'd go mad. But today, I think today was a blessing. Yes." She smiled. "Now, don't you forget to pray, Monroe."

"I'm an atheist, grand."

"Black people can't be atheists, Monroe. You're just trying to provoke me."

"Yes, grand. Love you, grand."

He watched her make her creeping way along the path, not going back in until she had safely passed the garden gate.

# Chapter Twenty-Five

The three of them sat on the back porch in silence, Roe and Hark on the swing-seat, Phyllis on the kitchen chair Roe had brought out earlier. Hark had retreated within himself now great grand was gone. Exposed as pregnant, Phyllis abandoned trying to flirt with him and went back to scrolling on her phone.

Eventually, at around eleven a.m., out of desperation Roe suggested a walk in the woods at the top of the Side. As he'd hoped, Phyllis said no – she only exercised if the activity took place in a gym, disconnected from anything actually useful like moving from place to place – so he and Hark went out, just the two of them.

As a boy Roe had often wandered among the trees, felt their magic and fantasized adventures. Everything was different now. Spoiled, maybe, though he didn't think that really mattered – or not much more than finding formerly beloved toys rotting and stained in a box in the garage. Hark seemed content to accompany him. Roe wished it was Cleve instead, but he no longer wished Hark away: they were all too connected now.

They reached what as a child Roe had thought of as

the summit in less than five minutes: it was only a hill after all; had never been a mountain. Everything he knew seemed smaller now, and what lay beyond far larger.

They went on a little farther, stopping where the hillside began to fall steeply away, plunging down into Black Bear Gully. Below, hidden by trees, the Illitabi rushed noisily. Large, old-style homes with river-facing verandas dotted the far side of the gully. These were the most expensive houses in Tanner's Cross, whose white residents' historic opposition to the black folks seeking to build all the way to the top of their own side of the gully had led to the Side remaining crowned by primal forest.

Shaded from the noon sun's blaze by ancient oaks and cypresses, Roe and Hark sat on last winter's heaped dry leaves and looked east. Roe tried to find the billboards that announced the restoration of the Tyler Plantation but couldn't: Tanner's Ridge cut off a chunk of the view to his left, and all he could see ahead and to the right was undifferentiated woodland. He couldn't even make out the Nooseneck. Strange, he thought, how rarely a view ever looked like a map. Hark didn't say anything.

"She called you Paul," Roe said eventually. "My great grand. When I was saying goodbye to her on the path."

"Yeah?" Hark said. "I didn't think she remembered."

"Yeah, she's got Alzheimer's or something," Roe said, not wanting to say the ugly words senile dementia. "On top of being about a hundred."

"Did you know Mister Ellison?"

"He died before I was born. I mean, like, years and years before. I guess I've seen photos of him, but... I remember she had a beehive, like the Supremes, and those white frame cat eye glasses."

"Okay."

Hark stared out at the view and didn't say more.

After a bit Roe texted Cleve, *My sister almost outed me to my grand.*

*Wow. Bitch.*

*I K R?*

*But she didn't actually tho?* Cleve texted back. He was lying on his side on the couch in the lounge. The indentation his mom left was beginning to twist his pelvis quite uncomfortably, but he was too lazy to shift position.

*She didn't*, Roe replied. *Twelve point five hours to go *sigh**

*750 minutes*, Cleve replied, after using his calculator to check.

*Not helping.*

*Soz.*

*No worries.*

With a grunt Cleve turned onto his back, took a selfie of himself sprawled languidly on the couch that he hoped was beguiling, and sent it. *Would like u on top of me.* When no reply came he added a nervous, *Or under. Wotever u prefer* and a smiley wink.

This time a brown thumbs up came back. Relieved, Cleve struggled up from the couch. The small of his back ached and his coccyx was numb. He yawned and stretched.

A call came from his dad, and he and Kenneth stumbled through a conversation about how everything was going well with Myrtle but he, Cleve, mustn't have too high expectations when they got back, it would be a journey, his mom would need all their support and so on and on. Then Cleve spoke briefly with Terri, and her mood too was lower than it had been the day before. Maybe, being a kid, she'd believed in the miracle in a way he hadn't. His dad mentioned nutritional counseling for the whole family.

Cleve rang off, half missing them, half wishing they'd never come back. He went through to the kitchen and fried eight strips of bacon, then found there was only the heel of the loaf to go with them. He spread it thickly with margarine, dumped too much ketchup on the flabby bacon, and ate the greasy result too quickly and without pleasure.

Now he felt bloated and nauseous.

He hadn't thought to buy more groceries on the way home because his mind had been full of the Bohemians. He knew he hadn't betrayed them – he cringed at the thought Karen had believed that even for a second. But when Spider brought out the shotgun a door had opened that led to a certain path, and Spider, Choc, Karen and the others had gone through that door and Cleve hadn't, and then it had closed. It would always be between them now. Some choices couldn't be walked back from.

He dragged the Big Ass out and into a shady part of the backyard, grabbed a juice and sat there, killing time. The short, yellow-brown grass was as spiky as an up-turned scrubbing brush, and the under-inflated paddling pool with its slick of scum-fringed water was somehow depressing. It was like he was watching his childhood evaporating. And he wanted it to, sometimes desperately, but even so...

He tried to imagine what would have happened if he and Roe had just kept going, driving to – where? Somewhere full of possibilities, like in a corny song. But there was Hark.

Cleve felt a sting of jealousy then. Hark was getting to be alone with Roe, getting to see Roe's home and meet his grandmother – great grandmother. Cleve had no relatives that old, and his one remaining grandparent, his grandfather, was unpleasant.

Just possibly he was also jealous of Roe being alone with Hark, the handsome mystery man.

Having slept poorly the night before, and there being nothing better to do now, in the dense warmth and stuffed with bacon Cleve fell into a doze.

He awoke two hours later with a crick in his neck, a

slanting slice of hot sunlight on his bare calf burning him
as if focused there by a magnifying glass. He struggled up,
went back inside and showered again, futile though it
seemed in such sweaty weather. He found a single Roe
hair on the edge of the bath and smiled.

After toweling down he checked his phone to see if
there were any new messages. There weren't. He wondered what Roe and Hark were doing, and felt restless.
He ambled through to the kitchen and put the phone
down on a work surface to plug in the charger. It at once
began to ring and vibrate like a panicky beetle. The ID,
spelling uncorrected, read "Row." Cleve snatched it up.
"Hey, cutie."

He could hear Roe's smile on the other end of the line.
"Hey." His voice was husky and low, as if he was trying to
avoid being overheard, or maybe he was trying to sound
sexy.

"How's it goin', dude?"

"Weird. My grand started calling Hark Paul for, like,
literally no reason."

"I guess he reminds her of someone. I've seen stuff
like that on TV, where old people literally think their
daughter's their sister or even their own mom, you know?
They kinda lose track of, oh, this person'd be ninety-nine
years old or whatever."

"I guess."

"Where is he now?"

Roe's voice fell further. "Up in my room. My sister
thinks he's gone, so the deal is he has to stay up there and
keep, like, totally quiet till we sneak out later. It was way
too complicated to have him meet the parents."

"The sunglasses thing for a start."

"Yeah."

"So where we meetin' up? Right in front of the gates
seems like a bad idea."

"Go along the wall to the left – facing the gates, I

mean – into the trees. There's a bit where it leans out and there's kind of a big iron girder thing to stop it, like, totally collapsing. Meet us there."

"Okay. Be seeing you."

Roe laughed softly. "Be seeing you."

"Oh, but wait. Shit."

"What?"

"Do I bring like, um, tools?"

A pause. "Screwdrivers, I guess. A crowbar?"

"Okay."

Cleve rang off, feeling tense.

# Chapter Twenty-Six

Walking the road alone in the bright moonlight was almost beautiful to Cleve. To be answerable to no one as he left the house had been a joy. Only the crowbar in his backpack spoilt it, because why would a young man be out at night with a crowbar unless he intended using it for breaking and entering? Intention wasn't proof, but combined with the company he kept, both old and new, it would condemn him in the eyes of the cops if they stopped and searched him. And weren't they right, after all?

Cleve was actually much more worried that someone he knew would happen along and offer him a ride than that the alleged black prowler would draw the police back to Coleman East for a second night, because if that happened he would have to accept the ride, ask to be dropped somewhere obvious like Barney's Balls, then trudge back from there on foot, hopefully without being seen by anyone else he knew and offered a second overshooting ride home.

He had considered cycling, but that seemed like it could easily turn out to be a mistake: if things went wrong and he had to leave the bike behind, its being registered against theft meant it would be traced straight back to him. *Thanks, Mom.* If the cops showed up he could say it had been stolen sometime earlier, but once you were a suspect it was hard to get away with something.

The trick was to not become a suspect in the first place.

The few cars that passed were headed out of town. Lowering his eyes against the glare of their headlights, he didn't know if he knew any of the drivers. No one flashed recognition or sounded their horns, and no one stopped or even slowed.

To his annoyance he reached the gates of the Tyler Academy a half hour early – a consequence of being both bored at home and too eager to get going and get it done.

Pulling experimentally at the padlocked chain, he peered through the wrought iron gates. Past the curve of the drive and skirted by lawns, the school stood on a slight rise, its multiple gabled roofs and ornamental spires a spiky black jumble backlit by the rising moon. To one side a square tower was enclosed in scaffolding like an Ilizarov frame for a broken femur. The science block being refurbished, Cleve supposed.

Farther off, the outlines of other buildings were visible. These were low, large and modern, a sports hall and swimming pool, maybe. Over towards the boundary wall to the left he made out an octagonal bandstand, and past that were maybe ponds: somewhere toads were croaking in large numbers.

Rubbing his face, which was sweaty and itching as though he'd pushed it into a spider's web, Cleve followed the wall round to the left, and in a few minutes found the place Roe had described where it cantilevered wildly outwards. A triangular fan of iron girders splayed out to support its sagging weight on the woodland side and prevent it from collapsing.

Cleve had a good sense of balance and reckoned he could climb along the topmost girder, which was at an angle to the ground of about sixty degrees, then step over the top without much difficulty. Tilted as the wall was, it would surely be easy to climb down on the other side (and up again afterwards.) He wondered briefly if guard dogs would be patrolling, but decided he had watched too many movies.

There was nothing to do now but wait. The cicadas rasped and the toads croaked, creating a dense shimmer of night sound. He wished he'd brought something to drink.

By contrast, Roe and Hark set out later than Roe had meant them to. His dad had invited another council member over for dinner, and his parents and their guest had sat up talking politics until nearly eleven. That was the time Roe had planned to leave. Instead he had had to wait another half hour before he could risk sneaking out with Hark.

Their combined weight on the garage roof made it creak tale-tellingly, but no one inside the house seemed to notice, and they dropped to the ground softly enough.

They began to make their way down the hairpins of Van Cleef Avenue, on foot and in silence. No one was about, and where lights were on, drapes and blinds were firmly closed. To try and make up lost time they walked quickly, and in the blood-warm night Roe soon began to sweat heavily. Walking seemed particularly tedious here: perversely slow compared with rolling down on his board. He texted Cleve they would be late, but the text came up as undeliverable.

Hark was soon dragging his feet, and his breathing became labored. "I need to just – take a moment, okay?" he wheezed, reaching for and leaning against a lamppost only a few bends down.

"Cleve'll be waiting," Roe said, but it was clear Hark couldn't walk any faster: he was already bending over as if he had a stitch.

Grudgingly Roe waited for him to get his breath back, and then they went on, much more slowly now. Roe put up with it: there was nothing he could do, and anyway to be seen rushing might have drawn attention to them.

They found Main Street deserted, and the trees in the town square were as still as if they had been cast in bronze. In Roe's backpack were a ringful of hex keys, an adjustable wrench, a box of jeweler's-type small screwdrivers and a twelve-inch metal ruler. The latter three items had required him to make a furtive visit to the garage and his father's toolbox earlier in the evening. Like Cleve with the crowbar he felt they branded him a criminal, or at least an incipient one. He could think of no convincing reason for having them in his possession if questioned.

East of the square was a block of office buildings, many tenantless and with signs proclaiming that long leases and favorable terms and conditions were available; then several blocks of run-down houses. Almost half of these had For Sale signs in their front yards, and several had an abandoned air. Rumor said some were meth labs, despite being all but under the noses of the cops.

In a little while they came to the church that marked the eastern end of the residential part of town. On a marble monument in front of it the old white families of the area were commemorated with dates that went back to slavery times: the Tylers, the Oglesbys, the Colemans. A continuity that it seemed ran on unbroken by war or slavery's ending.

Seeing the monument, Roe was proud he had been part of taking the Tyler statue down. It had been removed for "repairs" while the issue of whether to reinstall it was debated by the town council – the subject of his father's colleague's visit that evening. He and Hark walked on. Now belts of woodland ran along both sides of the road.

The Academy was a short way past the turn that led up into Tanner's Cross. Tanner's Cross was still the wealthiest part of Claypit, and was aspiring to become a gated community with its own security force, but hadn't got there yet. Maybe it never would. The withering away of middle-class jobs was affecting white people too.

Roe thought of the massed past, of small battles fought against injustice, small achievements blazoned then buried and forgotten, small lives that left no mark, and felt troubled and repelled. He found himself pushing the pace again.

Once they were away from the house he had planned to ply Hark with questions, but now somehow he didn't have the energy. Hark probably didn't either, and what would be the point anyway? Hark would as usual be evasive, and Roe couldn't make him answer. He supposed you could be a supernatural being who was also a bit crazy and a liar – what his grand would call a demon, maybe, though he didn't think there was anything demonic about Hark, as nor had she.

"When you said 'they'," he said eventually, "I mean, they who gave you the box. Who did you mean?"

"I'll tell you afterwards," Hark said. He was sweating heavily and sounded breathless, but was managing to keep up with Roe for now.

"I thought there wasn't going to be an afterwards," Roe said.

Cleve checked his phone: 12:38 a.m. In the shadowy nighttime wood the screen seemed dazzlingly bright, a glaring giveaway to anyone who happened to be nearby, meth heads or whoever. He turned it down until it was faint but still just legible, then waved it around. No signal. He considered trying to climb a tree in hopes of finding one, but in the dark that seemed too likely to result in a jab in the eye from an unseen twig or branch.

*I'll give 'em till one*, he thought, though trailing home alone at one a.m. without knowing what had happened would be a wholly unsatisfactory outcome.

At 12:55 he heard soft crackling sounds, as of some large animal pushing its way furtively through brush, and a minute later Roe and Hark emerged from the darkness, keeping close to the bulging brick wall as the undergrowth was thinnest and least obstructive there.

"You're late, dude," Cleve said, kissing Roe on the cheek.

"My parents were up till after eleven. We had to wait."

Cleve extended a hand to Hark, who this time shook it briefly. Hark's hand was warm and sweaty. "Dude."

They contemplated the fan of girders. Each was around fifteen feet long and six inches wide. The wall, twelve feet high when upright, here sagged to less than nine. The far end of the uppermost girder was bolted into the brickwork a foot short of the top. Stepping over the broken glass should be easy if they took care.

There was nothing to do but get on with it. Being Roe's school, it seemed natural for him to lead the way, going carefully, followed by a confident Cleve and then a wobbly Hark. The girder was solidly fixed and didn't bend or shift. Straddling the shards of glass was unnerving – slipping and sitting down on them made you wince to think of – but there was space to place your fingertips between them and support most of your weight that way as you lifted one foot over, cautiously moved your hips across, then drew your other foot after.

The brickwork on the far side of the wall was spongy and sagging, but it didn't actually disintegrate as one after the other they scurried down it to the lawn below, though falling mortar pattered audibly onto the dry leaves on the woodland side.

Following Roe, Cleve and Hark hurried slantwise across the gently rising lawn. Ignoring the modern buildings, he led them towards the main body of the school. Moonlight flashed on lead-paned, mullioned windows and revealed ivy-twined downspouts as they skirted round to the back of the turreted black mass.

"Where do you play quidditch?" Cleve snarked.

"Up yo ass," Roe replied softly as they passed in under a side arch and along a short passageway. Beyond was a graveled quadrangle with a sundial at its center and shingled awnings. "Here's where it's probably easiest to, like, get in."

He pointed to a row of four windows with sills at hip height that were set into the right hand wall of the quadrangle. Past them was a wooden door with a twisted black iron loop for a handle and a pointy-arched top that again made Cleve think of *Harry Potter*. He went up to the door and gently turned the handle. Locked. Hark joined him, wordlessly running his fingers along the frame, lightly touching the hinges. Cleve wondered how well he saw by night in his blind man's glasses.

Meanwhile Roe had produced the metal ruler from his pack and was working it slowly down into the frame of one of the windows. The wood seemed soft as if dry-rotted. He pushed one of the larger screwdrivers in next to it, and started carefully to lever up the window.

At first the wood splintered without the window moving, and the glass bulged ominously, threatening to crack, but then, with an unnervingly loud screech, it slid up a half inch. Hark and Cleve got their fingers in the gap and, careful to keep their movements symmetrical and in synch, hauled it up in the frame in jerking stages as Roe put his tools away.

A minute later they were stepping over the sill and into the passageway beyond. Trespass had now become criminal trespass.

The carpet underfoot was thick and there was a smell of furniture polish. This part of the school was reserved for staff: no boy ever came here. Given the other circumstances, Roe was surprised by how strongly he felt the force of the taboo; how it made his heart race.

"Where now?" he asked Hark.

Hark brought out his compass and consulted it. "This way."

Roe and Cleve followed him through an interior door into a spacious hall. Moonlight filtered in through a row of small, high windows, and it had parquet flooring. On the wall facing them was a large cork notice board with no notices on it. There were several doors, all closed. Above one an emergency exit light glowed green. To their right a wide, balustraded staircase rose to a landing where it divided into two flights going in opposite directions. A gilt-framed portrait of the school's first headmaster hung there, hawk-nosed and haughty in watered black silk.

"Up there," Hark said.

Roe and Cleve followed him as with an effort he climbed the stairs, taking without hesitation the right-hand flight.

"The library," Roe said.

Cleve now began to take in everyday details that the gothic setting had distracted him from noticing before, like fire-extinguishers and crummy old radiators. Under the staircase there had been a row of lockers just the same as at his school, and everywhere there was the smell of the floor wax they use in school sports halls and nowhere else on the planet, and boiled cabbage. It was, he realized, far more like Welt High than Hogwarts.

The library, which was along a short passageway at the top of the stairs, had a glass-paneled door with a brass label on it which read, when Cleve flashed his phone-light on it, "Bramwell Reading Room." Underneath it was tacked a laminated notice showing a cell phone with a diagonal red line across it. Like every laminated notice ever, it was curling away from where it had been stuck. The glass panels were threaded with safety wire, and the door was locked.

"In there," Hark said breathlessly.

"Do you, like, know how to pick a lock?" Roe asked him.

"No."

"Can't you – I dunno, magic it open?" Cleve asked.

"The box is dead, buddy. You saw it die. There's no more magic now."

Reluctantly Cleve unslung his pack and brought out the crowbar. It felt heavy in his hand. Feeling inept, he worked the claw end in between the door and the frame next to the lock. Though the lock was modern, the door was old and loose, and there was plenty of room to get the claw a good way in.

Cleve was about to lever it hard, hoping for a clean one-jerk break, when there came from below the creak of a heavy foot on a carpeted step.

Crouching down instinctively, he, Roe and Hark looked back towards the stairs.

# Chapter Twenty-Seven

From where they crouched they could see only as far as the landing where the stairs divided. A torch-beam stabbed up from lower down and played over the portrait of Tyler A's first headmaster. Someone who breathed heavily through his nose was coming up.

Gesturing to Roe and Cleve to stay where they were, Hark slipped over to the top of the stairs. Bending low, he quickly crept down a flight, stopping next to an ornately-carved newel post and squatting on his haunches. The post and the spindles shielded him from the view of whoever was holding the torch until that person stepped onto the landing.

Cleve and Roe watched, holding their breaths. Neither of them had believed the school would really have a watchman, but why wouldn't it, with so much poverty nearby, and meth heads prepared to do whatever was needful to feed their bottomless habits?

There was nowhere to run to: only back down the

stairs. And Hark's presence would make it impossible for them to claim that breaking in was a teenage prank.

A heavyset white man in a short sleeved blue shirt and gray pants heaved into view, waving his torch about vaguely. Maybe he had seen the window, which they had left open to make getting out afterwards quicker and easier; maybe he had heard them moving about inside. Stepping onto the landing, by chance he looked left first, sending the beam of light that way.

As he did so, Hark rose up and punched him hard in the side of his neck. It was a trained blow: one that aimed to reach its full extension a foot past the man's head.

"Fuck," Cleve said as, with a choking gasp, the watchman staggered sideways and fell back down the stairs, vanishing from view. Muffled thuds were audible as he rolled to the bottom, and the torch beam cartwheeled then went out. Cleve had seen enough fights to know a punch like that could kill someone.

Hark went down after him, moving fast and noiselessly, and Roe and Cleve exchanged worried looks. This was no longer a spooky what-if-he's-what-he-says occult thrill: sane or insane, Hark was a grown man on a mission, whatever that mission really was, and lethally serious about it.

Cleve realized he was now exactly where he had avoided being with the liquor store robbery; and Roe could claim no elevated motivation for this as he could for felling the statue: it was just criminal, vicious, and now possibly even murderous.

"Is he alright?" Cleve called in a weak, dry voice, exchanging a fearful glance with Roe and feeling sick.

Hark came back up fast. "Get it open," he said to Cleve, indicating the door to the library.

Cleve obeyed. All his thoughts now were to get whatever they were doing done, get out of there, forget he and Roe had ever seen Hark, and try to carry on with their lives as if none of this had happened. He thought of his cousin Vince, stuck in the Welt County Correctional Facility for half a decade. Was that his destiny too? And what about good student Roe? He would lose a future full of far richer possibilities than Cleve had ever dared hope for.

He forced the crowbar into the frame. Two sharp jemmies broke the lock. As the door swung open he murmured to Roe, "You wanna go check he's okay?"

Before Roe could answer, Hark swiveled his blind man's lenses onto the pair of them. "I told you he's fine," he said, though he hadn't in fact offered any such reassurance. "Come on."

Nervelessly Roe and Cleve followed Hark into the library. It was an old fashioned room, with a narrow balcony on three sides that was reached by a spiral stair. The built-in shelving was of golden oak; the freestanding bookcases were modern and modular. Under the arched windows to the right was a long desk on which a row of computer terminals sat. They had safety locks on their cabling. Laminated notices about not eating or drinking or trying to access forbidden websites abounded.

Hark hurried over to an anonymous door at the far end of the room. "Here," he said.

"That's the archive," Roe said. "It's just a big cupboard, pretty much."

Hark tugged on the handle: the door was locked. He turned to Cleve. "Open it."

Once again, Cleve went to work with the crowbar. This door was much closer fitting, however, and he struggled to get the claw in between it and the frame. His hands were slippery with sweat, and he felt a muscle tug painfully between his shoulder blades as he wrenched at it repeatedly and in a rising panic. Eventually, with a loud crack, the lock broke open.

The room beyond was small and windowless. Pushing

past Cleve, Hark groped for and snapped on a switch. Though only weakly fluorescent, the overhead lighting seemed painfully bright after the shadowy, no-more-than-moonlit rest of the building, and revealed tidy rows of anonymous box files on gray aluminum shelving.

Cleve and Roe watched as, using the compass like a fault-tracer, Hark moved up and down the rows, taking a moment to reach out and touch this or that box before moving on, all the while muttering, "C'mon, c'mon, c'mon."

The image of him punching the security guard in the neck replayed itself before Cleve's eyes: the abrupt sideways shift of the man's head. If he was dead then the same law of co-conspiracy or whatever it was called that would have applied to Spider killing someone during the liquor store robbery would apply here. And what were they even doing this for?

Hark pulled a document box down from a shelf at head height. The box was gray like all the rest, A4-sized, featureless and not new, and had some weight to it. He took it over to a small table and set it down. His hands were trembling as he popped the lid.

"I hope that man's okay," Roe said, as he and Cleve moved to join him.

"Yeah, yeah, don't sweat it."

Hark folded back the lid, which on its inner side was marbled like an antique book, then started to leaf through the papers within. All their edges were to some degree discolored with age. His lips moved silently as he quickly scanned each item he came to, then set it aside.

Roe and Cleve glimpsed letters on embossed headed paper that had been typed on wonky old manual typewriters; faded notes in elegant handwriting of the sort no one had done for half a century or more; a yellowing, folded up newspaper cutting that seemed to show no memorable story; a document typed on onionskin paper, the keys incising the letters like a stencil cutter. At the bottom of the stack was an A5 manila envelope. Its flap was held closed by a brass clasp, and on it were listed the names of those who had consulted it. Next to the names dates were stamped with one of those old fashioned library stamps that never quite got the numbers in a straight line. The most recent date was 1972.

Hark took a breath, turned the clasp, opened the envelope and reached inside. He drew out several more old letters, all handwritten, and a postcard that was face down. Seeing it, he exhaled.

As carefully as if it might cut or sting him, he placed the postcard on the table, still face down. He rubbed his hands together, then rubbed his face.

"The first one," he said. "And the last one."

"How is it both?" Roe asked.

"The centrifuge throws you out," Hark said. "Then the whirlpool draws you in."

From the breast pocket of his shirt he now produced the thermometer Cleve had given him and set it down next to the postcard. Pink and plastic, amongst the yellowing papers it looked incongruous, almost comical.

Like nurses bent over a patient in an operating theater, Cleve and Roe stood either side of Hark. The dustmotes released by Hark's search through the old papers set their noses itching.

The back of the card, which was unsigned and undated, and addressed to someone named Everett Livesy, Dept. Principal Tyler Academy, in a clumsy but painstaking hand, read simply:

*Claypit hospitality on a hot Saturday night.*

Taking a breath, Hark turned the card over.

"Jesus," Roe said. He and Cleve had half expected it to be blank like all the others in Hark's satchel, which similarly bore the legend *Jack Bean – photographic services: weddings, funerals &c, 122 Coleman Avenue*

*West*. They had expected, if anything, just another dead end in the mystery of Hark. But it wasn't blank, and what it showed tore a little of their innocence from them, innocence they would, perhaps, up until then have denied possessing.

It was a photograph of a lynching.

Cleve felt the hairs on the back of his neck prickle, and he glanced at Roe and tried to read his twitching eyes, and couldn't.

# Chapter Twenty-Eight

**B**oth Roe and Cleve had, of course, seen images of lynchings before. What their schools tended to repress, if not actually deny the existence of, social media and Google searches provided freely, and uncensored.

Then there was the cover of that Public Enemy single, "Hazy Shade of Criminal," that Roe's parents wouldn't discuss when, aged nine, he found it in their record rack: two black men, heads lolling unnaturally, hanging from trees above a white mob. What had his parents said? They must have said something, but he couldn't remember.

There were the images Cleve had been shown by Spider and Karen on Spider's laptop, mixed in with other attempts to shock – huge grubs being tweezered squirming and alive from people's nostrils; genitals rotted by sexually-transmitted diseases; swollen, elephantiasized limbs; and photographs, always black and white, of hung and burned black bodies, and white onlookers with strange, excited expressions on their faces.

*Illicit joy.*

The image on this postcard was also black and white, an old fashioned photograph. In the background was the pillared, porticoed façade of Claypit's town hall. In front of it a white crowd milled. The men were in shirtsleeves and high-waisted pants, and many wore hats. There were women there too, both young and middle aged. Some had dressed up in party frocks and fancy hats, and several wore white gloves.

There was one child visible in the crowd, a boy maybe ten years old and just in long pants. Fair haired, with a buzz-cut and skinny, he was looking up at where several of the adults pointed, confusion on his face at the carnival mix of horror and delight. It seemed that only the pointing men had noticed the camera: they mugged for the photographer while the others were caught as in a snapshot, or a documentary image.

From a branch overhead a man hung by the neck, a black man in a still-smart army uniform. His pants were round his ankles, though the shadowy nature of the image mercifully precluded seeing any detail of what had happened between his legs. His head was bent sideways at an angle that was impossible for a living man to endure. His mouth hung open, his tongue lolled bloatedly, and his eyes were closed.

It was Hark.

It was Hark. At that moment both Cleve and Roe were sure, though later they would become uncertain again, suspicious they had been somehow hypnotized into believing it.

That changed nothing of the reality, however: this had happened, here in the town square of Claypit. A man, a black man, had died horribly at the hands of a white mob. But even the word "mob" was misleading, because a mob is made up of individuals, isn't it? And you could see them: white people, white citizens who fixed flat tires for damsels in distress, who restored old furniture for the love of it, who fretted about their grandparents' health and their children's grades, who went to church, who sent their kids to school with apples in their lunchboxes. Who presumably woke in their beds the next morning as from a queasy, titillating dream. Who walked through the same town square the next day careful not to drop litter. Who might be civil, even pleasant towards the black citizens with whom they interacted daily.

Through that image the past flooded into the present, for a moment unbearably, a wedge and a connection between Cleve and Roe they would have done anything to disavow and evade, but could not. Cleve fumbled for Roe's hand, but Roe couldn't take it, not then.

"August 10, 1946," Hark said, though the postcard had been undated. Carefully he slid the fragile glass thermometer out of its pink plastic sheath. Inside was a thread of mercury and no more. Holding the tube over the postcard, he flexed and snapped it.

A tiny spatter of mercury spilled out onto the image, making a random shape. Hark set the broken halves of the thermometer aside and bent forward so his face was near the dot of shiny liquid.

"Mercury fumes are poisonous," Roe said.

But Hark didn't inhale: he blew, and his breath spread the metallic fluid out in an impossibly symmetrical web of silver filaments. These seemed to take on a life and energy of their own, continuing to travel outwards to the edges of the image, where they stopped without spilling over, covering it as by a glittering mesh.

Turning his head to draw breath, Hark blew on the postcard again, and as Cleve and Roe watched the image began to fade away, beginning with the hanged man, then the excited crowd at his feet, and the lone lost boy, then the tree branch; and finally the town hall behind them vanished too. As each element disappeared what was behind it was revealed, though both Cleve and Roe knew photographs didn't work like that.

In a short while the card was wholly blank and appeared never to have been used, just like the others in Hark's satchel.

Nodding to himself, Hark straightened up. He stood like a soldier at attention, chest out, looking straight ahead, as if awaiting a command. He rolled his head and his neck vertebrae crackled.

Nothing happened. The windowless room grew stuffier. Cleve and Roe shifted uneasily.

"So, um," Cleve began eventually.

"I don't understand," Hark said. "That was the last one, I know it was the last one. They told me the number. I did the number. Goddamn it." He tilted his head back and shouted at the ceiling, "I did it! All of it! In order like you said! Every shame their eyes fed on, every gloating white turn-on, gone! They don't own none of me no more! So what do I do now, huh? What?"

If he was expecting an answer, none came.

"We'd better go," Roe said. If the night watchman had only been knocked out he might have come round by now, and if he had a gun he would certainly be prepared to use it. Hark stood there impassively as Roe shoveled the papers back into the document box, then reshelved it in what he hoped was the right place. *No sense in leaving clues.*

With Hark trailing behind them, Roe and Cleve went back through the library and hurried down the stairs, Roe going first, using his phone for a flashlight. At the bottom of the staircase, like something out of *Clue*, the night watchman lay on the parquet flooring. Roe turned the light on him. An unfamiliar face, a vacation hire. His chest rose and fell, and that was reassuring, though he was still unconscious.

"I'm just gonna –" Cleve said. He knelt and rolled the man over into what he could remember of the recovery position, so at least he wouldn't choke on his own vomit. He drew in a clogged, sucking breath as Cleve turned him that made Cleve glad he'd bothered. Roe kept his light on the man so he could see what he was doing. When Cleve stood up, the man's eyelids fluttered as though he might be coming round.

Leaving him, they returned the way they'd come, stepping over the windowsill as fastidiously as if the paint were wet so as to avoid leaving fingerprints, and made their way out into the grounds. The moon was as bright as a searchlight but there was no one there to see, or so it seemed.

The toads croaked triumphantly as they crossed the lawn to the sagging part of the wall and scrambled back up it. More mortar slid to the ground as they climbed, but they moved fast and light, and thirty seconds later were making their way down the girder on the other side, arms flung wide like gymnasts on a balance beam.

"What now?" Cleve said once they were all back on the ground. "Where now?"

Hark shrugged. He was wheezing asthmatically.

"We can't go back to mine," Roe said. "My parents and sister are there, and we'd have to, like, go past a ton of houses just to even get there, then sneak in without anyone noticing, and I doubt he could haul himself up onto the roof."

"Mine then," Cleve said. Somehow it had always been going to turn out this way.

There were three of them walking the road now, and Cleve felt horribly visible. Hark was a suspected prowler, a homeless man who couldn't establish his identity, and black. Roe and Cleve had already been questioned by the police, and were now, in fact, criminals.

"You reckon we should dump the tools?" Cleve asked Roe as they hurried along as fast as Hark could manage.

"I can't just lose all my dad's screwdrivers and stuff," Roe said tensely. "He'd kill me. Maybe the crowbar, though: we actually used it."

Tugging the crowbar out of his pack, Cleve rubbed it over quickly with his vest to clean off any fingerprints. Then, awkwardly bunching the fabric round his hand so as not to leave any fresh ones, he lobbed it clumsily into some bushes. It bounced back off their springy twigs, but fell out of sight among the weeds so he left it.

As they walked, Cleve and Roe discussed making an anonymous phone call, the idea being to get an ambulance sent to the school for the watchman. Neither of them knew how easily the police could trace cell phones, though, or landlines – Cleve's parents still had one of those. Roe remembered seeing an old horror movie where a cop ran back and forth among walls of circuits before realizing – and shouting too late for the girl who was keeping the killer on the line, "The call's coming from inside your house!"

He had a signal now, and quickly Googled call-tracing, trying not to trip over his own feet as he did so, or slow his pace. Disappointingly, the time taken to trace a call turned out to be basically instantaneous for both cell phones and landlines.

"We shoulda called from the school," Cleve said.

"Except we didn't think of it and we can't go back."

"I know, but –"

"If we're seen now we're still like, basically screwed," Roe said. "We'd be the only suspects. So we can't."

Cleve nodded. Then, with an awkward hunch of his shoulders, he asked, "Would you be more bothered if he was black?"

"Would you be less bothered?"

"No."

"Well, then."

"I'm sorry."

"It's alright." Now Roe's hand found Cleve's, and took it.

The time was a little after two a.m. and there was no traffic on the road. They passed the billboards and went on. The asphalt was warm beneath their feet.

# Chapter Twenty-Nine

They reached Cleve's house a little after three a.m., apparently unobserved. Footsore and with adrenalin levels crashing they sat in the kitchen and drank orange juice and then coffee. All this time Hark said nothing.

Eventually Cleve said, "So what now, dude?"

"I don't know," Hark said. "I thought I'd just – go."

"Go where?"

"Where you go to when you're done."

Cleve found himself thinking vaguely of heaven and hell, which just then felt childish, obviously unreal. With life being the way it was, full of good luck, bad luck and blind chance, how could death turn out to be the door to an elevator that went up or down one time only, dumping you forever in the basement or giving you a permanent pass to the penthouse?

"So what happened?" Roe asked Hark. "I mean, like, in the photograph."

"Aw, Roe –" Cleve said.

"I think we've earned it."

Hark sighed. "See, there's shit you can't put together

because *you* weren't together by then, and –" For a while his jaw moved but he didn't say anything.

"You don't have to, dude," Cleve said. Roe shot him a look. "Well, he don't."

Hark made a small, weary gesture as if to say it was fine. "I went off to fight," he said. "Hitler and Hirohito – Stalin was on our side then. I'd gotten hitched just six months before, to a fine gal from the Side, church-going, always real well turned out, nice, you know? But when the band blew she knew how to cut a rug. She kept me on the beam too: I managed to impress her old man enough he gave his consent even though I wasn't nothin' but a mechanic. It was a fine wedding. Fine.

"That was early '45. Hitler was winning in Europe, and it started to bother me more and more – the sense you gotta do something if you can. 'Cause sometimes what's evil is clear. All able-bodied men not in exempt professions had registered for the draft by then. It was kinda weird though, 'cause after that you *couldn't* volunteer, it would've messed up their systems or somethin'. You just had to wait. But when I got my papers I thought, good. I left my gal expecting and I went to war. Thought I'd get to fight or at least be handy fixin' up tanks and jeeps.

"We was trained up in the South. Basic trainin'. Some of them Northern colored boys didn't know what hit 'em. For me all that cracker folderol was just something to get past –" He wasn't looking at Cleve as he said this, but Cleve still blushed. "Best believe they didn't feel easy seeing us armed, no, sir.

"Well, they beat up on us some but they didn't kill us, and we got our rifles and our postings overseas. We was in Belgium first, then down through France and into the Reichland itself. Mopping up, mostly – not frontline stuff, but they left snipers behind: you had to watch your ass. And sometimes there'd be Nazi units got cut off still roaming about and killing. The tide had turned but it was war, brother."

Cleve refilled Hark's mug with coffee. Hark sipped and went on:

"The white people there was all real pleased to see us – even the Germans by the end, on account of the Russians was so vicious. Any German woman they come to they'd rape, so they'd run to us. That was a queer thing: these big-eyed blonde fräuleins cryin' 'Hilf mir! Hilf mir!' Hitler treated them Ruskies subhuman, like he did the Jews. The untermensches, you dig? So the ladies were friendly, and as a black man you got treated decent – human – and it made me wonder – made us all wonder – why we was fightin' for a freedom we didn't get to enjoy back home. Well, you know all that, no doubt."

Roe and Cleve nodded.

"Hitler was beat, Japan was nuked flat. I got my demob. I'd been writing Ellie all that time, though being as we was on the move she mostly couldn't write back. I suppose she got my letters out of order if she got 'em at all. She'd found out she was pregnant just before I left for basic training but she wasn't showing. I was in a hurry to get back to her before the baby came. I sent telegrams, but I didn't know if she knew I was on my way."

"How old were you?" Roe asked, half believing, half playing along, as you do when you're with an actor in one of those educational historical recreations, seeing how convincingly they can keep it going.

"Twenty-four. Ellie was nineteen. It was August, and I rode the dog from New York – that was where the ship put in. I was saving my pay for things for the house and baby, though I reckon it's bad luck to plan too much for a baby before it comes. I had a real sharp suit I got made up for me in Harlem, but Ellie had never seen me in my uniform, and I was proud to wear it, so that was how I was going to arrive. Just me in my uniform, my satchel and some gifts for her and my folks. I – I don't remember what they were."

He rolled his neck. The occipital condyles went *clickclickclick*. The satchel hung from the back of one of the dining chairs, brown and gleaming.

"I – I sent on the suit and the rest of my gear. It was hot, you know? Southern heat, like a cow breathing in your face every way you turn. Almost sweet. I'd been in Belgium, France and Germany, I'd been in New York. I'd been stuck on that bus for a day and a night, and there I was, on a Saturday night in Claypit. Steppin' down from the 'hound in the square was unreal, all the things I'd seen mixed up with all the plans I'd made, with memories, and my mind was open wide."

He took another swallow of coffee, rolled his neck again. *Clickclickclick*.

"My thoughts was all on Ellie, but a buddy of mine, Arnie – a white guy, we palled up in Belgium and stayed tight – he was catching another 'hound and headin' out west – we'd got bent in New York, and Arnie said let's raise one last glass to the Hun and Little Boy and Fat Boy."

"Who?" Cleve said.

"The bombs we dropped on Japan," Roe said quietly.

"Oh, yeah."

"Well, Claypit being segregated I declined, but I walked him to where the white bars were, shook his hand and left him there. I could've done with a drink myself, but after bein' overseas segregated bars just didn't sit right with me. Where we said goodbye there was an ice cream parlor didn't used to be there, freshly done up, all gay colors an' neon. And there was the White sign, front and center, and round the side, deliberately mean, the Colored one. It was scooped out the same tub but couldn't be handed out the same window. You know the Nazis was inspired by our segregated ways?" Hark said. "Der Führer admired our southern states."

Cleve and Roe nodded wordlessly. Hark rolled his neck a third time, and dread began to crawl over them.

"I woke up to reality pretty quick. My white buddy was gone and Main Street was the same as ever: black north, white south. I turned around and headed for the Side, sorry I'd come even that far, my mind on my wife. Got some smiles from the colored gals on account of my uniform, and some white scowls that said who the eff did I think I was."

Hark bared his teeth joylessly. "Before the war I'd never left Claypit. Now I was a changed man. Yeah. And it burned them white boys like radiation. The main drag was live back then, not like now, and it was as if the whole town was out that night, black and white, and a handful of Indian, Chinese, whatever, who mostly drifted to the dark side. Outside a juke joint called Polka Dottie's I came on two young things, one yaller, one dark, both of 'em pretty and wearing matching summer dresses, white gloves and them little white hats – pillboxes, with fascinators – and they were being hassled by a group of young white toughs from the mill. Paper Boys, you dig? Well, I had to step in, tell them ofays to take a powder."

"Ofays?" Cleve asked.

"White cats, buddy. There was five of 'em, drunk as skunks and looking for a dust-up, and they didn't like that I was in uniform, no sir, they did not."

Hark fell silent then, seemingly going within himself. His eyes being hidden behind the blind man's shades, for a moment Cleve thought he had fallen asleep, and shot Roe a should-we-nudge-him look, but then he went on:

"At first it looked like they might respect the uniform, never mind who was wearin' it. But truth to tell it made 'em madder. Their jobs was war work – they fed the presses putting out propaganda – so they could duck the draft. They were exempted, legit, but they knew how that made 'em look to other men. To any man who served. And to women. And maybe they could smell on me that things was set to change."

The room they were sitting in was gone now: there was just Hark's voice, his tale of Claypit, seventy-one years ago. "One of 'em pulled a knife, but I took it off him quick-smart and that gave the others pause. From then on it gets kinda fractured. It goes into splinters. Like if you smashed a mirror, then threw the pieces up in the air and tried to catch your reflection in 'em."

He stood up abruptly then, and crossed over to the kitchen window. Leaning heavily on the sink, he looked out at the night. Moths bumped blindly against the glass, eager to come inside. "Well, you saw the picture," he said thickly. "Twenty-seven prints got made. I found twenty-seven."

"Yeah, but –" Cleve blurted.

"Someone smashed me over the head with a bottle. Blood ran down in my eyes, and it was cold and hot at the same time. They got me down on the ground, and then it began. Yeah," Hark added quietly. "Then it began. Kalei-doscopically. And then, after a thousand years, it ended, and that was another beginning because nothing ever ends, you dig? Nothing dies. The worm twists and bur-rows forever. And everyone gets their own ancestor box in the end. But I guess you know that now. And I guess everyone who was there that night is passed now. They're down in the ground and their skulls grin or their skulls scream. And I'm tired now and I want to get free. Go home, if there is a home for a man who travels in wood."

# Chapter Thirty

"So what can we do?" Cleve asked, after Hark had taken a moment to gather himself.

"I don't know," Hark said flatly. "I've never done this before."

"Maybe there are other postcards you don't know about," Roe said.

"That was the information I was given."

"But could it be, like, wrong?"

Hark shook his head. "They don't get shit like that wrong. It's molecular to them. Mathematical. Like, if there ain't two Os it's not oxygen, you dig? One O is something else. No, that was the last one. And I know the negative is gone. It burned in 1978. I saw it; I was there. And all my power, all my energy is gone. Here at the bottom of the spiral, where the battery's drained flat."

"But there must be something," Roe said, the dread he and Cleve had felt before now a clawing despair. Hark would never be released, they would never be free of him. He was history itself, proof they would never be able to walk hand in hand through the streets of Claypit, or through any other streets, or even unwitnessed in the primal woods, side by side and simply and singularly themselves, their skin color reduced to mere opticality.

Yet did either of them truly want that? To have no history, no past; to deny disquieting connections in order to escape from pain?

No: it had to be faced, faced up to, faced down. And in some way their love – and yes, it was love then, or at least the beginnings of love – was made heroic by the journey they had become a part of, through Hark. "There must be something," Roe repeated. "Some chance we can..."

Hark turned his mirrored lenses on the two young men, and they were shy and vulnerable and yearning. "There's no such thing as chance," he said. "We didn't meet by chance. Something about the two of you –"

"I dunno, dude," Cleve said. "It seems pretty random to me."

"It was unlikely," Hark said. "Vastly, extremely unlikely. But unlikely isn't random."

"Coincidence," Roe said, quoting Sherlock Holmes, "is the breeder of false theories."

"Yeah?" Hark said. "Maybe so."

He brought out his compass and set it on the table. Now the needle was immobile. He flicked it. The needle quivered but didn't rotate even slightly, and when he turned the compass case round the needle turned with it as if soldered in place. It now had no letters at the cardinal points, just black dots. Even so, Hark returned it to his breast pocket. "You don't abandon equipment in the field," he said, as if in answer to a question.

"When we pulled the statue down, you said it, like, dragged you off course," Roe said.

"Yeah."

"But what if it didn't?"

Suddenly Hark was alert. "Go on, little brother."

"What if when they sent you they knew what was going to happen?"

"You said they know pretty much everything," Cleve chimed in.

"So it was meant to bring us together?" Hark said.

"Maybe," Cleve said. "I mean, I guess, but..." He shrugged: the thought didn't seem to get them anywhere. Then, abruptly, he asked, "Why were you watching my house, dude? I mean, the night before we went to the Tyler place, that was you, right? You were standing on the far side of the road, and you saw me and stepped back out of sight."

"Yeah, I was – disorientated. Off course, I thought, and running out of charge. In my mind I saw your house and somehow I knew it was someplace to get to, even though the compass wasn't pointing that way. It was like knowledge on another level, maybe a deeper level, so I followed the moon line and then the star line. But when I got here, there seemed to be nothing to do. So I scoped it out for a while. Then I saw you seeing me and I went back to the plantation house. It seemed like a kind of anchor, or the center of a web. And by then I was being followed by the thing that got through when I arrived, and I had to make sure I was keeping ahead of it."

"And then we came out to where you were," Cleve said.

"The center of the web," Roe echoed.

"A black boy and a white boy," Hark said, "kissing – yeah, I saw that – in the ruins of the big house of a plantation left over from slavery days. That's some heavy history you were fightin' just to be there. That's some heavy energy."

"It was almost, like, just a dare," Cleve said. "You know: go check out a haunted house."

"Innocent, almost," Roe said. "Like kids."

"Not kids," Cleve said.

"No." Hark nodded. "But young. Young compared to mineral eternity. Young to me."

"I guess everyone in that photo would be dead by now," Cleve said.

"They'd have to be into, like, their nineties," Roe said. "Most would have to be over a hundred."

"Except that boy," Cleve said.

"How old would you say he was then?"

"Maybe ten?"

"He'd still be eighty-whatever," Roe said, "and that's assuming no cancer or heart disease or being hit by a truck et cetera."

"I wonder what he thought about it," Cleve said. "I mean, later on, you know?"

"Seeing all the grownups acting like it was some fucking church social," Roe said, his voice thick and catching.

Beyond the horror of ruined black bodies, which he tried never to look at directly, Roe had always been most intensely disturbed by the faces of the white people in those photographs. That Public Enemy cover had given him nightmares, and he had resisted trying in any way to conceive the minds behind those faces: they were the enemy, pure and simple. But that boy, that boy with a mind which was at that moment being violated by what his eyes were seeing, hadn't – couldn't have – chosen to come to that carnival of hate; had been dragged by a father, a mother, an uncle, an excited older brother.

But so what?

So everything. Maybe.

Cleve's hand was warm in his, and Roe felt the stronger for it, though everything else in this impure world was at that moment unbearable. Or no: just barely bearable. "Hark," he said, "are you my great grandfather?"

Hark brought his hidden eyes to bear on Roe. "Aw, well," he began, then trailed off awkwardly.

"My great grand called you Paul. She knew you."

"Time doesn't work that way, not when you're dead,"

Hark said. "There's no woulda coulda shoulda, you dig? You can't uncut the cards. So no, I never was that."

"What I'm saying is, if there's family on my side, then couldn't there be family on the other?" Roe looked at Cleve, and Cleve looked back and his chest tightened. "Couldn't that be the connection, the one last thing? The thing that balances out the equation. That completes the molecule?"

"One last thing," Hark said thoughtfully. "One last…"

# Chapter Thirty-One

"Witness," Cleve said. "One last witness."

"Who?"

"My granddad."

"He still alive?" Hark asked.

"Just about."

"And you think he was that boy?"

"I don't know," Cleve said. "I mean, that would be the connection, right? That he was in the photograph too."

"Did he ever –?" Roe began.

"He never said nothin' about it that I ever heard , but you wouldn't. I mean, would you?"

"Except maybe to a therapist," Roe said,

"They didn't have therapists then."

"Um, I think Freud –"

"– and even if they did, he couldn't've afforded one. And anyway, he was kind of a man's man, he wouldn't wanna sit there cryin' or whatever."

"Which side of your family is he on?" Hark asked.

"He's my dad's dad, an Olsen."

"A family that's been here for generations."

"Yeah. We was farmers once. He never liked my mom

or us kids, though, so we don't see him much."

"Where does he live?"

"You know the place out on the freeway? What they call a retirement community?" Hark shook his head. "He lives there now. It's kinda grim, but my pop ain't got the money for nothin' better, and even if he did I reckon he'd rather spend it on us than him."

Yeah, his dad was okay, Cleve considered.

"After my grandma died – of lung cancer, from smokin' sixty a day – he was gettin' so he couldn't cope, fridge full of rotten food, hoarding, all that. We cleared the house out one time, got skips, everythin', but he filled it up again real fast. That's the kinda thing you can only do once, then you figure the person wants it that way so you leave off. But the neighbors called the county on account of the stink an' the rats, and he was removed 'for his own safety,' as they say. Actually I think he was relieved. I mean, he couldn't ta wanted to live like that, or I don't reckon so..."

"How long's he been there?" Roe asked, thinking of his great grand and her horror of the facility. She had said racism was rampant there. Roe had assumed she meant the staff, but Cleve's grandfather was the descendant of someone who had taken part in a lynching; someone so unashamed they brought their child to witness it.

"Three years, coming up on four," Cleve said. "We visit on his birthday, Thanksgiving, stuff like that. Well, not my mom."

"I need to see him," Hark said.

"What for?"

"I won't know until I see him."

"You think he *is*, like, the last witness?" Roe asked.

"I'll know when I'm there."

"If I can borrow Dale's truck again we can go first thing in the morning," Cleve said. Excitement was coursing through him. This could be a resolution. This could set him and Roe free from the stranglehold of history at the same moment as it set Hark free to go on to wherever. He turned to Roe, and Roe's eyes were aglow – he felt the possibility of liberation too, it seemed; and Cleve was filled with an overwhelming desire to kiss him, to clamber on top of him, to take him in his arms and hold him close. Instead he said, "Um, what about your folks?"

"How do you mean?"

"Well, while I'm waiting to go round to Dale's they'll be gettin' up, won't they? And they'll freak out if you're not there. And you can't exactly call 'em up and say, 'Oh, don't worry, I snuck out in the middle of the night because, um. Oh, and by the way just ignore the break-in that happened at my school the exact same time I was outta the house.'"

"Shit," Roe said. "You're totally right, obviously." By now very tired, he had been thinking how in a little while he would fall into bed with Cleve; how they would curl up like cats and sleep, no more than that, but for the first time in his life since being a baby, so for the first time he could remember, not alone. Now he was deprived of that simple pleasure, and it felt like he would never get back to it – or in fact get to it, because he had never been there yet. "How do I even *get* home?" he groaned.

"You could borrow my bike," Cleve suggested.

"I haven't been on a bike for, like, literally a decade."

"You skateboard, dude. That's wheels, and balance. And riding a bike's like, well, riding a bike, right? I mean, you never forget, supposedly."

"How long do you reckon it'd take me?"

"You mean if you don't wind up face-down in a ditch?"

"Ha ha. Yeah, assuming that."

"Maybe an hour. And it's 4:25 now."

"Okay." Roe sighed. However worried he knew his parents would be, he was reluctant to leave that room and go out into the uncertain night alone.

No better or more practical option presented itself, however, so he forced himself to get up from the table, and he and Cleve went out and round to the front of the house, where Cleve's bicycle lay on the parched lawn by the drive.

Cleve had left the porch light off so they would be less likely to be seen by any passing driver, or by the Rippels next door, and there in the shadows they kissed, passionately and lengthily, and arousal surged through them, and they longed to go further but there was no time then, and no right or practical place. Hark was waiting inside and would soon enough grow restless; and though they didn't know it, in some liminal way Roe's parents were awaiting their son's return too.

Reluctantly they broke the kiss and Cleve helped Roe straddle the bike. Every movement he made now seemed sexual to Cleve, and comically oversignified – Roe's awkward mounting of the upthrust saddle; the curve of his tensing thighs against the tight denim of his shorts; his butt perched high on the saddle, Cleve's palm briefly in the small of his back – and then just plain comical as Roe wobbled down the slight incline of the drive towards the highway, his arms rigidly extended in front of him, the gears jerking and clicking as the chain jumped from one toothed cog to the next, then finally caught.

"Come down to where I dropped you yesterday," Cleve called softly. "Be there for nine a.m."

Roe waved acknowledgment but didn't risk looking back, as even briefly taking one hand from the handlebars made him swerve perilously.

Cleve watched him pedal away. Soon he gained in confidence, lifted his butt, pumped harder on the pedals, picked up speed, and was swallowed by the night.

Cleve sighed and went back inside, to Hark.

# Chapter Thirty-Two

Once the houses of Coleman East were behind him, Roe pedaled faster. The road was lonesome here, and thoughts of watching things among the trees crept in, fears both childish and not.

Cycling was faster and less effort than riding a board, and inflated rubber made for a smoother ride than rigid polyurethane, but the bike's tires were flabby, and soon he felt his thighs begin to burn. Funny, he thought, how little one sort of exercise prepared you for another.

After fifteen minutes or so he found himself passing the Peach Street truck stop. A single light cast a glow on a lowered blind in one of the dilapidated trailer homes out back; otherwise it was in darkness. Here the road ran slightly downhill, and he had built up enough speed to freewheel for a while, but the whirr of the chain set a dog barking somewhere, so he began to pedal again, to quiet the sound.

Soon he was nearing the billboards advertising gracious plantation living restored, and he felt a sudden urge to stop and try to burn them down. As he hadn't even a match on him, never mind a lighter or any sort of accelerant, the urge was easy to ignore. But he imagined the blaze, visible for miles around, a spectacular symbol of one black man's refusal to accommodate the overwriting and erasure of historical truth. Then he imagined being caught pedaling away as fire trucks rushed to put it out.

*Vandal, robber, arsonist.*

He thought of Cleve, and wondered why one body was drawn to another so strongly it was like they were two parts of a mechanism that had been designed to interlock; why that should happen, and why it should feel miraculous. He wondered if straight people had the same thoughts, the same sense of wonder. He supposed they took it for granted: after all, every romcom told them it would turn out that way.

As he passed the third billboard Roe heard the roar of a vehicle up ahead, coming on fast. Tightening his fingers on both brakes far too sharply, he pulled up in a clumsy skid that almost sent him flying over the handlebars, and he flashed to a time as a kid when he had landed face-first on the asphalt and chipped both his front teeth.

Breathlessly he hauled the bike off the road, threw it down in the long grass, and crouched behind a clump of bushes as a pickup hurtled by, heading east in a hurry. Someone escaping something, maybe, or eager to get home and be in bed, or just opening up the throttle on the flat. He waited till the red of its taillights had vanished before setting off again.

It took him a further forty minutes of straight cycling to reach the bottom of Van Cleef Avenue.

Roe turned in and began to pedal up the first of the residential street's relentlessly rising zigzags, but soon his thighs were straining, and he found himself going so slowly he could hardly keep the bicycle upright – and that was even once he'd remembered to switch down to the easiest gear.

Realizing he'd actually go faster on foot, he dismounted and walked the bike the rest of the way up the hill. The sky was starting to lighten by the time he reached Cedar Close, the first glint of birdsong had begun, and his eyes ached.

Roe sneaked the bike along the side of the garage no one came round except to put the trash out on refuse day, which was his chore anyway, leant it against the wall, then came back round to the front. Glancing about him to make sure no early bird or night owl neighbor was watching, he clambered onto the rain barrel and hauled himself up onto the garage roof as quietly as he could, trying to not kick the guttering as he swung a leg up onto the warm tarpaper.

His window waited, open wide. As he climbed in over the sill he didn't think he'd ever been so tired.

Yet being back in his bedroom was strange. It was so exactly the same as it had been when he left with Hark last night; as it had been two nights earlier, before he had met Hark; or three nights earlier, before he had met Cleve, and when the Tyler statue still stood on its tomb-like plinth at the Main Street intersection. With its Marilyn Manson poster on the wall, its X-Men and Batman action figures (that his father disparaged as dolls) lined up on the shelf above the bed; with *Wuthering Heights*, *Pride and Prejudice* and *David Copperfield* stacked on the bedside table next to a broken Felix The Cat alarm clock, it was the bedroom of a boy dreaming about his life beginning. And now it had begun, in ways that were strange and thrilling and even frightening.

He shucked off his vest, shorts and socks, and lay back on the bed in only his briefs. The Joker, Catwoman and the Riddler looked down on him. He had always thought he would look good in the Riddler's question-marked bodysuit and bowler hat.

From the hall downstairs came the faint, reassuring tick of the grandmother clock. His dad wound it each

Sunday evening, using two keys, one to winch up each weight.

His mom would call him down at 7:15 a.m. like she always did, school or no school.

It was now 5:40 a.m.

He was still a virgin.

The sky was showing pinkly at the window.

He sighed. With only ninety minutes' sleep, breakfast would be an ordeal. And after his parents went to work he would have to think of a way to leave the house that wouldn't cause his sister to suspect he was up to something.

With a grunt he arched his back and stretched his arms out over his head. There was a hint of Cleve's cologne on his skin from when they had hugged goodbye. Something with citrus and musk in it, or cheap imitations of them, anyway.

Well, not the citrus: lemons were cheap, right?

What was musk anyway? Something to do with musk-rats? That didn't sound right. Or glamorous.

Closing his eyes, Roe exhaled as slowly and fully as he could, and as his chest sank he sank into sleep.

"Roe? Roe!"

It was his mom calling up the stairs, jerking him awake. "Breakfast in five!"

"I'll be down in a minute!" he called back, croaky-voiced and resentful as he dragged himself up from his sweaty bed. He felt unrested and hard eyed, and his thighs and arms ached from the cycling. Sniffing an armpit, he wrinkled his nose. Wrapping a towel he had fished from his dirty clothes bag round his waist, he staggered from his bedroom barefoot, heading to the bathroom to grab a shower.

He was just in time to shove past his sister, who was standing in her bedroom doorway in a fancy satin dressing gown, her hair carefully wrapped against the evils of condensation, and was holding a knock-off Louis Vuitton wash bag bulging with a woman's mysterious array of toiletries.

"Losers weepers!" Roe shouted as he rushed past her into the bathroom. Locking the door behind him, he shucked off his underwear and turned the shower on. Phyllis was already banging on the door. "Roe!"

"I can't hear you!" he called.

Thump thump thump.

"I'll be, like, literally two minutes!"

Roe stepped into the lukewarm water and cranked up the pressure, squeezed out a too-large glob of coconut shower-gel and quickly lathered his body. Once she got in the bathroom Phyllis could take more than an hour, doing what he couldn't imagine, so he felt both natural justice and household efficiency were on his side. Their parents had an en suite, so this daily battle was between siblings only.

Back in his bedroom he moisturized briskly, pricked his Mohawk into springy symmetry, and pulled on fresh underwear, avoiding the more raggedy pairs. *When I live alone I'm gonna get briefs that are way briefer than these*, he thought, turning sideways on to check himself out in the wardrobe mirror.

He pulled on a tight black tank top with a faux fascist red lightning jag down the front, wiggled into black denim shorts, and shoved his feet into a pair of retro hi-tops with pumps in the tongues. These were held together by duct tape, which annoyed his mother, who favored cheap and new over decrepit but hip when it came to her son's wardrobe.

The shower had livened him up a bit, but the instant he parked his butt at the family breakfast table Roe's energy crumbled, and he found himself mumbling replies to his parents' routine questions like the worst, most lumpishly clichéd teenager imaginable. The orange juice tasted so acidic this morning that he could feel it burning holes in his stomach lining; the eggs seemed unpleasantly greasy, with creepy bits of underdone albumen in them. It was weird, he thought, how lack of sleep was so instantly sickening. He struggled to perform normality, and found himself wishing Phyllis would come down and draw attention away from him with some obnoxious or combative comment.

Eventually the meal was over. His dad left for work, then his mom. His sister still hadn't come down. Leaving her place set, he cleared away the rest of the breakfast things, resentful at having to empty the dishwasher before he could load it up again. How did people stand the nightmare futility of mundane things needing to be done over and over? Why not just kill yourself?

He went out onto the back porch and looked across north Claypit, which was already stewing in the glare and blaze of the morning.

Way out west was a line of bare mauve hills. He supposed they must have a name, but he didn't know it. They began somewhere beyond the freeway that, along with the warehouse-sized out-of-town superstores, had done so much to choke off local businesses.

Roe pictured mobility scooters moving slowly up and down endless Sprawlmart aisles, customers filling their baskets. Everyone knew such stores were parasitical and killed community spirit, yet people gave themselves over to them willingly, guzzling down a crazy excess of sugary, fatty, low nutrition foodstuffs, swelling up like Cleve's mom, a literal embodiment of poverty.

A glance at his phone told Roe it was now 8:30 a.m. He heard Phyllis emerge from the bathroom, and then her bedroom door close. He felt an unexpected impulse to go up and – what? Apologize? Try to share what he had been through the last couple of days? He realized he hadn't asked her what she thought about the statue coming down, and now he felt guilty for assuming that she had no more than considered herself and her pregnancy upstaged by his criminal act of restitution.

I'll be an uncle, he thought, and found he liked the idea. He wondered if it would be a boy or a girl.

Most of all he wanted to share that he had met someone. Phyllis wouldn't care he was gay – she was no more religious than he was, though she kept quiet about her fading faith. He wondered if whoever had got her pregnant was black or white – or Asian, for that matter, or Hispanic or Arab. She always acted Jill Scott militant about wanting a good black man, but maybe that was more about who she saw herself ending up with after multicolored adventures along the way. He wondered if it had been a hard decision to keep it. He wondered if she would like Cleve, and realized he wanted them to meet, and that her opinion would matter to him. Funny how being gay made the reactionary shit radical, he thought: to want your partner to meet your family and be well-received in defiance of millennia of human history.

Maybe afterwards, he thought, and with that thought came another: there might not be an afterwards. Because it struck him that this meeting they were going to today could somehow go badly; could even be dangerous. Hark had punched that security guard down the stairs, and hadn't cared then or later.

Uneasily he let himself out of the house and fetched Cleve's bike. He left a note on the kitchen table, for Phyllis to find when she eventually came down:

*Be seeing you, sis.*
*Love u and looking 4ward 2 my nephew slash niece.*
*R x*

# Chapter Thirty-Three

**B**eing sleep-deprived, Cleve hadn't managed to fake up some crucial errand he needed Dale's pickup for when he went round to the Rippels that morning.

Fortunately it hadn't mattered. "Enjoy!" Dale called as Velma handed Cleve the keys in a virtual rerun of the day before. "Gals give the eye to a guy in a truck!"

"Now, Dale –" Velma turned to chide him.

Hark was now finding it difficult to walk, so Cleve lent him a cane that had belonged to his maternal grandfather. Varnished, nubby and shod with brass, Myrtle claimed it was an antique, but it probably wasn't. They set off earlier than they needed to, as you always do when there's nothing else to do, and reached the rendezvous point on Main Street ten minutes early. Roe was already there, waiting with Cleve's bike.

Cleve pulled in. Roe swung the bike onto the back of the truck with a grunt and climbed in up front next to Hark.

Cleve pulled out again. Both he and Roe were squinty-eyed for lack of sleep, and short of talk, and for some reason this morning Cleve struggled to force the stick from one gear to the next, which consumed what little remained of his attention and energy.

When they reached the intersection where the statue of Colonel Tyler had once stood and stood no more, Roe said, "Can you pull over?"

Without bothering to indicate, Cleve did so, jerking to an accidentally abrupt halt under a tired old cypress and stalling the engine. "Sorry," he muttered.

The morning sun was bright and already pitiless, and though the tree's leaves scattered shade on the truck's hood and windshield, everything else was glary and tiring. A beat-up blue Chrysler coming down China Row gave way to a white SUV with tinted windows that was coming up Paper Street. An elderly white man in dark glasses, a white flat cap, a check shirt and the sort of cargo pants where the waist is apparently just below the nipples, was walking a small dog. "So, um, what are we doing?" Cleve said.

"There." Roe pointed.

Cleve looked, and then he saw: by the not yet open drugstore was what was probably the last public payphone in Claypit. He realized then that he had totally forgotten about the night watchman, who for all he knew still lay at the foot of the stairs in the main hall of the Tyler Academy.

"You want me to do it?" he offered.

"Um, well, I could, if you want," Roe said. "But you sound more, um..."

"Criminal? White trash?"

Roe looked embarrassed. "Um."

"It's okay," Cleve said, forcing a grin. "*I* can say it."

He got out and crossed to the payphone. Trying to remember how they worked, he first lifted the receiver and listened for a dial tone. Despite its battered appearance, there was one. The coin slot gave him pause: he had no change. But a notice inside the curved kiosk hood stated that 911 calls were free. Glancing round uneasily, he punched in the number, waited, and then, when a male voice answered, blurted, "There was a break-in at the Tyler school last night. The watchman got hit in the head. You should send an ambulance."

"Who is –?"

Cleve hung up and went back to the truck, started it up and pulled out faster than he meant to, with a screech that made the elderly dog walker look round. Cleve wanted to kick himself. But would the police care enough to try and find witnesses to someone making a call from that particular payphone at that particular time?

If the watchman was dead, then probably.

Beyond the intersection, Main Street ran due west for miles. They passed Barney's Balls and O'Flaherty's, both at that hour closed, several blocks of mostly shuttered stores, three abandoned basketball courts, several light industrial units, each of which had a few cars parked in front of it, and finally a closed-down factory that gave no clue as to what it had manufactured. A sun bleached sign read "PYLOR."

In other circumstances Cleve would have riffed on the name – Piles? Hemorrhoid cream? Wasn't pyloric sphincter a word? – but he was dog-tired, and though the sun was at their backs everything ahead was somehow dazzling, so he said nothing.

Dale had asked Cleve to put some fuel in the truck, so he pulled in at a gas station just past the town boundary and put in thirty dollars' worth – twenty of Dale's, handed him by Velma; ten from the money his dad had given him – choosing a pump where a pulled up U-haul meant the clerk couldn't see his passengers from the pay station.

Hark and Roe stayed in the truck while Cleve went to

pay. He brought them back some Cokes and candy bars – thanks to his lack of food shopping, he and Hark had had nothing to eat that morning. The sugar and caffeine were poison, but gave them all a little fake energy.

To get to the senior facility you had to take an anonymous right-hand turnoff just before the interchange. If you missed it and ended up on the freeway there was no exit for miles and miles. On their first visit they had overshot, and Cleve's dad had cursed for forty minutes straight as they looked for a place to get off the freeway and turn around. Inevitably the needle had started bumping on empty, and the warning light began to blink just as they were funneled onto the up ramp.

Cleve didn't miss the turn.

The road was dusty and straight and ran parallel to the freeway. One hundred sixty years ago black sharecroppers had attempted to farm there, on the impoverished land resentfully – spitefully – assigned them after the white south lost the war. Then the clay works came, and though the work was hard and dangerous, the sharecroppers abandoned their farms for the mines en masse. Cheap tract homes were built round the works, and the black people moved into them.

The clay was worked out by the late 1950s, and the mine closed down, but no one wanted to return to the land. Many who had worked in the mine drifted into lives of perpetual disability and, slow decades later, prescription pain-medication addiction. The most recent blow to north-west Claypit had been dealt by the sub-prime housing crash, which left street upon residential street as deserted as if the inhabitants had collectively looked back and turned to salt.

Land out this way being all but worthless, a company that specialized in low-cost facilities for impoverished seniors lobbied the town council for financial support in setting up there. A vote was taken, and by a modest majority the council awarded the company a fifteen-year contract and a grant to come to Claypit.

As Mayor Oglesby said, it wasn't a private prison but it was something.

In the short term it led to construction work; in the longer term to minimum waged care work. Those applying from "bad" addresses in the Pits were rejected even for that, staff being drawn mainly from a smaller Hispanic community that would once have picked peaches.

The facility, which currently accommodated – or, as one report baldly put it, "warehoused" – fifty-seven seniors, had been the subject of several investigations over the years, following allegations by worried loved ones concerning shoddy care and even abuse. However, since the company did a job no one else wanted to, and cheaply, the investigations lacked stringency, and the facility's doors remained open.

The abandoned farms had long sunk into the parched and dusty earth, swallowed as the pyramids had been swallowed by the desert sand, leaving only here and there sagging, half-buried lengths of barbed wire and the odd fence post to mark their former presence.

In this bleak, untenanted landscape the senior facility stood alone. A bunker built of concrete and yellow brick, it was bounded by a waist high chain-link fence on all sides save the access road it fronted onto. The fence divided unloved dirt on one side from unloved dirt on the other to no apparent purpose; certainly there was nothing there that could be called a garden. Maybe it was to deter the demented from wandering off; maybe to deter coyotes from wandering in and predating on the incapacitated seniors.

A couple hundred yards beyond it, passing cars glittered on the freeway. Perhaps that was the lure that had caused the fence to be erected: the possibility of escape;

the fantasy of thumbing a ride to somewhere, anywhere else. Or perhaps the fence was there to allow the administration to claim the center had "grounds," and so was a good, guilt-free place to stow an unwanted, impoverished and dependent relative.

The parking lot had no shade, and here the cars of visitors baked in the sun. The seat-leather burned any bare skin that touched it when you got back in after making even a brief visit.

That early it was deserted.

Cleve knew from previous visits there was a staff lot round the other side that had some shade – even the worst-paid workers needed a car to get out here; the bus service had been discontinued before he was born. His dad had parked there one time, and an administrator had rushed out to row with him even though there were plenty of free spaces. The point seemed to be that if you left a relative here then you were a shitty person, and you had to be reminded of this by being treated like shit.

Red-faced his father had given in to the power of notices. "Staff" here, "Visitors" there, as immutable as actual facts.

Cleve thought of Hark and the ice-cream parlor: "White"; "Colored." Almost impossible to defy.

Unable to face needless conflict, and wanting to avoid institutional attention, he turned into the visitors' lot, pulling up randomly across two spaces. As a gesture of defiance this was, he knew, pitiful: he had never seen more than two or three vehicles there, even on public holidays when the guilt rays were at their strongest. He swallowed the last of his Coke. By now blood-warm, it hit the bottom of his stomach like a lump of acid and left his mouth sticky, making him want to rinse it out or at least spit.

Under the sun's glare they crossed the lot and made their way round to the entrance, which was a glass sliding door on the side of the building facing the road, and was shaded by a concrete awning supported by a pair of splayed, brushed metal uprights, the building's one concession to architectural style. These were flanked by two small orange trees in tubs. Their leaves were dust-smothered, and it was hard to imagine anyone wanting to taste the few stunted oranges that hung from their branches.

Beyond the sliding door was a reception desk and past that, Cleve knew from previous visits, was a day-room with windows that looked out towards the hills. In between was a wall of frosted glass, with a door you needed to be buzzed through.

He took a breath. This was where Roe and Hark being white would have been really useful, because then, once Cleve presented his ID, the receptionist would accept the flimsiest statement on his part that they were family. Okay, yeah, Roe and Hark *could* be his in-laws – what was that statistic he'd seen about the rapidly rising number of mixed race marriages, even in the South? – but still she would be suspicious, and might refuse them entry. She might even join the ranks of crazy white women he'd seen on social media calling the cops on black people for swimming, eating, reading in libraries, sitting, viewing properties for sale et cetera.

Well, Roe *was* family. That was a fact. And wasn't Hark somehow kind of related to Roe?

Maybe if he said, "This is my boyfriend, actually," the receptionist would be so shocked she'd forget to think they were up to something bad. Maybe she'd even think it was cute.

*Yeah, right.* She'd probably cross herself, as against vampires.

He sighed and thought about trying to sneak round the outside of the building. Tempting though it was, it clearly wasn't an option: they'd be bound to be seen by someone, and then the staff really would call the cops, and that would be infinitely more embarrassing than trying to sweet-talk the receptionist.

With Roe on his right and Hark on his left, Cleve approached the entrance. The door slithered aside to admit them.

# Chapter Thirty-Four

Despite the conditioner's persistent hum, the air in the reception area was humid and close, and tainted by food odors that combined unappetizingly with medicinal smells and the tang of bleach. The walls were a pale yellow, the linoleum was gray flecked with white, and the doors and furnishings were of the same cheap blond wood that was used throughout Cleve's school.

"Yeah, um, so try and act normal," Cleve murmured to Hark as they approached the reception desk, though he was aware that it was the Mohawked Roe who probably looked more like trouble to the receptionist, his rebel hair likely suggesting an intention to pilfer prescription painkillers. "Sunglasses, dude," he said to Roe, who hastily took them off.

Hark, of course, kept his on.

A heavyset white woman in a white uniform sat behind the desk. She looked up at them inquiringly over a pair of half-moon spectacles. Now Cleve was with Roe he noticed white people were white in a way he never had before: before, they had just been people. Her gray-blonde hair was scraped back into a bun and she wore no make-up, though she sported a pair of outsize hoop earrings intended to suggest, Cleve suspected, that she was really a "fun" personality. In front of her was a booklet of puzzles, partly filled in; to her right a computer, the screen of which had gone to sleep. From beyond the door to the dayroom came the sound of TV chatter, a scattering of studio audience applause.

"Can I help you?" she asked suspiciously.

"Good mornin', ma'am. I'm Cleve Olsen. We're here to visit my grandpa, Ron Olsen."

"Did you book an appointment?"

For a moment Cleve was flummoxed. He knew perfectly well no one ever booked appointments because the facility never had too many visitors. "Uh, is he okay?" he asked. He supposed it just possible his grandfather had had some sort of medical drama and was drugged up as a consequence, or was  having a catheter changed or something else gross and invasive.

The woman – her badge gave her name as Kimberlee – looked him over, trying, he guessed, to make up her mind as to what course of action would be the least effort for herself. He got out his wallet and produced his driver's license. "It's been a while since my last visit," he said as he showed it to her. "I'm feelin' kinda guilty about it."

"Mm-hm."

"I mean, we don't know how long he's got. And my mom, she's, um, disabled on account of her knees, so it's hard for her to get out here."

Kimberlee turned in her swivel chair and produced a visitors' book from a drawer. She opened it, turned it to face Cleve and handed him a biro. "Names and addresses," she said.

"Thank you, ma'am." Cleve carefully printed his name and address. Roe's handwriting was more fluid than his, but also more scrawly. Hark's was old fashioned, in the style they used to call copperplate, and he gave Roe's address as his own. Cleve saw he had written "Paul Harker" in the name box. Roe gave his relationship as "friend"; Hark as "uncle".

Kimberlee glanced at the book indifferently. "You can go through," she said, indicating the security door. They went over to it and waited for her to buzz them in.

Beyond was the dayroom. A TV high on one wall was turned to a morning chat show. Pale blue padded chairs with easy-wipe seats were scattered about, and on some of these seniors sat, men and women, mostly white, a few black and brown, all of them torpid and dull eyed. Several looked round as Cleve, Roe and Hark came in. Then, not recognizing them, they turned away again. Some, Cleve supposed, wouldn't recognize their own children or grandchildren, and so would feel abandoned even when they had actually been visited.

It didn't seem like a place that would keep the brain going.

To one side a vending machine sold snacks, a monetizing opportunity for the company that ran the facility, as visitors were offered nothing but a water fountain for refreshment. The seniors, of course, weren't allowed to handle money.

Through a room-wide picture window, across the dusty land out past the freeway, the hills lay low and lavender. Almost a pleasant room, it was somehow bleak. Perhaps it was the lack of any personal touches, as though some machine had decided the minimum that was required to keep a body going, and the staff had fallen in with its assessment.

In a pot by the door a dying fig struggled on. Cleve imagined a staff member bringing it in, then getting fired, probably for being too human, leaving it behind, and no one else bothering to water it.

His grandfather wasn't there.

"Uh, this way," he said to Roe and Hark.

His grandfather's room was one of eight off a feature-less side-corridor. Hark's cane clicked as he walked, and he leant on it heavily, as if he was turning into one of the residents.

Cleve knocked on a door and, hearing no reply, opened it and looked in. His grandfather wasn't there either. He could be in one of the shower- or bathrooms of course, but there was no sound of running water. Cleve knew there was a porch that ran along the back of the building, where you could go and sit. The door to the porch was off the dayroom. They went back and out that way.

The air outside was hot and tangy with dust, but at that hour the porch was still in the merciful shade the side of the building provided. Only one resident was out there, an elderly man sitting on a wooden bench that faced the hills: Cleve's grandfather, Ron Olsen. Thin and frail-looking, he wore a floppy white sun hat, very dark dark glasses, a white tee shirt and over it, despite the broiling heat, a chunky-knit gray cardigan; too-baggy navy track pants, and white trainers with easy-fasten Velcro straps.

"Hey, Grandpa," Cleve said as they approached the old man, who turned his head in their direction. His eyes were as hidden as Hark's and he had no particular expression on his face. Suspecting an onrush of senility, Cleve added, "It's Cleve, your grandson." Then, "These are my friends, Roe and Hark."

"Mister Olsen," Hark said.

Roe waved feebly, feeling awkward, and effeminate in a way he never normally did. His interactions with elderly white blue-collar men were at that point in his life basi-cally nil.

The old man went back to staring at the hills. Cleve sat next to him on the bench; Hark and Roe pulled up some nearby plastic lawn chairs. Ron Olsen's lower jaw ground constantly – judging by their yellowy-brown waywardness he still had all his own teeth – and he had a slight tremor.

Cleve looked round at Hark and Roe. Preamble seemed impossible, so he said, "Roe's my, um, friend. Hark's come about a photograph."

"Photograph? What photograph?" Ron Olsen asked without interest.

"Um, one from when you was a kid," Cleve said.

"I don't have nothin' like that. When they forced me out my home they threw it all in a skip. Trashed it. I don't have no keepsakes."

"It was all pretty much trashed already, Grandpa," Cleve said mildly.

Ron Olsen made a rumbling noise in his throat. "Yeah? So what you come for, then?"

"It's about something you saw," Cleve said. "When you was around ten years old. They took a photograph and made a postcard of it. We reckon – me, Roe and Hark – that you're maybe the last person who was there who's still alive."

"I don't know what you're talking about."

"Yeah, you do," said Hark.

The old man's head jerked round as if he were a puppet. His dark glasses swiveled onto Hark's. "Do I know you?"

"You know me."

"Yeah? I don't remember too good nowadays. Where I know you from?"

Hark reached out and took one of Ron Olsen's hands in his. Cleve's grandfather withdrew his hand sharply, as if he'd been shocked. "Goddamn it," he said sharply. "What was that? Something ain't earthed."

"Earthed," Hark echoed.

"I don't know you," Ron Olsen said uneasily. "Never

did. Never."

Hark rolled his head. The vertebrae in his neck crackled alarmingly. "The thing is," he said, and now he rose from his seat to stand over the frail old man, "and I'm sorry, I really am, but I reckon I need to take your eyes."

# Chapter Thirty-Five

Cleve jumped to his feet. "What the fuck, Hark?"

"I'm truly sorry, old man," Hark said, looming over Ron Olsen. "But I reckon to be free I got to take your eyes."

"Aw, dude, you know I can't let you do that," Cleve said. Hark was a lot weaker than when he'd punched the watchman in the neck, but you don't need much strength to gouge someone's eyes out – or not physical strength, anyway.

Roe too was on his feet, wavering between running to get an orderly, never mind how impossible it would be to explain what was going on, and staying to prevent a sordid, macabre tussle during which a frail, elderly white man might be blinded by an insane black man.

Then Cleve's grandfather chuckled, a mirthless, unexpected sound. "That's an old wives' tale," he said.

"What?" Hark said.

"The dying image, caught in the lens."

"I don't believe so," Hark said, and he leant in so close he was sharing the old man's breath.

"You're too late," Ron Olsen snapped, and with fingers buckled by arthritis, he fumbled off his sunglasses. "I got me my moon-discs, see." And they did see: his eyes were pearled over with cataracts. "I can stare at the sun and I wouldn't know."

"When?" Cleve asked.

His grandfather shrugged. "How would I know, stuck out here? Since you last come, anyhow."

"Huh." Hark exhaled. Cleve and Roe watched him as you'd watch a tarantula: an immobile and venomous creature that might move fast.

Slowly Hark straightened up. He stepped back from the old man and, with a grunt, sat down on one of the chairs. Once they felt sure he wouldn't attempt a last mad lunge, Cleve and Roe sat too. Ron Olsen replaced his dark glasses.

"You knew which photograph we was talkin' about," Cleve said.

"I guessed." Ron Olsen turned his head towards Hark. "You the grandson?"

"The – descendant," Hark said.

"Then I guess you're owed, if anyone is."

"I guess so."

"It was my brother took me. Vern. You wouldn't know about him, Cleve. He was eight years older than me, and a bully. Came in talking 'bout how there was gonna be a necktie party over in the town square. I didn't know what that was."

"Tell me," Hark said.

"Here's the thing: I'd give you my eyes to not have seen it."

"Too late."

"There's things cast a shadow that never gets lifted. Marriage, kids, church, all the things that tell you life is good, that there's a plan and purpose, you do 'em, but none of 'em lets you unsee what you saw: what it showed you about life, about people. About reality. The inside splits off from the outside, and it kinda shrivels away. Vern died in Vietnam," he added. "He got his from the Cong. Is that justice?"

"Maybe," Hark said.

"I never talked about this with anyone," Ron Olsen said. "Not ever, Goddamn you. I didn't want to be there. I was supposed to be in bed. But he come in my room and his eyes was so bright, so I went with him. That's about the only answer to why he was there and why I was there, and I don't suppose it'll be enough for you."

"No," Hark said.

"I don't understand," Cleve said.

"Course you don't. But there's an ecstasy to it," his grandfather said. "See, an object of hate is as sweet to the heart as an object of love. That's human nature. It ain't about color, though I guess it looked that way that night. I mean that, that was our own particular American hate. What you'd have to call white hate. But I seen them churches on TV, them ones full of skulls in that African country, what was it called, where one half turned on the other, neighbors hacked up neighbors, kids, old folks, everything."

"Rwanda," Roe said.

"Rwanda, yeah, that. Racks and racks of skulls." To Hark he said, "Can I touch your face?"

Gently Hark took the old man's vein-wormed hands and lifted and placed them. With tremulous fingertips Ron Olsen explored Hark's features. "Young," he said quietly. "Thank you." He returned his hands to his lap. "For a while there I was thinking you was a ghost."

"I don't believe in ghosts," Hark said.

"The only ghosts is memories," Ron Olsen said. "The haunting kind, anyhow."

They sat in silence for a while, each alone with his thoughts. It was both an ending, and not. Suddenly very thirsty, Roe went and got them all polystyrene cups of water from the dispenser in the dayroom, bringing them out on a plastic tray.

Cleve's phone went off, and he got up and stood to one side, quietly sharing with his father the surprising information that he was visiting his grandpa, and, perhaps by way of proof, the news that the old man's sight had failed.

Hark sat with his head bowed as in defeat. "There must be something we can do," Roe said.

"Do?" Cleve's grandfather said. "There's nothing to do now."

"Mister Olsen, did they let you keep *anything* when you came here?"

"Just one box. You speak well. Are you from round here?"

"I go to the Tyler Academy."

"Rich kid."

"Kinda. Not really. What was in the box?"

"Not much. I don't recall – I was pretty far gone by then. My Julie had passed, and..."

"But old things?"

"Junk. Well, they called it junk. I call it stuff I need to keep balanced. Yeah, some of it was old. Real old. Cleve!" he called. Cleve looked round from where he was still talking quietly on the phone. "Help – Roe – here go get my box. It's under the bed."

Cleve quickly finished his call, and after shooting a glance at Hark that was still wary, he and Roe went inside and through to his grandpa's room.

There was nothing under the bed except some twists of dust, but on top of the wardrobe they found a tin trunk, four feet long, three wide and two deep. They lugged it down together – it was heavy – and, taking a handle each, carried it to the porch between them and set it down next to Cleve's grandfather. The old man seemed to have been crying. Hark seemed not to have changed position, even a tiny bit.

"It's locked, Grandpa," Cleve said.

Ron Olsen rooted in his cardigan pocket and pulled out a fob with a fishing fly on it and a few small, old keys. He felt his way round to the one he wanted by pressing his thumb against their teeth, and held it out to Cleve. Cleve had to wiggle it about for what seemed like ages before he could get the lock to spring, but he managed eventually, and lifted the lid.

The contents of the trunk were packed in like Tetrominos, so as to leave no spaces, and were a mix of things that looked personal and stuff Cleve suspected had gone in because it was the exact right size to fill a certain gap. It was almost art, and undoubtedly severely OCD. Some of the "treasures" you could see were pretty much junk: a tarnished tin cigarette case; a clear resin paper-weight with a small tarantula inside; an alligator-skin glasses case with a split and a broken hinge. Playing cards had been used as dividers to prevent the contents from moving about if the box was tilted. Cleve tugged one of the cards out. It was the queen of spades, with a color photograph on it of a girl with a black bob hairdo in just her bra and panties. The colors were all slightly off, like in old magazines: too red, too pink.

"It's like Joseph Cornell," Roe said.

"Who's that?" Ron Olsen said.

"He was an artist who made these, like, he called them memory boxes."

"Well, I don't remember what's in there."

"Can we, like, um, dig in?" Cleve asked.

Ron Olsen shrugged. "I can't see so what do I care? Just don't ask for explanations. And pack it all up again when you're done."

Like archaeologists at a dig, Roe and Cleve carefully started to unpack the box, knowing as they did so that there was no hope of repacking it anywhere as neatly, and

that it would be pretty much impossible to cram everything back in.

There were old letters kept in their envelopes, carefully tied round with a ribbon. There were marbles, some
misshapen. There were blown fuses and a couple of
screw-in Christmas tree light bulbs. There were match-
boxes empty of matches. One had a dead beetle inside,
whether by accident or on purpose, who knew. There was
a plain white candle-stub. A small brown bottle had the
word "tincture" handwritten on its label. Whatever was
inside had seeped out and stained its surroundings a
cochineal red.

Cleve imagined himself combing through all this after
his grandfather's death, thinking how few answers he
would find amongst these bits and pieces, kept for
reasons obscure or nonexistent. Even the letters, which
he assumed to be to or from his grandmother, love letters
maybe, might be no more than replies to rants sent to the
local paper about garbage collection. Only at this moment, through Hark, was the past truly accessible, truly
alive. And still Hark might be a fantasist.

"What's this?" Roe asked, tugging out a flattish, rectangular box about eight inches by four by two. It had
slightly rounded edges, and was covered in a black papery
plastic the texture of snakeskin. There were button levers
on the narrow sides, and a hinged lid was set into it to
which was attached a hook that looked like it could be
levered up with a fingernail in order to pull it open.

For the first time since they had opened the box, Hark
raised his head and looked interested. "It's a camera," he
said. "You open it up and the box kinda accordions out.
Give it here."

"No, I can do it," Roe said, suddenly proprietorial. He
stood it up on its shortest side, lowered the lid like a
drawbridge, and the camera mechanism within stretched
out obligingly. The accordion boxing that connected the

tin-framed lens to the main body of the camera was made of some sort of paper, and had splits in it where it had deteriorated over time. A small, glass-fronted metal cube had been soldered to the housing of the lens, a flash, Roe supposed as he studied it, pleased by its steampunk aesthetic.

"That camera? Vern gived it me," Cleve's grandpa said. "It don't work, though."

Roe, Cleve and Hark exchanged looks. "D'you think maybe…?" Cleve murmured.

"There's only one way to tell," Hark said, and there was a catch in his voice. "You reckon you can rustle me up a thermometer, buddy?"

Cleve nodded, got up and went inside. In one of the corridors he found a nurse's station, at back of which bedpans and urine bottles were stacked. A quick search of a drawer produced a thermometer. Concealing it cupped in his hand, Cleve went back out to the porch. They were still the only ones there, and the shadows were shortening rapidly as the sun rose.

"What are you doin'?" Ron Olsen asked.

"Testing the lens," Hark said. He laid the camera on its back so the accordioned paper made a ziggurat, and the lens was the apex where the sacrificial altar would be.

"Testing it?"

"To see what it remembers."

Hark snapped the thermometer above the lens and the mercury spilled out fast and bright. It spread randomly over the meniscus, running down into the edges of the square metal frame. Hark bent his face to it and this time he inhaled, drawing the fluid back up towards the lens's convex center.

There, in minute silvered negative, the mercury created the image on the postcard that they had seen in the archive room of the Tyler Academy. Then Hark exhaled and the image broke up.

The mercury now crazed the surface of the lens in a symmetrical silver mesh.

"At last," Hark said.

He blew softly on the glass, and with a soft sound like sifting sugar it disintegrated into particles smaller than grains of sand, fell away and was gone, leaving a round, black, tin-framed hole.

As the others leant in like a conjuror's audience to study the camera and the vanished lens, Hark sat back. When they looked round, he too was gone.

# Chapter Thirty-Six

"What happened?" Cleve's grandpa demanded as Cleve and Roe looked about them in confusion. There was nowhere Hark could have slipped away to: no fence or outbuilding, no dip in the ground where he could have concealed himself. He hadn't had time to get to the corner of the main building either. The cane leant against the chair he had been sitting on.

"Hark's gone," Cleve said thickly.

"Gone where?"

"Back," Cleve said.

"Forwards," Roe said. And at that, both he and Cleve felt a piercing sense of loss.

Remembering his grandfather's tears, Cleve asked, "Did he tell you who he was?" When the old man nodded Cleve asked, "Did you believe him?"

"Yeah, I believed him."

"Why?"

"Because he said when he looked down – when he was up there; when he was *up there* – he saw my face,"

Ron Olsen said. "He said it was the one face that was nothin' but sad. And that was true. That was true..."

The old man's face crumpled and once more he began to cry, softly at first, and then in great heaving sobs, and Cleve and Roe put gentle hands on his hunched, bony shoulders and sat with him till he was done.

"You can take the box," Ron Olsen said, blotting his eyes with a balled linen handkerchief he had produced from a cardigan pocket. "I won't need it no more."

"We'll come visit again real soon," Cleve said, and he stood before his grandfather hand in hand with Roe, and that felt like something, for all the old man couldn't see it. There were a thousand questions Cleve wanted to ask that he knew he never would. And he knew that was okay. For the first time he was faintly aware of the sound of the far-off freeway traffic.

Cleve and Roe repacked the box, managing with an effort to force the lid back down on the now-bulging contents until the catch clicked. There was nothing to say now but goodbye.

There was no one on reception when they came through from the dayroom, carrying the box between them with the cane balanced on top of it. That was a relief, as explaining Hark's disappearance from the building – from the entire area – would have been extremely difficult. The door to the outside world slid open as they neared it.

Back in the parking lot they lifted the box onto the back of the truck and set it down next to Cleve's bike, then got in up front. The seat leather was burning hot, and they slid their hips down awkwardly so the under-sides of their thighs, bare past the hems of their shorts' legs, and the backs of their exposed upper arms avoided contact with it. Cleve started the engine, backed up, turned out of the lot and headed in the direction of town.

"Can we go to the library?" Roe asked.

"Sure. Why?"

"We know the date, right? Hark told us: August 10, 1946. We can check out the newspapers."

The librarian, a gaunt, spinsterish but friendly white lady, was pleased to help two young men keen to dig into Claypit's history, and showed them how the microfiche reader worked with an older person's excess of detail. "See, you can move it sideways, like this, as well as down and up," she said, spinning one knob then another. "One day we'll have it all online, but you know how it is..."

She added that regrettably some issues were missing. They thanked her and she left them to it. Roe and Cleve pulled their chairs in and began to scan the crowded, sometimes blurry pages. August 10 was a Saturday. The *Welt County Times* came out on a Thursday, so they searched ahead for the August 15 edition, half expecting it to be one of those the library didn't have.

But there it was.

The front page was headlined blandly, *Holiday Mood Marred by Violent Incident*. Side by side they read the text:

> *Tempers frayed on Saturday night following an altercation between a Negro and several white mill workers. The situation escalated until Paul Harker, 23, recently demobbed, was taken to the town square. Rumors having circulated that he had been approaching white women on Main Street, and police officers' attentions being diverted elsewhere owing to the thieving of farm equipment, citizens took matters into their own hands.*

That was it; there was nothing else. No photograph, no further details on page two or anywhere else.

"Wow," Cleve said. "What a crock."

Roe reached out and switched off the microfiche lamp. Looking round, he saw the library computer was unoccupied. "Let's try..."

They went over to the computer, found it had an internet connection, and typed "Paul Harker lynching Claypit 1946" into the search engine. The *Welt County Times* report didn't come up, but an article in the *New York Amsterdam News* did, under the blunter title *Another Colored Soldier Lynched in Uniform*. Advertisements for hair and beauty products told Cleve this was a newspaper for a black readership.

Here the story was recounted much more as Hark had told it to them, with the two young black women who had been harassed by the white men quoted as eyewitnesses:

> *One of them said to us, "This is a Klan town and don't you forget it'," reported Lanie Mason. Amongst many other outrages, this follows the brutal blinding of Sergeant Isaac Woodard by South Carolina police chief Linwood Shull. The NAACP is taking up the case.*

Accompanying the article was a portrait photograph of a smiling young black man in army uniform. The reproduction was blurry, but –

"It *is* him, right?" said Cleve.

"I think so," Roe said, doubtfully. The longing to disavow what had happened flooded through him – not to disavow the all too real horrors of the past – but to deny that the past could reach out into both his and Cleve's lives as it seemed to have done: into their hearts.

A stranger might say that the man who called himself Hark had read this exact same article; that he had happened to strongly resemble Paul Harker; that he was a curious sort of conman who didn't want money, who just wanted to convince – to connect emotionally, like those fraudulent mediums who want to appear to be of use while offering only bromides, bullshit and clichés, moving on before they can be uncovered. But though there was no proof – no magical ancestor box, no cryptically lettered compass, no sinister dead creature to puzzle zoologists, no photograph – Roe didn't think Hark was a conman.

He thought about his great grand. So far as he knew she had never been called Harker: she had always been an Ellison, and no one had mentioned, or at least not in his presence, that she had been married before.

Maybe they had thought him too young to be told about what had happened to her first husband, which was an irritating idea.

"Can I, um," Cleve began, then tailed off.

"What?"

"Do you reckon I could meet your great grandmother?"

Roe frowned. "I guess," he said.

"I mean, if you think it's a crappy idea, if you think she'll – I dunno, freak out, or have a stroke, then don't worry about it," Cleve said.

Roe shrugged. "I guess you took me to meet your granddad," he said.

The sense rose in him then that it would perhaps be a part of completing whatever this was, this interpenetration of past and present, race and class, economics and geography, segregation and integration and whatever lay beyond it; and that discomfort must be struggled with if you want to reach comfort.

"Okay," he said. "Okay."

They parked Dale's truck, with its Confederate flag decal, on Main Street, just past the turn into Van Cleef Avenue, and made their way up on foot. It was a little after lunchtime and no one seemed to be around, though in their different ways both Roe and Cleve felt self conscious and looked upon.

Glaringly aware of both his whiteness and his poverty, Cleve at least didn't have to experience the fear of potential violence that Roe had felt sneaking about in East Coleman, and he was coming in by the front door like a proper guest, not being sneaked in like a dirty secret.

They turned into Cedar Close and began to make their way along it. Roe pointed out his house as they passed it by. "You can meet my sister after, if you like," he said.

"Cool," Cleve said. "Yeah, I'd like that."

As if she had been expecting them, they found Roe's great grand at her garden gate. Today she was all in white, and wearing a turban, and to Cleve she seemed like a priestess, both handsome and alarming, and her expression was unrevealing. "Who's this?" she asked her great grandson, not quite looking Cleve's way.

"Ma'am," Cleve said, bobbing his head and blushing.

"This is Cleve, grand," Roe said. "He's my, um..." He tailed off, but his hand found Cleve's and took it.

The front of the old lady's house was trellised and grown up with heavy-bloomed roses, yellow and white. Past it, farther up the hill, the treetops of the Side rose, ancient, eternal. "Lord," she said.

"Don't freak out on me, grand," Roe said.

"I warned Earl and Angela about that school."

"Schools don't make you gay, grand," Roe said. "God does."

"Humph."

"We wanted to ask you about Paul, Miz Ellison," Cleve said.

"Paul Harker," Roe added.

His grand gave him a look so strange he was almost afraid, then looked away from both him and Cleve as if into the distance. "That man," she said.

"He's gone on now, ma'am," Cleve said. "He's free."

"Free," she echoed. "I pray it's so. Yes, I pray."

She turned her gaze back onto the two young men still holding hands in front of her, bold in both their innocence and their knowledge. "Well, I suppose you had better come in," she said. "I don't care to talk on the step."

She turned and began to make her way back to the house. They passed through the gate and followed her slowly up the path.

# Chapter Thirty-Seven

They sat on Roe's great grand's front porch and sipped lemonade, and she told them small stories about Paul Harker, then forgot she had done so and why they were there, then forgot Cleve was Roe's boyfriend and got prayerful all over again, then got partway used to it.

Over the weeks that followed they met each others' parents. Each set had much the same response: that two young men so different from each other could only want to spend time together because they were lovers, and so nothing explicit needed to be said. That freedom from having to make an explicit statement meant Roe and Cleve could exist for a time outside judgment, and the impulse of others to judge was softened by the simple passing of time; by people getting used to their unusual relationship.

Each had had to endure a parallel moment of cognitive dissonance in front of the other's parents. Cleve, in Roe's eyes so graceful & confident, so deft in his movements, was flush-faced, awkward, even lumpen in the formality of the Jones parlor, almost upsetting a vase, which Roe had had to catch. And with Cleve's amiable, unpretentious parents, the normally talkative and mentally wide-ranging Roe had groped for "suitable" topics, even trying to stumble through a conversation about football with Cleve's dad that had woefully failed to convince.

These initial encounters, cringeworthy on both sides, bound Cleve and Roe more closely together: *they* saw the beauty, the wit in each other, and if that was in defiance of the world's opinion, well, wasn't that the point?

Of the siblings, Terri liked Roe at once. Phyllis took a while to accept Cleve's presence in her family's home, but his sweetening of Roe's sourness won her round, and the longer he and Roe were dating, the more sincere the relationship was proved to be, to the doubting and at times hesitant families on both sides.

Neither Roe nor Cleve had any desire for their respective families to meet each other, however: there was a limit to how much awkwardness you could stand in any given period of time without dying inside.

The people around them got used to their association too. By the end of the summer Roe could skateboard to Cleve's and get amiable waves from near neighbors like the Rippels as he clattered along. The fact that Cleve was connected to a councilman's family earned him civil treatment from Roe's neighbors on the Side, though he never ceased to feel self-conscious and disreputable as he trudged up the hill to visit.

Both Cleve and Roe felt most at ease hanging out at Eriq's mom's café in the Triangle, where they became regular fixtures. Every so often she pressed inspirational books on them by black gay writers like James Baldwin and Audre Lorde, and about activists like Bayard Rustin and – for which they were more immediately grateful – gave them free Cokes, and didn't mind them holding hands and even kissing so long as they were in one of the booths.

Sometimes they would go up into the woods on top of the Side, spread out a blanket and read books, and in between chapters they would make out.

A week after their visit to the senior facility, Cleve's grandpa died in his sleep. Roe attended the funeral, which was the first time he met Cleve's father and sister. Cleve's mom stayed home. They and some aunt who no one seemed to know were the only mourners.

The Tyler Academy burglary was reported in that week's *Welt County Times*. The watchman, Eddie Holtzer, had been knocked unconscious and suffered concussion, but seemed set to make a full recovery. He couldn't describe his assailant, and the police had no clues as to what had motivated the break-in.

Roe's classmates, Eriq, Mikey and Will, were quietly told they would be allowed to return to school that fall with no marks on their permanent records. Roe came out to them, and they took it in their stride, pretending that Eriq's mom hadn't tattled a month earlier and that it was still big news.

The statue of Colonel Tyler was not replaced. Instead the contextual plaque on its base was expanded to incorporate a few, in Roe's father's view still overly neutral, lines of historical context.

Spider got three years in Welt County Penitentiary for the attempted robbery, Choc eighteen months. Patty and Tag were cautioned as minors. Rick and Rob got suspended sentences, Rob because he was on the basketball team, Rick owing to his crippled leg and the pity he was careful to arouse as he struggled up to the witness stand. Karen quit her job at the tattoo parlor and dropped out of sight. And so the Bohemians really were over.

Cleve's mom was getting her addiction under control and had even lost a little weight. Mayor Oglesby was stepping down; Roe's dad was contemplating running for office. Phyllis's pregnancy was progressing smoothly. She was avoiding knowing the sex of the baby.

As time passed, Cleve and Roe talked less of Hark, and more of future plans. And more and more those plans involved each other.

And that was the summer that Roe met Cleve, and Cleve met Roe, and both of them met Hark.

## The End

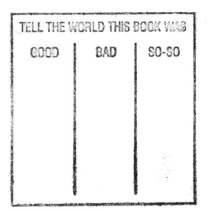

TELL THE WORLD THIS BOOK WAS

| GOOD | BAD | SO-SO |
|------|-----|-------|

# About the Author

**John R Gordon** lives and works in London, England. He is a screenwriter, playwright and the author of eight novels, *Black Butterflies*, (GMP 1993), for which he won a New London Writers' Award*; Skin Deep*, (GMP 1997); and *Warriors & Outlaws* (GMP 2001), both of which have been taught on graduate and post-graduate courses on Race & Sexuality in Literature in the USA; *Faggamuffin* (Team Angelica 2012); *Colour Scheme* (Team Angelica 2013); *Souljah* (Team Angelica 2015); and his historical epic of same-sex love in slavery times, *Drapetomania* (Team Angelica 2018) won the prestigious Ferro-Grumley Award for Best LGBTQ Fiction.

He script-edited and wrote for the world's first black gay television show, Patrik-Ian Polk's *Noah's Arc* (Logo/Viacom, 2005-6). In 2007 he wrote the autobiography of America's most famous black gay pornstar from taped interviews he conducted, *My Life in Porn: the Bobby Blake Story*, (Perseus 2008). In 2008 he co-wrote the screenplay for the cult *Noah's Arc* feature-film, *Jumping the Broom* (Logo/Viacom) for which he received an NAACP Image Award nomination; the film won the GLAAD Best (Limited Release) Feature Award. That same year his short film *Souljah* (directed by Rikki Beadle-Blair) won the Soho Rushes Award for Best Film, among others. He is the creator of the *Yemi & Femi* comic-strip, for teen readers.

As well as mentoring, dramaturging and encouraging young LGBTQ+ and racially-diverse writers, John paints, cartoons and does film and theatre design.

www.johnrgordon.com

Also available from Team Angelica Publishing

*Prose*

'Reasons to Live' by Rikki Beadle-Blair
'What I Learned Today' by Rikki Beadle-Blair
'Faggamuffin' by John R Gordon
'Colour Scheme' by John R Gordon
'Souljah' by John R Gordon
'Drapetomania' by John R Gordon
'Fairytales for Lost Children' by Diriye Osman
'Cuentos Para Niños Perdidos' – Spanish language edition of
    'Fairytales', trans. Héctor F. Santiago
'Black & Gay in the UK' ed. John R Gordon & Rikki
    Beadle-Blair
'Sista! – an anthology' ed. Phyll Opoku-Gyimah,
    John R Gordon & Rikki Beadle-Blair
'More Than – the Person Behind the Label' ed. Gemma Van
    Praagh
'Tiny Pieces of Skull' by Roz Kaveney
'Fimí sílè Forever' by Nnanna Ikpo
'Lives of Great Men' by Chike Frankie Edozien
'Lord of the Senses' by Vikram Kolmannskog

*Playtexts*

'Slap' by Alexis Gregory
'Custody' by Tom Wainwright
'#Hashtag Lightie' by Lynette Linton
'Summer in London' by Rikki Beadle-Blair
'I AM [NOT] KANYE WEST' by Natasha Brown